MONSTROUS BOOK 1

<u>Changeling</u>

By
Robert. P. Martin

Robert. P. Martin

Dedicated to my lovely Jules

CHAPTER 1 – WHAT'S IN A NAME?

I shiver slightly and blink in the harsh light from a too bright bulb above my head as the third sensor is pushed tightly against my neck, just over my carotid artery. It's been a few days since I saw anything more than a candle flame and the sudden brightness feels like small daggers pricking at my eyeballs. Mistress Kiko licks her lips, absently running her forked tongue across her sharply filed, vampire-like fangs. Sitting back across the small metal table between us, she nods to herself, satisfied with her work thus far, her frightening visage still something to behold up close, even after all this time. I find myself trying hard not to stare at the two horns pushing up out of her forehead, some work of surgical devilry only God knows why anyone would want to have implanted in them, but to look into her eyes for long is harder still. Whatever contacts she is wearing have made her pupils into slits, doing homage to a snake or some such reptile I can only guess at. I turn my gaze slightly to the left. A laptop, with a number of different coloured lines rippling across the screen, is open on the table next to me. Aside from the table, the laptop, the two of us and the chairs we are sitting on, there is little else in this room other than a small metal ashtray, a camera in the top corner of the room by the door and a large black mirror on the wall to my right.

Kiko stares at me with those cold, dispassionate eyes, watching me squirm under her gaze, like a lizard anticipating its next meal, waiting for it to try and run. There is a steady beeping coming from the laptop, which I can only assume is my pulse being picked up by the sensors. I am not sure what all the lines on the screen mean but I suspect that they will show the hateful woman sitting before me what might be going on in my head and whether it matches what comes out of my mouth, as I have two other sensors already attached to either side of my forehead.

The thin, worn clothes I am wearing, do little to warm me in this cold, claustrophobic little room, and I have to keep my bare feet lifted off the ground as the granite floor beneath me feels close to freezing. I am all too aware of the scrutiny bearing down on me behind those predatory amber eyes and suspect there are other eyes watching behind the black glass too. I try to see it as just one more test. I have been through so much in the last year … at least I think it's been a year, it's been so long since I saw the sun or even a clock, but this test, this one is the most important. If I get this right, if I can prove myself here and now, I just might get to leave this terrible place, but if I fuck it up…. Please God don't let me fuck it up.

The beep coming from the laptop starts to pick up pace and I force myself to breathe deeply and calm down. Mistress Kiko is still looking at me, her long, greasy black hair framing her pale, marble-like features, telling me nothing, her thousand-yard stare inscrutable, and I wonder how long she intends to maintain this uncomfortable silence between us.

The armoured material of her protective clothing creaks slightly as she adjusts herself in her camouflage fatigues, relaxing back and lifting the chair's front legs up off the floor, casting a ghastly shadow on the wall under the bulbs' light. A small smile plays on her lips, like she already knows I have failed, that she is already planning some diabolical punishment for me. Let there be no mistake here, Kiko is a 'sadisutikku meinu', who seems to enjoy nothing more than toying with and torturing those in her care.

Unfortunately for me, I am one of the people she seems to

have a particular taste for hurting. Maybe it's because of Richard and how he is with me, maybe she just doesn't like me, or maybe it's because she is a Bonafede, grade A psychopath. Either way, most encounters with her usually end up with me spitting blood and covered in bruises, spending days curled up in my cell like a whipped dog. I am hoping this time, things might just go my way for a change. Richard had already given me fair warning that this meeting was coming several weeks ago when I had shared his bed. His quiet, genteel voice had whispered it to me close in my ear after he had taken his time with me, telling me that I had been chosen for an important mission, that it was time to prove myself a valuable asset to the company. Though that was before the incident, and before I was sent back down here for more training.

I scratch at the thin silver collar around my neck, an aid for my incarceration and part of my training, or torture, depending on your point of view. It sends a little shock through me at my lingering touch that jerks my fingers away from my neck, a little reminder, a little warning. I flinch and clasp my hands together. Trying not to show weakness in front of this woman is making me as nervous as a cat in a bag by a river. This is all part of the test of course; slaves are not permitted to speak without being spoken to first and I await Mistress Kiko's first question with coiling trepidation in my stomach. I suspect she can smell my fear, that she knows just how sick I feel inside, regardless of what the lines on the screen are showing her.

Finally, she clacks the chair back down to the cold stone floor and pulls a large, brown, manila envelope from inside her clothing, placing it with deliberate slowness on the table and sliding it across to me. A moment later she pulls a silver cigarette case and lighter from her trouser pocket, deftly plucks one of the pre-rolled cigarettes from inside the case, lights it up and blows several plumes of smoke in the air above and around me. She gestures lazily with the cigarette towards the envelope on the table, giving me unspoken permission to open it. As I reach down to pick it up she suddenly slams her free hand down on top of mine while sucking hungrily on the cigarette and causing the ember to glow red hot. I try to stop myself from trembling, expecting the worst, but I don't move a muscle to stop whatever it is she plans to do. I have been trained to be submissive to her and so I fight all my instincts to pull away.

For a long, drawn out moment, I wait for Kiko to burn me, but instead she simply turns the butt around and passes it across to me, holding it out as a gift, while gently stroking my other hand with her finger tips that she has pinned to the table with her own. I snatch the cigarette out of her grasp with my free hand and take a long slow drag as she releases my other hand, the nicotine doing wonders to still my fraying nerves. Kiko smiles all the more, her grin now showing those shark-like teeth of hers in all their terrifying glory. I bow my thanks and take the envelope from the table still wary of what is going on, unsure what she might do or say. Finally, my mistress clears her throat and speaks for the first time since she bid me to sit,

"Tell me your name?", a pause as she tilts her head, watching me watching her. A simple question but not such a simple answer. The name I had been born with was Naruhitto Yamamoto. I had always known what I wanted to be. The son of a soldier and a psychologist, my father had instilled a sense of pride in the country I was born and raised in, wanting to protect those less fortunate than myself as well as experience the thrill of putting myself between them and those who would seek to harm them. My mother had taught me about the good and bad that was inherent in most people, as well as the few born without empathy or compunction.

At eighteen, rather than going to university, after passing my A-levels, I had enlisted in the police, joining the highway interceptor team of my local county. Dedicated to my duties and vigilant like my father, by twenty-two I had already made sergeant in the Serious Organised Crime Unit, a special branch of the police force where officers from around the country were hand-picked to join it, based on their abilities and arrest records. Before long, I was promoted to detective and given my own team, part of a small task force working to stop human trafficking and vice in and around the city of London. I had been privately investigating a man named Darren Winters, CEO of the Europa Corporation, aka the 'yakkai no kirainahito', as I now call him inside my head, the shitfaced bastard responsible for putting me here, for everything that has been done to me.

I was looking into him off the books, after he was released from police custody despite being caught, literally with his pants round his ankles. I suspected him of being behind a European wide human trafficking ring, after arresting him during a raid on a West London brothel, a raid I had led as the commanding officer on the ground. I was certain that bribery or blackmail had taken place to ensure his release. Despite my discretion in investigating him privately, someone must have informed him of my enquiries and he had ensured, with a kind of ruthlessness that had astounded me, that I would never get the chance to take my findings any further....

They came for me during the night while I slept. I awoke to sudden pain and heaviness in my limbs, a group of terrifying shadows, men dressed like dark nightmares with grinning skull masks, pinning me down, telling me I was fucked. Something sharp was jabbed into my neck and sudden cold and numbness had swallowed me as whatever they had injected me with dragged my mind down into unconsciousness in mere moments.

I had come too in a dark cell, naked, lying on a scratchy wool blanket that had been thrown over a small wooden pallet. To wake in such a place had been disturbing enough itself, but as I looked down to appraise myself and my situation, I had realised something was terribly, indescribably wrong. I was changed, altered beyond imagining... I had screamed and cried for a long time, until my throat refused to do more than a hoarse croak. Nothing would ever be the same. Darren Winters had destroyed me.

Naruhitto no longer really existed, he was just a voice that floated around inside my mind, an angry ghost trapped in another person's body. I had been beaten, collared and shown my own grave as well as a photo of my home, now little more than a pile of rubble and ash. The woman sitting in front of me now, had declared herself my Mistress and given me a new name. Kiko liked to use names from the British royal family, or so Richard had told me, maybe it was more amusing for her to give slaves the names of Queens and Kings, and well, a slave is what I am.

I finish the cigarette, taking one last, long drag, sucking the ember right down to the filter before stubbing it out in the small bronze ashtray before me. "My name is Elizabeth," the words come more easily than they once did, my voice no longer my own, even this they had taken from me but I speak the lie as though it was utter truth. It is the name they have given me, along with this body.

CHAPTER 2 –
THE MISSION

"Whom do you serve?" An easier question with more than one answer. I serve her, I serve Richard, but ultimately, we all must serve the Company.

"I serve whom my mistress commands, I serve Europa as she does, as my master does." I don't know if this is what she wants to hear but since she has not thrown the table aside to punish me, I assume my answer has been enough to satisfy her. The only reaction, a shrug from Kiko as she turns her reptilian gaze to the monitor.

"Open the envelope and place the contents face up on the table Elizabeth." Not a question but a command, not even bothering to look at me as she speaks. I obey with as much deliberate slow precision as they were passed to me, despite wanting to rush, to get this over with as quickly as possible. I have found that fighting nervous instincts is the best way to behave around Kiko. She seems to despise weakness as much as someone daring to stand up to her, as I have learned to my detriment on many occasions already. I tread a fine line with every response, every gesture.

I remove and place three photographs before me on the table. The first photo is a side view of a rather good-looking woman dressed as though heading for work in a smart jacket and skirt, classy heels and long, blonde hair blowing behind her, she was crossing a road towards a park. It looked as though she had no knowledge that the picture had been taken, I suspect someone had taken it from a car parked around twenty metres away, judging from the angle it had been taken at, the size of the other cars and the people in the background.

The second photo is grainy black and white and looks like CCTV footage taken from a high ceiling at a forty-five-degree angle. It is of a gang of masked raiders, each holding weapons, two with shotguns, one with some kind of hand cannon like a magnum 45 and the fourth figure looks to be holding an AK47 assault rifle. They are clearly a gang of heavy hitters and are pointing the guns in different directions at a group of people cowering on the floor around them.

I place the third photo face up on the table beside the others. The first two had elicited little more reaction than a mild, almost professional curiosity from me, but the third photo makes my heart skip a beat, my breathing quickening with sudden icy dread filling me. This photo is of a lady of fifty years, she is sitting in a wheelchair beside an old-fashioned fireplace and out-of-date wallpaper with sequential black and white flowers on the walls behind her. She is staring through a large window at a little garden with a bird table and weeping willow in the foreground, a slightly bemused expression on her face. I know every line of worry forever etched on her forehead, every freckle dotted across her cheeks and I know these things because I am staring at a photo of my mother.

Maria Yamamoto looks older than I remember and I feel a wrenching feeling of loss and grief flow through my very being. I am overwhelmed with memories of her, as though I was a child once more… Waking me with a loving kiss on my head, passing me a packed lunch in a little brown paper bag and waving me off to school, of her warm embrace whenever I was scared or upset, her gentle brown eyes, so wise and kind… Oh Mum, oh God, why do they have a photo of you?

Kiko's eyes are boring into mine, her mocking smile daring me to do or say something. It is taking every inch of training and willpower not to throw the table aside and strike at her with everything I have. It would be futile of course, and only result in my collar activating and bringing me to the floor in agony, anything that happened after that would likely be far worse than what has come before. To dare to strike my mistress would mean a fate where death would be a kind release.

The laptop's beeping has become loud and rapid and the lines on the screen are waving all over the place. I close my eyes and try with all I have inside me to forget that last photo, to centre myself once more and concentrate on just breathing, in and out, slow, deep breaths. I listen to the beeps become slower and softer and when I open my eyes once more, I find I can still feel that anger and rage bubbling somewhere within me but for now it lies out of reach of the monitors and Kiko's keen scrutiny. I am a willing servant once more and so I take one last calming breath and I wait for her to tell me what it is she wants of me.

"The woman in the first photograph is Megan Archer, twenty-three years old, graduated top of her class in computer programming at Warwick University. She currently works as a web developer and freelance programmer for a high-tech security company in the city of London. However, it is suspected that she is, in fact, a mercenary hacker for hire and may even be the infamous 'White Rabbit', leader of the terrorist group known as 'Wonderland'." At the mention of the White Rabbit I feel a tingle of recognition go through me. I recall several incidents involving e-mail and phone hacking scandals relating to high ranking politicians that the Wonderland group had exposed and taken credit for a few months before my capture. As Kiko goes on, it seems that they have raised their game considerably over the past year.

"Most recently it is believed that the Wonderland group was able to hack into a safety deposit facility in the heart of the city run by Steadman and Mason themselves. Several members of the group burst through the main doors armed to the teeth and forced people inside at gun point to relieve themselves of

any money and jewellery they had on them. They then pro-
ceeded to the vault and raided the safety deposit room, carrying everything onto the roof. By the time the police arrived,
they had thrown the entire contents of what they took from the
depository and all the valuables they had taken from the people
inside, off the roof, onto the street below. They then made their
escape by base jumping off the other side of the building, leaving total chaos in their wake. It actually led to days of rioting and many other businesses were broken into and looted by
locals caught up in the madness. The total cost of their little
escapade cost the government and local businesses hundreds of
millions of pounds."

By now my attention is truly taken as I try to imagine the
sheer chaos of the mob and what that would have been like for
the police to try and stop. I picture riot shields and burning cars,
shrieking men and women in masks, rubber bullets, tear gas. It
would have been a terrifying thing to be caught up in on either
side. What I can't understand is why an organisation like Europa
even cared about such goings on when their own business was
so morally reprehensible. Kiko seemed to read my mind, or perhaps, the genuine confusion written on my face as to why she
was telling me all this and continued,

"You think this company is only interested in the flesh
trade Elizabeth? Come now, considering your intellect I would
have thought more of you. You know who the father of the CEO
of this company is? You know his ties to the very government
you swore to serve in good faith? They are willing to pay a great
deal of money to have anarchic little cells like Wonderland disappeared off the map permanently."

She smirks at me as she tells me this, relishing in how uncomfortable it's making me. If what she says is true, the corruption she is describing goes right to the heart of the government
itself. Would they truly be willing to pay organisations like Europa, off book, to assassinate and dispose of trouble makers? And
if the threat was that serious why not use actual spooks? But

then, if you have politicians working for you whose business, if made public, could cause more rioting in the streets, even a tearing down of the state, perhaps you might be willing to hire someone with no link to government to deal with it for you, using people who were utterly dispensable, who didn't technically even exist, people like me?"

I feel tears running down my cheeks and wipe them away, desperate not to show weakness in front of Kiko. If this is true then I had been serving a corrupt regime even before my capture, something I had suspected when Winters was released in the first place, but I had no real idea just how high up his influence might reach. My sadistic mistress has just fed me a most bitter pill to swallow.

"And so, we come to the crux of the matter dear Elizabeth. You have the skills, having worked both as a highway patrol officer and for special branch, and now the looks and wiles, thanks to the Europa Corporation, to infiltrate the Wonderland gang through Megan Archer. You see it seems she has quite the selective taste in women and you are exactly it…." a pause as she lets me take that little morsel of information in with obvious discomfort.

"You will gain Miss Archer's confidence by any means necessary and find out all you can about the gang, joining them as a new member if you are able to convince them you can be trusted and, in doing so, learn where they next plan to strike and where they are plotting to do it. I think you could prove very useful as a driver for whatever they might have planned next. Only next time our agents will be waiting to bag and tag the lot of them before they are able to bolt down any other rabbit holes." At this last statement Kiko pulls a grin that shows most of her hellish teeth. She is truly relishing my recent downfall and what I will have to do to ensure my mother's safety. But I have to ask, I have to know... I pick up the photo of my mother from the table, memorising every detail of her before it begins to blur in front of my tear-filled eyes,

"And if I refuse to do this?" My hand is trembling as I stutter out the seven words that could seal my fate and that of my mother.

"The company policy is that such a refusal would be most inadvisable Elizabeth. I understand your mother suffers from early onset Alzheimer's disease correct?" At my almost imperceptible nod, Kiko continues, "such a fascinating disease, reducing the sufferer to little more than a child, do you have any idea just how easy it is to hurt and terrify a child Elizabeth?" The question is rhetorical as Kiko does not wait for me to answer. "You have seen some of what we are capable of doing here, I think Mr Winters would want you to watch me take my time with her. Oh, the fun we would have together Elizabeth. I must say it is my dearest wish that you refuse."

I can feel a rage boiling within me again at Kiko's words. I have never truly hated anyone in my life before being brought to this place, but at the mention of what she would do to my mother my feelings for this woman are such that I actually visualise myself wrapping my hands around her throat and choking that smug grin right off her face and the very life out of her devilish eyes. She wants me to try it, daring me to fight my way out of this nightmare. Without even realising, I have pulled the sensors from my head and throat, crushing them between my fingers. A tense silence has filled the room, an indrawn breath waiting to be released or a fork of lightning that precedes the sound of thunder, for a split second I can't tell which it will be.

I swallow and reach down deep inside myself for some anchor, some way to control my anger, if I can't, I will be sentencing both my mother and myself to something truly horrific.... At last, I recall a memory from when I was a just a boy. I reach out across time to my father, the calm discipline and solid way in which he did everything, teaching me martial secrets passed down through generations of our family through the art of Iaido. Before beginning any training, we would always kneel and bow over our swords, calming our minds to prepare for what was to come. I seek that inner peace I had once known with him by my side and slowly, moment by moment, I can feel my rage cooling, no longer a roaring bonfire of hate but becoming a glacier, as cold as ice. I swear to myself that somehow, I will get out of this mess and when I do, there will be time enough for revenge.

"So be it.... I accept the mission," it comes out of my mouth in a hoarse whisper, dragged kicking and screaming from the depths of my being.

"Good for you Elizabeth, I didn't think you had it in you," the words uttered in response carry a grudging respect from my tormentor and she stands, her leather armour creaking, heavy boots thudding to the ground with finality, a bargain struck, a bargain sealed. She wastes no more time discussing the matter with me, picks up the laptop and slaps it shut. Without so much as a backward glance Kiko stomps out of the room leaving the door wide open. I cast a wary eye at the floor, and sure enough, a green light begins to glow between the stones, lighting a path from the room, a path I am expected to follow. If I don't, the collar will begin to cause me pain, wait too long and I would be writhing on the floor in agony, barely able to crawl in the direction it wants me to go. I sigh deeply, resigned to my fate, place my bare feet back on the cold ground, stand swiftly and follow the green glow from the room.

CHAPTER 3 – ASCENSION

I keep my eyes to the floor and continue along a well-trodden, gloomy corridor, following the green light where it wants me to go, past other cells, some of the occupants are already in bed sleeping off exhaustion from their daily chores, others are staring listlessly into space, the look one of total despondence and hopelessness, indeed they have the look of the damned and it is fitting, for this place is hell on earth. Some cells I pass are empty, including my own, but the lights continue past it round another bend, leading straight to the elevator where a guard awaits, clad in similar combat gear to Mistress Kiko, his face hidden behind a blank metal mask, only the eyes can be seen watching my shuffling and bowed approach. I hear a terrible scream echoing from behind me and freeze in place momentarily, unable to help myself, turning my head back towards the sound, a terrible lurching, roiling in my stomach wondering which poor bastard is being tortured, guilty at the knowledge that it is not currently me. I begin to feel pins and needles in my fingers and toes, quickly turning to icy pain leeching up my arms and legs. There is nothing I can do to help whoever that is, in fact, yesterday it was me, and that thought alone hastens me on my way, the pain easing and fading away as I continue ahead.

The guard turns on his heel, opening the elevator door for me without a word and I step inside, the doors closing automatically behind me. The whirring and grinding of gears announce my ascension from the depths, I watch the numbers climbing on the control panel, wondering where I will be let off. Despite the fact I am rising up, I feel a sinking feeling inside as I pass floor after floor, past the servant quarters, past the work rooms and laboratories, and up into the executive levels. I only ever go this high up for one reason, I am being taken to Richard. I look down at myself, I am filthy, my clothes are stained and worn from three days of being in the pit and I doubt I smell much better. Richard will not be pleased to see me like this and I wonder why he has sent for me when I am in such a sorry state.

Floor ten and the elevator comes to a grinding halt, dropping several inches before coming to rest, briefly filling my mind with the mental image of suddenly dropping back down through the lift shaft and coming to a grisly end back at the bottom, back in the long dark. The doors open with a slow and silent grace in comparison to the ascent and I find myself in another world from the one I have come to know, Richard's world.

The green lights, now moving along the wall, lead me into a stylishly decorated apartment filled with black leather sofas, tasteful oak furniture and various artworks on the walls. My first few steps leave grey smudges in the thick cream carpet in my wake. Despite my misgivings about being here, just the feel of the thick comfy fibres beneath my toes is almost enough for me to fall to the floor and weep in relief. It had taken me months of 'training' before I was allowed to leave the cells for the servant's quarters, before I was finally 'given' to my master, but several weeks ago I had been sent back to the cells for an unforgiveable infraction. I had tried to help when another servant was being beaten for a simple accident, she had tripped and spilled a decanter of wine in the corridor. One of the guards had reacted with immediate and extreme violence, throwing her against the wall and kicking her hard in the ribs and stomach. Without thinking what I was doing I had run to her and stood between them. It was one of the worst mistakes of my life.

I was beaten with even more force than her, ending up with several fractured ribs, for daring to prevent the guard from carrying out his duty, and then I had been sent back to that awful place where I had first woken to this nightmare.

Just the thought brings back that first dark day to mind. Having woken in the cell to my predicament and new body, I had screamed and cried myself hoarse. I had been ranting and babbling to myself, curled up in a ball on the floor when Kiko came for me. At the sight of her demonic visage entering the cell, I had felt my mind fracturing, wondering if I was dead and had woken in hell itself. With so much fear and anger rolling through me I had flung myself at her in a blind rage, forgetting all my training, no real sense of what I was doing, I was so overcome with hate and despair.

Of course, my attempts to attack her proved futile, I was weak and disorientated, barely able to stand, let alone swing a decent punch or kick at her. She swatted me away like I was little more than an annoying insect, then pulled an electric baton from her waist and struck me in the stomach with it. I had collapsed around it, folding in on myself, consumed with pain and shock. I think I blacked out for a few moments because as I came back to myself, I found she was pressing her knee into my back, pulling my arms behind me. Within moments she had bound first my hands behind my back, then my legs together. I was screaming incoherently at her, spitting and wriggling, trying to bite her until she shoved a ball gag into my mouth and tied it round the back of my head. It was all over in moments, what little was left of my pride had been taken away so quickly I could barely grasp the dire circumstances I had woken up to. But worse was yet to come...

She had smiled down at me bearing those hideous fangs of hers, not even saying a word, with almost inhuman seeming strength she picked me up bodily from the floor and slung me over her shoulder like I barely weighed a thing. I was carried, shamed, naked and humiliated from the cell block, into the lift and taken up through several floors. She carried me down a sterile looking corridor with gleaming metal walls and silver floor tiles, the swinging and motion of moving upside down leaving me feeling sick and dizzy and fearing what was coming next. She turned suddenly into a large conference room, I could make out half a dozen chairs surrounding an oval grey table with a number of strange looking objects on it, then she had dumped me rather unceremoniously into a black office chair, calmly tying me to it with ease and obvious experience, so that I could not speak or move. Her task accomplished, she blew me a kiss and strolled from the room with a casualness that belied what she had just done.

I was left for some time sweating and shivering nervously in that room, before eventually being joined by a balding, well dressed looking gentleman with a handlebar moustache, wearing a pin striped navy suit and matching waistcoat. I had guessed him to be in his early fifties, from the amount of grey in the hair he had left on his head and in his moustache. He was carrying a laptop briefcase and placed this with calm precision on top of the table, proceeding to pull a white laptop from it and plug it in to one of the many sockets surrounding the room and then sitting down just a metre from where I had been tied up and left by the female demon from down in the cells.

The old bastard had cleared his throat, introducing himself as the building's administrator. He then began by advising me that a few things were necessary to process me correctly now that I had woken from my surgery. I recall little of what he actually said to me in those first few moments of meeting him, as I was silently screaming at him through the gag in my mouth and desperately pulling at my bonds, my blood chilling to ice at how matter of fact he was being, given my condition before him. He had slapped the table in anger when I refused to listen to his little speech, I was turning my head this way and that, looking for anything I might be able to use to cut or remove my bonds. His sudden aggression got my attention long enough for me to see him pick something up from the table and show me what looked to be a cross between a gun and a drill, with a large metal needle sticking out of the end. The sight of it terrified me, as I could only guess what he intended to do with it. He wheeled himself over to me on his chair, not even bothering to stand, and grabbed my right arm with his free hand. I was flinching, begging through my gag not to do whatever he was intending to do but he paid no heed to my muffled cries. Instead he shook me and warned me to be still, informing me this was to put a tracker in my arm, not some torture device as I might have feared. It will sting, he advised, but only for a moment. This did little to calm my jangled nerves, at the thought of such an invasive thing being carried out on me, on top of all they had done to me already, within moments of waking up into this new nightmare of a life.

When I refused to do his bidding, he simply slapped me hard in the face. With my head turned to the side, I felt the sting of the needle piercing through the skin of my arm, into the muscle underneath. I felt a sudden sharp pinch deeper in my arm, then the offending needle was pulled back out. A smug air of confidence about his business, the administrator placed the gun-drill back on the table and picked up what looked to be a thin silver hoop or necklace. When I think back to that time, I should have been far more fearful of this seemingly innate object. If I had known just how much it would bind me to this place, to how much of my freedom I would lose.

The administrator twisted and pulled at the silver hoop and it came apart, reaching around my head, he placed it upon my neck and I heard an audible click as it was secured tightly in place. Having completed these two tasks he wheeled himself back to the table and with as little concern as he had shown on arrival, he explained to me just what he had placed around my neck and that he was going to give me a demonstration of its purpose, that being, to train me to be submissive and do what I am told.

It is no exaggeration to say that something broke inside

my mind at his words. On top of what had been done to me, my worst fears were being made reality. This was the stuff of horror stories and I half expected the ageing gent in front of me to suddenly sprout horns like the woman who had brought me here and rip the mask of his human face off revealing some horrifying demon beneath. But, of course, he was no demon, just an unscrupulous businessman doing his job. He gave me a taste of what the collar could do and I came too on my side, still tied to the chair, my cheek resting on the floor, dark blood from my nose dripping scarlet onto the tiles. The pain had been excruciating, burning me inside-out, I don't recall how long it lasted but it had felt like it was never going to stop. For a time, I just blinked and breathed, staring at the room sideways-on, seeing nothing but chair and table legs surrounding me....

Eventually I was hauled back up off the floor by the demon from the cells. She had presumably returned to the room at the administrators' behest. I did my best to scream bloody murder at her through the gag, but achieved little more than choke on more of my own blood inside my mouth, feeling it trickle down my throat and chin. Kiko took a seat herself, leaning back in the chair, resting one arm over another chair next to her, totally relaxed, while the administrator tapped something into his laptop which lit up a white screen on the wall in front of me.

The first thing to appear was a video message from Darren Winters, his image enlarged, taking up most of the wall in the conference room. He had filmed it on some tropical beach, I could make out palm trees and a sizeable yacht just offshore in the background. He was dressed in a ridiculously loud Hawaiian shirt, with white shorts and a white Panama hat covering his completely bald head. He had been holding a bright pink cocktail in his hand, with one of those umbrellas and a curly straw sticking up out of the glass. He looked for all the world like a cliched advertisement for a fat, wealthy, middle aged Brit abroad. He was grinning like a damn fool, not a worry in the world and he gave his little speech with completely undisguised relish.

"Welcome detective! Welcome to paradise, I trust you are enjoying your stay? No? Well I expect it's all come as quite a shock, but don't worry that will pass in time. As you can see, I have had some of our finest surgeons working day and night to craft you into something a little more pleasing on the eye. I wanted you to know there was no hard feelings, you were just doing your job. However, I can't say that I was happy about that little investigation you were carrying out on me, so I thought I would just nip the whole situation in the bud before things got out of hand.

First and foremost, I am a businessman, not someone to waste an opportunity, and rather than simply have you killed for being a meddlesome little fucker, I thought this would be much more fun and lucrative in the end. By now you are probably thinking of all the horrible little things you want to do to me, but let me assure you detective, I thought of them first. I will leave you in the capable hands of my team on the ground there with you. I do hope you enjoy your stay with us. Once you're all settled in, I am sure we can find something useful for you to do. Oh and do have a look at these pictures I have for you, I took them myself you know, and no, you don't have to thank me, it was my pleasure."

The video cut off at this point, Darren Winters' smug face begging me to punch my fist through it, the last thing I see before the computer switches to a number of images which only made my heart sink further. My house, burned to ashes, a graveyard in the rain, then a close-up picture, zoomed in on my own gravestone, Naruhitto Yamamoto, 1994-2017 RIP.

I had started sobbing through the gag at this point, my tears blurring my vision. Unable to take anymore, I had fainted, blacked out again I guess, but was slapped back awake just moments later by the demon from the cells who introduced herself as my new mistress. Kiko had then told me my new name, explained that Naruhitto was dead and that I belonged to her now. She had untied me from the chair, releasing the bonds from my legs but leaving my hands still tied behind my back and marched me from the room and back to the dark place below, her sharp fingernails, grown and shaped like claws, digging into my arms all the way.

Later, when I was back in my cell, my thoughts swirling down deeper and darker corridors of my mind, he had come to me. Richard appeared, like some stage magician, seemingly out of thin air. Dressed in clothing more suited to a black-tie event, he had asked if he could join me and without waiting for a reply had banged on the cell door and a guard had stepped forward, unlocking the door for him. He had stepped into my dank little cell and perched himself rather gingerly on the edge of my pallet-bed. I had shrunk up against the corner of the room, the scratchy blanket pulled up around me to cover my shame. He had looked upon me with such pity in his eyes that I had nearly burst into tears but I think I had cried it all out by that point. Instead I just stared back at him, my eyes large and owl-like, straining to see him clearly in the dark, wondering what on earth such a man was doing here in this place.

Unable or unwilling to meet my intense gaze he had turned his head to the rest of the room, taking in the little ceramic sink and dented bucket just a few metres from where he sat, the extent of my world under my present circumstances. He had wrinkled his nose at the sight, unable to hide his dismay or disgust at his surroundings. While he was pinching his nose and closing his eyes, I had studied him in the dark. I couldn't help but picture him as some rich playboy on his way to a charity ball. He had taken three deep breaths before beginning, before he told me of the bargain he wished to strike with me.

A sponsor is how he described himself, he wanted to sponsor me in actual fact. In return for his patronage I would not be touched or abused sexually by any of the guards. I would get certain privileges too, more food and water in my cell and, once a week, a chance to stay in his rooms, use his shower and he would provide a freshly cooked meal for me. In return I would be expected to be a companion to him, to provide him with friendship, the kind of friendship that a raised eyebrow indicated was the exact sort of thing this place was built for.

I had balked at the proposition he had laid before me. I was barely coming to terms with the idea of the body I had woken up in, but I was also no blind fool. It was obvious why I had had my gender reassigned, given the place I was in and the people responsible. If it wasn't Richard, sooner or later it would be someone else and I doubted I would be asked for permission a second time. Still, I could not bring myself to reply to his offer. I had begged him to just leave me alone or to free me. He had apologised that he could not free me, that he would explain another time. He had left then, telling me he would return in a month and give his offer one more time. In the meantime, his sponsorship would begin, I was under his protection, for what it was worth.

Those first days and weeks had been the worst of my life and I had thought many times about trying to commit some form of seppuku if the chance permitted. Of course, when Richard finally came back with his offer once more, it had seemed like a lifetime since his first visit in that lonely little cell. In his absence I had not been sexually abused in any way, just as he had promised and I hadn't completely starved either, but physically, and mentally, I had been beaten and subdued, locked in solitary confinement at times for God-only-knew how long, half drowned, once even hung by chains in a huge meat locker, until I thought I would be left to die and my body carved and eaten by the crazy sadists running the place.

More recently I had been given more mundane but physically exhausting and utterly pointless tasks, like being made to clean the floor outside the cells for hours on my hands and knees, with nothing more than a bucket of soapy water and a toothbrush to do it with. In short, he came to me when I was broken and beaten, as he knew I would be I suspect. And so, I accepted his offer, the thought of what the guards and Kiko would do to me if I lost his patronage so terrifying a proposition I could not even comprehend doing anything else. He had smiled sadly at my answer and advised he would send for me once I had passed my initial training...

So much had happened since that day I had said yes to Richard's offer. And for a time I had believed the worst of all that had been done to me was over and in the past, but the last three weeks of my life had been hellish beyond anything I had experienced before. I was certain at times that I would never be allowed to leave the cells again, that I would die down in the pit alone, bowed and broken. I can only assume that Richard had intervened on my behalf and convinced the company that I was still worth something to them, that I might still prove useful, for I was sure that Kiko would never have agreed to consider it otherwise. And now, well, Richard would want his due....

I cross the apartment, following the lights through the open planned lounge into the kitchen. I can smell the scent of wondrous aromas wafting from the same direction I am heading. I can detect the heady tang of cooked meat, of herbs and spices blending together in the air, making me salivate and my stomach growl in protest at its emptiness. I pass through an archway, leaving the kitchen to my left and find myself staring at an empty dining table and chairs. Well, the table isn't exactly empty. There is what appears to be a roast dinner with all the trimmings plated and waiting for someone to come along and eat it, a generous amount of red wine already poured into a glass beside it, a single white rose sitting inside a tiny vase in the centre of the table. The green lights are pointing me right to it.

I don't wait for an invitation, my most basic instincts are kicking in, and I have barely eaten in days. I draw the chair back and scoot myself in, snatching up a plastic knife and fork from the table, I waste no time before I begin consuming the feast before me. The sudden light touch of a hand between my shoulder blades nearly makes me jump out of my skin and I force myself to swallow the chewed up potatoes and peas in my mouth rather than spit them out across the table. Just as quickly, the hand draws away and I hear Richard make a tsking noise behind me. I turn my head to face him as he rounds the table, taking me in.

Richard's tall, lean form is towering over me, his clean shaved and chiselled face staring back at me with barely concealed disdain at my appearance. "That's quite a mess she's made of you." His voice is precise as he makes this statement, upper class politeness trying to mask what he really wants to say. I nod in agreement, as I begin shovelling another mouthful of succulent food inside my mouth, hardly bothering to chew it. Richard is holding out his right hand, examining the well-manicured fingers that he touched me with, his usually handsome face is screwed up, like he had just found something very unpleasant to be under those nails. I wonder what face he must have made when he saw his carpet.

"Do me a favour Lizzy? When you are done wolfing down your repast like a ravenous dog, I would greatly appreciate it if you take a long hot shower, gods you smell worse than the latrines at my old boarding school." I nod again with genuine gratitude at the thought, before turning my attention to the glass of wine, swigging several large gulps, sending a hot oaky taste straight down my throat and then returning to the plate of food, now already halfway through. Richard sighs theatrically before turning away towards his bedroom, likely finding my table manners to be a little worse for wear after my time in the cells. "Come and find me when you're done, and do be a dear and clean your teeth too won't you?" I swallow a piece of Yorkshire pudding soaked with gravy and finally find my breath to answer. "Your will sir". He nods once, his back to me and leaves me to continue filling my face with his fine food and expensive wine.

Ours is a strange relationship, even for this dark place.

Richard is technically my owner or sponsor as he calls it. I am not entirely sure what that means but, as such, he gets certain rights to me that the guards, and even Kiko, for all their wanton violence, are not allowed to visit upon me. He could choose to simply force himself on me if he wanted and I would be powerless to stop him, since my collar could knock me out at his order. Instead he chooses to play this odd game with me, as though we are courting each other, making me meals, wanting deep and meaningful conversations by asking me my opinion about politics and philosophy, science and religion. He refers to me as his companion rather than his slave and I fear that he has deeper feelings for me than what someone in his position should. He told me not long after I first came to him, that he too was a prisoner here. He confessed to me that he was the architect of this whole place, that he had thought he was creating some grand underground hotel, above an old coal mine inside this mountain. He had lived on-site during its construction, believing it would be something that could make him famous in the world of architecture, but halfway through the works completion, he had started to become suspicious that his design was being twisted in ways not of his making. On confronting the board members of the company, he been advised, in no uncertain terms, that he could never leave, something many of the other workers on the build had also discovered as each part was finished, any that protested too loudly had disappeared mysteriously, never to be seen again.

Europa had been very careful about who had been allowed to come here, Richard himself had been a single man with no family to miss him if he never showed up again and the builders and craftsmen that helped build the whole facility had been brought in illegally from war torn countries around the world, desperate for work and willing to do as they were told for the chance to earn money to send back to their families. Those that hadn't gone missing had found new jobs as guards or had been kept on as work or maintenance men, keeping the place running like a large hive of insects.

Despite not allowing him to leave, Richard is still held in esteem here, as he is needed in case they ever have to build deeper into the mountain or repair any of the clever constructs he has come up with to ensure the structure never collapses beneath the weight of all the rock above it. In short, Richard was indispensable to Europa's plans here and whatever appetites he might need to have sated to keep him happy and willing to work he is given freely. However, I am not so indispensable and if I am to survive this place, I must play my part, that of the dutiful servant girl who will do as her master commands, because if I don't, my fate could be so unpleasant that I cannot even fathom it.

I wipe the last vestiges of gravy and apple sauce from my chin with a pristine white napkin next to the plate which I had studiously ignored until every last mouthful of food had been consumed. I take a moment to cradle my stomach gratefully and lean back in the chair, just breathing, trying not to think about what is to come before I can leave this place. Leave... ha, I can scarcely believe it, not yet. I get to my feet and head to the bathroom and it's enough to make tears fall from my eyes at the sight, as I am greeted by a beautiful white marble bath and sink, gleaming silver taps and a wet room shower, with Roman-like columns at each corner of the room. Smooth black and white under- floor heated tiles warm my frozen feet. This is a world away from the bleak, dank cell and servant's quarters I have spent months living in below.

I peel off my tired dress and drop it in the basket by the sink and step naked to the shower, turning the chunky silver tap, which is coming straight out of the wall, and wait for the water to start heating up. As soon as it's hot enough, I step under and immerse myself in the steaming water. Staring down at my feet, I let the water soak through my hair and watch as it runs down my legs, changing from almost black to clear before slowly swirling down the drain in the middle of the floor. The feeling of the hot water running down my back is even better than the meal and I find myself groaning in pleasure...

I have no idea how long I stand under the shower but by the time I get to actually washing myself, my fingers have started to go wrinkled. I pick up the shampoo from the shelf by the shower and cake my tangled hair in it, massaging it all into my scalp before rinsing it back under the water, it feels damn good that's for sure and I am beginning to smell like a human again. I wash the rest of my body with my eyes closed, trying not to think about what has been added to me and what I have lost.

By the time I finish washing myself, the bathroom looks more like a sauna and I have to rub the steam from the mirror above the sink to see my face. The pale half-Japanese beauty staring back at me gives me a sense of unreality, as I still find it hard to believe this is really my face. The dark green eyes, unusual for someone of my heritage, look haunted and drawn from weeks of little sleep or food but the shower and meal have done a lot to give my cheeks a healthy glow. My shoulder length hair looks jet black when wet and pieces of my fringe are plastered to my forehead, still wet from the shower. I don't look down any further, I still can't bear to see myself naked, instead I turn and grab a towel from a heated rail next to the door and dry first my hair, then my body, keeping my eyes shut throughout, doing my best to think about anything else.

Once dry, I use the new toothbrush left out for me on the sink and scrub furiously at my teeth for far longer than necessary with some expensive whitening toothpaste Richard has left for my use. After rinsing my mouth, I cast my eyes about the room and, sure enough, Richard has also left me some nightwear out and a dressing gown is hanging off the back of the bathroom door. I dress hurriedly, slipping into the matching blue silk chemise and underwear and finally drawing the white towelled dressing gown around me. After weeks of privation and torture at Kiko's hands this feels like a five-star spa resort. Of course, I reason that this is all part of the mind games they play in this fucked up place. I am expected to be grateful that I can wash and eat normal food like a human being instead of being treated like an animal, and I am, more's the pity.

Finally, unable to find any more reasons to linger I head to the bedroom and find Richard waiting there. He is sitting half on the bed propped up against some pillows, doing his best to look learned, spectacles resting on his nose, brown parted hair dropping foppishly across one side of his face, his head buried in some fascinating work of literature that would likely bore me to tears. He turns to look at me as I enter the room and his face lights up at seeing me standing there. He puts his book down and peels the glasses from his head, placing them down carefully beside him on top of the closed book. I have no wish to engage in any pleasures of the flesh with him and I find myself longing to just dive onto his bed and luxuriate in the sheer comfort of the mattress, wrap myself up in the duvet and sleep for days.

Richard catches me turning my gaze from him to the bed and back, smiling with his perfect white teeth, he pats the bed beside him and invites me to join him. I waste no time in thinking about it, rounding the bed and practically falling onto the side reserved for me. Leaning back against the pillows with my legs out before me I close my eyes, sigh deeply and feel my whole body sink gratefully into the mattress. Richard laughs out loud at my reaction, "Damn it all but I have missed you Elizabeth," this statement is said with no sarcasm and I can only conclude he is telling me the truth, so earnest is his gaze when I turn to look at him as he speaks.

"I have certainly missed your shower," I reply, for this is true as well, and I feel he deserves at least one utterance of truth to pass my lips tonight given how much indulgence I have just enjoyed, "and your cooking of course".

"Yes, well, you looked like you needed a bit of fine dining, I daren't think about the kind of slop they serve you down in Kiko's little house of horrors."

"We're lucky if we get anything at all to eat down there," I mutter in response, turning to look out of his window into a computer generated, forest landscape in winter. Like so many things in this weird place the beauty here masks the true reality. Since we are inside a mountain the only thing I should be able to see outside the window is more rock and dirt, instead it looks like I can see for miles, the vista, a beautiful white forest dusted in snow, stretching off into the distance towards a pale orange sunset, something I thought I would never see again until my interview with Kiko was over.

As always, my thoughts take me to a dark place in my mind at the mere thought of Kiko, souring my mood and reminding me of everything I have lost along the way to get to this point in time and place. I look down at my open palm and squeeze my fingers tight, making a fist with them and then letting them back out. Whatever they have done to me, these are still the same hands I had before, and like someone clinging to a rock in the rapids, I use that to anchor me in the present, drawing my mind back from the abyss. Somewhere in here with me, Naru still exists, his memories are still there, of all that we once were and could have been and he is waiting and hoping that somehow, we will find a way to escape this life. But for now, I have to push him back down, he won't like what's coming and I don't want him to see or feel any shame in it. Tonight, I must be Elizabeth and rightly or wrongly, she belongs to the man sitting next to her.

I feel Richard's gentle touch against my chin, turning me back to face him and wiping a tear away that I hadn't even felt from my cheek. "Well, you are here now, fed and clean." He breathes in deeply and theatrically through his nose as he says this and continues, "and you smell much better too." His smile seems genuine as he stares deeply into my eyes, an unasked question lingering in his gaze. I lean towards him, pressing my forehead against his before kissing him gently on the lips.

Permission given, Richard wastes no time before reaching

across my stomach and pulling at the cord holding my gown in place. Once undone, I lean forwards and allow him to pull the gown down off my shoulders and lift my arms out of the sleeves. I raise myself a little off the bed and throw it onto the floor behind me.

Richard's breathing has quickened and his eyes are roaming my body, his hands following soon after, stroking and squeezing me sensuously and intimately. He shifts his weight and leans back, pulling off first his jumper, then unbuttoning and removing his shirt, dropping both beside the bed and revealing his slim physique underneath. I wait for him to come to me and he pulls back in close, his left hand slipping up under the chemise, his clever fingers alighting on my breast and gently rubbing at my nipple, while his mouth closes back over mine, his tongue seeking my own, snatching my breath from me, breathing it in, tasting me.

His other hand goes low and begins tugging at my underwear. I lift my buttocks slightly off the bed to give him better purchase and he pulls hard, one good tug taking them right down to my ankles. I kick them away as his fingers delve between my legs, to the place that shouldn't exist. I swallow and gasp at the same time as they slip inside me, his touch awakening the technology implanted within and making small waves of pleasure emanate through my body. Not yet satisfied with his view, Richard stops for a moment and pulls at the chemise covering the top half of my body. I sit forward and raise my arms, allowing him to pull the whole thing off over my head leaving myself completely naked under his gaze.

As I lean back against the pillows his head follows me down, first kissing at my neck and ear, then working his way down my chest until he is level with my breasts, before kissing and licking at both of my nipples one after the other, all the while his left hand is probing me down below, forcing more and more gasps from my mouth as the chip implanted deep within my body creates the feeling of the build-up of an orgasm inside me. Richard's own breathing is deep and urgent and he pulls away again to snatch at the belt holding his trousers together. Within moments he has worked his way loose of first his dark-blue chinos, then his designer briefs.

We are finally, completely naked together and he presses himself up against me, our flesh touching in the most intimate way, then he lifts himself up over my body, his knees pushing my legs apart, his penis now fully erect and seeking what is between them. I stare up into his striking light-blue eyes as I don't want to look at what is about to happen between us.

I feel him enter me, slowly, inch by inch. There is a little pain there as his girth opens me up, stretching my insides, until he has pushed his entire length deep inside me. I try to cry out but his mouth envelopes my own, swallowing my cries and breathing in my gasps as he begins to move himself rhythmically and slowly in and out, grunting his pleasure which is now mimicking my own. I reach up and clasp his side, my legs wrap around his hips, clinging on and waiting for this strange dance to reach its crescendo. I don't know how long he holds us both there on the cusp of orgasm but after a time I feel him swell inside me and my own body responds, firing out waves of pleasure and heat as we both climax together.

For a moment I can't even think, my body shivers with goose bumps and Richard eases himself down on top of me, kissing my face and lips with gratitude and pulling himself back out from inside me, almost sighing as he does so. "I really have missed you; you know?", he says once more. "I would never have guessed," I reply, somewhat sarcastically I'll admit…

CHAPTER 4 – NEW BEGINNINGS AND ENDINGS

I sleep deeply, wrapped in Ricard's embrace, our naked bodies warming each other beneath the duvet. The feeling is like floating on air after sleeping on a pallet of wood and straw in my cell, nothing else but a scratchy woollen blanket to warm me. I wake to find Richard's hand cupping my left breast, one of his legs hooked around my own, his penis, fully erect and hard, pressed up against my back. He is still asleep, breathing loudly by my ear and I try to stay still and quiet rather than wake him. I am hoping to leave this place today, the thought is almost an impossible one, one I had dare not believe before now.

Richard advised me last night that they would be sending me off on my mission in a few hours, one of the reasons he had sent for me despite my dirty and dishevelled state, he hadn't wanted to miss one last chance to fuck me before I leave, who knows how long I will be gone, or if I will ever come back here after all. Richard stirs a little in his sleep and pulls away from me, unwrapping himself from the embrace and turning over to face the other way. I whisper a silent prayer of thanks to who-ever might have been responsible for this sudden turn of luck, quickly slip out from under the duvet and make my way to the bathroom to relieve my bladder and clean myself up, picking up my discarded dressing gown as I pass.

While sitting on the toilet I can begin to feel the tingling in my fingers and toes that warns me of the coming onset of pain from my collar, I don't have long before I need to be back next to Richard. A quick wash down below, a flush of the toilet and I rinse my hands briskly in the sink, I don't have time to dry them so instead I wipe them dry on my robe as I dash back to the bedroom. I pause to stare at the new incredible view out of the window, a gorgeous turquoise sea at sunrise with corral and multicoloured fish darting all over, greets me. It takes me a few moments to realise it is the Australian Great Barrier Reef, I had never actually visited there myself but I had always planned to go before I turned thirty for an extended holiday, something else I doubted I would ever get to experience now.

Richard has woken in my absence and is standing naked next to the window, gazing at the sea, as enraptured by the view as me. He holds a hand out, barely turning from the window and I go to his side, my hand reaching his and squeezing tightly. His other arm reaches around my shoulders and pulls me in close to him. "It's beautiful," I mumble, genuinely awestruck at how lifelike the view is in front of us, I almost feel like I could reach out and touch the water. "You should see it up close, it really is something," he replies wistfully, his thoughts mirroring my own, I doubt he will ever get to see it again in reality either. Richard's hands lower to my waist and tug the cord of the gown free, peeling it back off me, letting it drop to the floor. His full attention has turned to me, looking my naked body up and down and clearly liking what he sees, his face one of wonderment. I had hoped we were all done with my duties but it seems I am not quite out of this yet.

He begins by kissing me on the lips, but this time I know he is expecting more from me, as I feel the light pressure he is applying building on my shoulders, he is directing me wordlessly to go lower and so I obey, as I must. I imitate his moves of last night, kissing first his neck, then chest, working my way down his smooth, hairless body, pausing to kiss and lick at his nipples as he did to me, then going lower still until I am on my knees before him.

I close my eyes to the sight of his erection before me, reach out and grab hold of him with both hands, feeling and tasting his tip with my tongue and lips. Months of feminisation 'training' have taught me what to do to ensure I please him. I start by licking and sucking around the tip of him, before working my way down his length with my tongue. I can taste the sex on him from last night and it's not the most pleasant thing I'll admit, but since being brought to this place, I have tasted far worse things that pass for food and still eaten them. I draw most of him deep inside my mouth, almost gagging as he rubs up against the back of my throat. Meanwhile my hands have not been idle, I grope and play with his testicles, earning all manner of grunts and gasps from above me, as well as a number of expletives with my slave name thrown in for good measure. I almost laugh at the power this has over him, as it once had over me. What is it about a blowjob that can leave a man inspired to write whole novels and streams of poetic nonsense about the woman prepared to do it to him? I work back and forth at him, licking and sucking until he can't stand anymore and has to pull me back up to face him. Unable to help himself now, his lips find mine and he gets a full mouthful of what I have just tasted, though not seeming to mind in the slightest.

Determined to reciprocate, he backs me up against the bed until my legs are touching the mattress. He pushes me playfully and I fall back on to the marshmallow-like duvet and this time Richard's head moves towards a set of different lips. He kisses my thighs first, while his fingers slip inside me once more, releasing the waves within me, making me groan in pleasure myself but this time his tongue darts inside me as well, his mouth nibbling and sucking at the soft flaps of skin on either side of my custom-made vagina, his tongue locating my clitoris.

Sudden intensity, heat and gasping, I am upside down and inside out, I can't breathe. I feel spasms inside me, jolts of electricity zigzagging around my body, I am crying out in ecstasy, unable to stop myself. A moment, a pause, as Richard climbs on top of me and slips himself back inside me, and then it starts again…. Waves of heat, pain, joy, pleasure, it all mixes together and I can't hold it all in, I am squirming trying to pull him out of me, I need it stop, but I don't want it to end. Like a wave crashing against the shore, I feel us climax together, rolling in the surf, smashing against the beach, the sound of the ocean suddenly the only thing I can hear besides our short, shallow, gasping breaths. "Kuso," I whisper, "just… kuso."

Richard is staring at me strangely, like some love sick puppy about to watch its human leave for work. In all our times together, it has never felt like that, I have never truly just gone with it, surrendered to him like that. Perhaps it's because I know I'm leaving, or because I wanted to give him a good send off, something to remember me by? Maybe this place is making me as fucked up as the people running it. I try to gather myself, I am in bits, frightened about the intensity of what just happened between us. This man is still my master and I need to remember that. He may not have a say in whether he can leave but he is highly regarded here and he did help to build all this. He could still have chosen not to have a slave for himself or not to use me like this, yet when he leans in to kiss my cheek I don't turn away, I lean into it, reach out and cup his face with my right hand and stroke him softly behind the ear. "Orikosan," I say, "orikosan". A voice from further back in my mind, Naru's voice, whispers his rebuke, "Traitor, slut, baishunpu"…

CHAPTER 5 – EXIT THROUGH THE GIFT SHOP

I should have paid more attention to what was happening. I was so busy staring into Richard's eyes that I didn't see the needle coming. He must have had it under one of his pillows or down the side of the bed. After patting him like a well-behaved dog, something I am not sure he took too very kindly, after all I was supposed to be the pet, he had suddenly stabbed me in the arm with a syringe. I barely had a chance to become angry about this sudden development, as whatever he injected me with was as potent and fast acting as the drug they had stuck me with when this whole bizarre nightmare had begun.

And so, I have woken up to find myself fully dressed, in clothes befitting a woman in her early twenties going out on a warm summer night, along with my ever-present silver collar, something I feel for instinctively as I begin to rouse my mind from the drowsiness of the drug. I am now wearing a light-blue summer dress with little anchors all over it, a small grey cardigan over the top and grey canvas plimsoles on my feet to match. I am strapped into the backseat of some kind of Humvee car, the windows are blacked out, the engine is rumbling along pleasantly, it feels like we are going at some speed, as I can hear the whooshing sounds of other cars passing in the other direction every now and then. There is a black screen separating the rear seats from the driver and the doors are very much locked.

So, I guess Richard doesn't like doing goodbyes? I sniff at myself, smell some kind of dainty, flowery perfume, in fact I smell and feel clean and fresh all over. The thought of Richard washing and dressing me most intimately while I was unconscious, before carrying me to this car and dumping me inside, is enough to make me wonder what the hell I was starting to think back in his bedroom. I recall something called Stockholm syndrome that I learnt about from my mother and again during my early days of police training. Something about the abductee coming to love their jailor?

In all honesty I don't know what my feelings are towards Richard at this point, I know if I allowed Naru fully into my mind he would have a different view entirely. In many ways, Richard is as much a victim of Darren Winters and the Europa Corporation as me, trapped in that place for years, is it any wonder he would have needs that he can't fulfil like he would be able to in the real world?

I suppose it could have been a lot worse for me, Mistress Kiko had introduced me to some of her pet projects early on in my training, a means of ensuring my full co-operation when I had been proving to be a rather troublesome slave. Understandable given the rude awakening I had suffered as far as I was concerned. But when the collar, the beatings and the starvation had not been enough to bend me to her will, it was being shown around her private sanctum that finally did it for me. The poor people in that place, my God, I had never prayed for salvation before that day but seeing what had been done to them would haunt me to my dying days... And there were things I knew that I had somehow blocked from my mind that I had seen there to prevent me from a deeper madness.

I pull my mind away from the spiralling dark thoughts and memories that are threatening to overwhelm me, say a whispered prayer for those still being held down in the dark and for myself, finally I would see the sun again, see the world again, albeit through a rather tinted lens.

I look to my left and discover an over-the-shoulder, dark grey cotton handbag on the seat next to me. It contains a number of essential items for survival back in the real world. Among them I pull out a driving licence, declaring me to be Miss Elizabeth Shaw, there is also a bank card, with the same name, a basic looking black smart phone, as well as some red lipstick and a small hand mirror. I crack the mirror open and stare at my face, just to see if I am still the same person I was before I was drugged, force of habit, I guess.

Someone has done a real number on me. My makeup has been applied expertly, my eyebrows plucked with precision, along with eye shadow, eyelash extensions, concealer, glossy red lips. I can scarcely believe my eyes staring back at the model-like beauty that has been bestowed upon me. I suspect I will never be able to recreate this look myself without professional help, despite my many feminisation lessons over the last year or so. I notice even my fingernails have been manicured and painted a similar blue to the dress I am wearing. Is this all Richard's doing? I suspect he might have had help, one of the other servants perhaps?

The envelope that contained the pictures is under the handbag as well as a ten-inch tablet with a sticker on it that says 'play me', in Richard's handwriting. With little else to do I click the button on the side and it lights up to reveal a frozen video message of Richard's face with a large white triangle superimposed over it just waiting to be pressed. I turn the tablet onto its side and the picture tilts and grows larger, taking up the whole screen, then I simply tap the screen and wait to see what my master has to say.

"My dear, I hope you are not too offended over how we parted. I know how you feel about Shakespeare but, to quote the bard, 'parting really is such sweet sorrow'. In short, I will miss you terribly and I shall recall our last hours together with great satisfaction. However, whatever my feelings towards you, we must do as the Company commands and so you had to be sent out the way you came in, 'exit by the gift shop' as it were eh? I wish we could have had more time but events march on regardless of individual desires and our jailors really are very keen on capturing this Wonderland bunch before they cause any more chaos out there in the real world.

You will find on your phone, a number of useful telephone numbers if you need assistance with your investigation. It also contains your bank pin number for the card we have given you. Inside your handbag you should also find a key card for your new apartment and a set of keys for the motorbike I have selected to be your mode of transport. Yes, I was listening when you recalled how much you enjoyed riding, and as part of your cover, the Company have set you up as a motorbike courier, allowing them to monitor your movements around the city and providing you with a nice alibi for getting around town in a hurry.

There is a weeks' worth of food and a wardrobe worth of clothing already waiting at the apartment, all picked by me I am sure you will be pleased to note, and you will find that your target just happens to live on the same floor of the apartment complex where you will be staying. Not that I am telling you how to do your job but I imagine an accidental bump into your new neighbour on her way in or out of the building might be a good way to break the ice and I am certain if you flash those intoxicating green emeralds of yours in her direction she will become as enraptured in your gaze as I am. Well my dear Lizzy, I wish you luck and good hunting. Take care and do be a good girl won't you."

The message ends here and I click the tablet back off. I had listened to Richard's words with dark mirth at his take on the situation. From how he spoke it was like I was being sent out for some kind of sporting holiday, not risking my life for a bunch of sadistic bastards who would string myself and my mother up by our short and curlys if I fuck up. I delve deeper into the handbag and pull out the bike keys, the make says Yamaha, good, it seems like he really was listening to me, the thought of getting back on a motorbike and pulling back the throttle, the feel of the acceleration as you hold on for dear life, is enough to take my mind from the crazy task that I am being sent out to do, if only for a moment.

I lean back and get comfortable, no real idea how long this will take, how long I have been unconscious, even what the actual date might be. I will find out soon enough. Until then I will take my chances to rest where I can. For now, I am leaving Richard, Kiko and that hell far behind, whatever fate I have laid out in front of me, I never want to find myself back in that awful place. So I close my eyes and listen to the Humvee's huge three litre engine rumbling over the tarmac and dream of a time when I was a boy, when the sight of my father coming home after months out on tour, was enough to overwhelm me with happiness, when my mother would make me homemade lemon meringue pie with custard and ice-cream, the day I rode my first bicycle up and down the road, make believing I was travelling at light speed like some spaceship in a science fiction movie. These thoughts had helped pull me through when I had succumbed to despair in my darkest hours within that facility and I use them now to send me on my way into the world of dreams. And slowly, but surely, I drift back to sleep...

CHAPTER 6 – NO PLACE LIKE HOME

The sound of a honking horn jerks me awake. I crack my eyes open and carefully wipe the glue-like sleep from them, trying my best not to ruin the make-up job that had been so expertly carried out on my face. The car has come to a stop and I can no longer hear the engine rumbling. There is a definite click-clunk to either side of me from the rear doors of my mobile prison, indicating I hope, that I can finally get out and see where I am. I try the door to my right and, sure enough, it opens on a silent hinge as I pull the handle towards me and push the door open. With my other hand, I pick up the bag with all my essentials, drawing the strap over my shoulder and tuck the tablet inside too. With one last deep breath I twist myself and place my feet on solid ground, pulling myself up and out of the car.

A sense of unreality hits me as I am confronted with the hustle and bustle of London's busy streets. The sheer volume of things going on around me is almost overwhelming to my senses after so long underground. Shielding my eyes to the sun, I shut the car door almost without thought and before I have even taken a step, the black Humvee screeches away up the street back into busy traffic, leaving me to stumble back to the kerb out of the road and try to get my bearings.

From the look of the local shops I am in a wealthy area of London, somewhere near Knightsbridge or Kensington by my reckoning, old memories floating to the surface, unused for so long, my old police training for noticing things around me kicking back in. It doesn't pay to stand around for too long in London, you start to stick out like a sore thumb. I pluck the driving licence back out of my bag and remind myself of the address I need to get to, turn my new smart phone on and tap the address into Google maps. Within a few moments my route is mapped out as just ten minutes walk from my current location. Making a mental note to turn left a few roads up, then take the third right, I start walking in the direction the little blue navigator triangle is pointing me.

Once certain I am heading in the right direction, I put the phone back in my bag and do my best to look like any other ordinary person just making their way along the busy streets. Meanwhile, my heart is hammering inside my chest as it dawns on me that I am actually outside, that I can actually see the sun, the real sun and then there are the questions I haven't dare ask myself during my incarceration, that begin to push to the front of my mind: 'How long have I been gone? How much has changed in the world, in the country? Do all my friends and family truly believe I am dead? Am I even Naru anymore, or am I Elizabeth now after all? I send a mental query into the depths of my mind, searching for Naru, I can feel him there somewhere I am sure, but he has remained quiet as a mouse since his little outburst in Richard's bedroom.

'Naru?'... Nothing... The lack of an answer and the fact that I am even having to ask it disturbs me, have I finally cracked completely in two?

I am coming up to the first turning, doing my best not to make eye contact with anyone, pressing on with a decent pace. As I pass a newspaper stand, I can't help my eye from being drawn to the date on the front of one of the broadsheets. Though I have been calculating in my head, seeing the date hits me like a blow to my chest and I have to stop and catch my breath, except I can't catch my breath, I'm breathing too fast, I can feel it coming, a panic attack, I know I need to breathe deep and slow but I can't. The thought keeps going around in my mind, 'It was July 2017 when I was taken and the date on the paper said twenty first of May 2019'. I have been gone for nearly two years....

Someone is escorting me towards a shop window, a man in a suit asking me if I'm alright. Fuck, I'm so fucking far from alright. Those bastards, shitting arseholes... and they aren't done with me yet, not by a long shot. 'Get a grip Elizabeth, get a fucking grip or you're going to faint'. 'Naru?'

"Miss, miss? Can you hear me? Just breathe, just breathe. Christ, shall I call an ambulance?"

My hands have curled in on themselves like claws, I am on my knees, staring at a very expensive looking pair of black brogues. Somehow, though, I am breathing more deeply, my mind is clearing, the panic making way for a slower boiling fury. I wave the passer-by, who has stopped to help me, away. I tell him I'm fine, I'm fine it's ok. I stand, albeit a little shakily and lean back against the wall between two shops, feeling a little sick and dizzy, but largely just embarrassed at what a scene I have made.

For some reason I am really craving a cigarette. A few other concerned citizens are standing nearby, initial looks of worry changing to nods and whispers, then turning away, moving on. The man standing next to me, who stopped to help, is still holding my arm and I have to reassure him several more times before he finally lets go. I thank him, tell him really, I'm fine, it's passed. Finally, accepting my word, he moves on, his good deed done for the day, his head held a little higher for having stopped to help someone in distress.

After a few more minutes, the world has moved on and forgotten all about my little panic in the street. But I haven't, I won't ever forget... Darren Winters, wherever you are, I am going to find you one day and make you pay for what you have done to me, somehow, somehow I will, I swear it, fuck you, you bastard, kutabare!...

A few minutes later, having stopped to buy a packet of Lucky Strikes and a disposable lighter, lighting and smoking one of them as I walked the rest of the way along the route to my new home, I find myself standing in front of a tall apartment complex in a very smart looking part of the city. There is even a damn bell hop on the door, tells me his name is Nathan, and welcomes me to the building after I show him my ID and tell him I just moved into apartment twenty-three. He explains that I can collect the mail from my post box in the lobby and that I am on the fifth floor, pointing the way to the lift, telling me to ask if there is anything I need, so I ask if there are stairs instead, I really don't like lifts anymore. Just around the corner, behind the pillars on the left, I am told by the ever helpful and cheerful Nathan, who is smiling at me like he wants to get my number, small dimples appearing in his cheeks. I thank him politely and turn away, pretending not to see that look.

By the time I reach the fifth floor, I am sweating a little and have to catch my breath, damn I am so out of shape, something I will have to remedy if I can, probably didn't help starting up smoking again either. I pull hard on a heavy fire door and exit the stairwell into a very plush looking corridor with dark grey carpet and light grey walls, every front door I pass is solid, black oak, with a card entry system on the side and a little spy hole in the middle.

Number twenty-three is the third door on the right and I find myself simply standing and staring at the door for some time before I come out of my daze, reach into my shoulder bag and pull out the card key for the apartment. I swipe it against the door, a little green light flicks on by the door handle and a faint click announces the lock has disengaged, so I pull the handle and step into my new home.

Inside the room is bright and airy, white walls and light grey carpet, wooden-parquet floor in the kitchen area with black cupboards and marble worktops, it's an open plan space and I can make out most of the apartment in a single glance, a white washed door at the back of the apartment and another to the side, presumably leading to the bedroom and bathroom respectively. Most of the furnishings look like they have come straight out of the Ikea catalogue.

All in all, its simple but clean and functional, nothing tasteless or hard on the eyes. I head to the fridge, it's a Smeg, with an ice making machine on the door, a little fancier than my little sink and bucket back in the cells. I open the door and can see that it's been well stocked with fresh vegetables, juices and milk. In the door there is a bottle of white wine, Sauvignon Blanc, one of Richard's favourites. There are also two bottles of beer on the bottom shelf and without a second thought I grab one, shut the door and crack the lid off against the corner of the kitchen worktop. I take one slow, grateful swig, letting the ice-cold amber nectar slide down my parched throat. Oh damn, nearly two years since I had a beer, it's the best fucking beer I have ever tasted!

I head over to the window, bottle in hand, draw the curtains and to my surprise there is a set of French doors leading onto a small balcony. I unlock the doors and head out onto the balcony, staring out over the street. I can see the top of the shard and the Gherkin off to my left in the distance. I can feel the wind on my face and I turn into it, closing my eyes and just basking in this new freedom I have been granted. I raise the beer bottle to my lips once more and tip my head back, taking another swig of cold fizzy joy. Not done yet I pull another cigarette out of my bag and light up, lean back against the outside wall and sigh deeply...

CHAPTER 7
– SUICIDAL
TENDENCIES

I am looking up at a beautiful clear blue sky, only something doesn't feel right, mainly because I appear to be lying down on my back. Did I black out? What was I just doing? Someone is holding onto me with an iron grip, their arms tight around my chest, a woman's voice, breathing rapidly, concerned, telling me they've got me, they've got me, it's all going to be ok. I have pins and needles in my arms and legs, I blink and turn my head to the right. I am on the floor of my balcony, the bottle of beer I was drinking is empty, sitting on the ground with a cigarette butt stubbed out in it. I try to speak but it comes out wrong, more like a groan. Have I had a stroke? 'Naru? Naru can you hear me?' What just happened? Have I been drugged? I try again, "I'm, I'm ok, really, just let me up, please?"

The woman releases her grip and steps away from me. "Do you want me to call someone?" she asks from behind me. I tuck my hair behind my ear, out of my eyes and get shakily back to my feet. I seem to be making a habit of needing strangers to come to my aid today. As I turn to speak to the lady who was holding me it suddenly dawns on me that I have no idea how she got in my apartment. What the hell is going on? I scratch nervously at the top of my head and finally face her. It takes all my concentration to keep the oh of surprise off my face as I find myself staring into the dark brown eyes of one Megan Archer, AKA, very possibly, the White Rabbit.

"Look no matter how bad it is, there's always hope, you just can't give up on life, we only get one chance at it after all." The words come out of her in a rush, almost pleading with me. She keeps looking over my shoulder as she says this, as though she is expecting something to happen.

"I... I don't understand?" I reply, "how did you even get in here?"

"Look I don't know the reason why you were balancing on the edge of that balcony. I was just watering my plants over there," she points at her own balcony that is full of small plants and herbs a few apartments over,

"I looked up and I saw you climb up on the edge of this balcony but you had this look on your face, you looked straight at me and it was the saddest look I have ever seen, I just, I knew if I didn't do something you were going to jump. I called out to you but you just ignored me and turned to look down at the ground. I ran to your door and I was all set to start banging on it and shouting out but it was open and unlocked. I just walked right in and well, I snuck up on you, sorry about that, I snuck up on you and just grabbed you, I figured if I tried to say something, you would jump before I got to you."

From the look of total confusion on my face, she must think I'm crazy. Was I standing on the edge of the balcony? All I remember doing was lighting my cigarette and putting the beer to my lips. A dark thought begins to take shape in my mind. Naru... he hasn't been talking to me. He seems angry at me and I wonder, shit, has he given up, did he want to throw us off the balcony, end it all the moment he got the chance? I wonder if he can't live with the shame of what I did to survive back in that dark place. In the old days, in Japan, such a dishonourable thing that has been done to me would have meant I would have been expected to take my life, as I had briefly considered myself in those dark early days of my indenture. My father had raised me to respect the old ways, honour, duty and loyalty were basically the family motto. I can accept that Naru is angry about what has happened but what I don't understand is why he would give up without a fight. I don't care what happens to me anymore but I need to make sure my mother is safe and if I can get this damn collar off then maybe, just maybe I will get my chance at revenge. I try to send these thoughts down to wherever Naru is lurking, down into the darkest corners of my mind. Please, Naru, please, help me figure this out, help me beat them, don't give up...

I marshal my thoughts and do my best to give Megan Archer an embarrassed smile. "It really isn't what you think. I'm just, well it's embarrassing but I am a bit of an adrenaline junkie. I was just daring myself; you know? To look down and not freak out." It's the best lie I can come up with under the circumstances but I feel like it is failing to convince my would-be rescuer.

"Is there someone I can call, a family member, a friend?"

"Honestly I'm fine and no I don't have anyone to call either. I just moved here after all. I think I might have given you entirely the wrong impression of me." I try to make light of the situation, shut the French doors and move casually away from the balcony. I can see the anxiety easing from Megan's face at this and when I dump my body theatrically onto the sofa she actually almost manages to crack a smile. "You're sure you're ok?" She says, still searching my face for the lie, trying to read me and my intentions. I cross my legs up on the sofa like a buddha and place my hands together as though in prayer. "Honestly, I am fine and thank you for stopping to help, it's nice to know I have a neighbour who is so concerned for my welfare, Namaste." I try my best beaming smile and get a small, sceptical one back in return.

Great, thanks Naru, the lady we are supposed to be seducing thinks I'm suicidal or crazy, or maybe both. My first day on the job and I have royally fucked it all up. I turn my head, listening for a phone to start ringing. But the phone doesn't ring and

Megan Archer is still standing there, as though waiting for me to do or say something more, and I realise suddenly, that I should be introducing myself, that I'm not supposed to know her name yet. And so I pat the sofa next to me and do my best to start telling the practiced lie I had come up with on the way here. I say,

"So, can we start again? I am Elizabeth, I have just moved to the city for a fresh start, a new life, no looking back, you know?" Megan draws nearer and eases herself very carefully onto the sofa beside me, not quite relaxing but determined to see this through it seems.

"Anyway, I was lucky enough to inherit a small fortune from my father so figured I would go to the centre of where it all happens, see the city up close, get a bit of excitement in my life. I'm going to be self-employed, do some courier work, dart around the city on my motorbike, maybe meet someone and have some good times together, not take life too seriously. I am pretty sure I don't have jump out of a fifth-floor window on my to do list." She listens to me with a kind of hyper-alertness, not unlike Kiko when she was interrogating me. Fortunately, I have become quite proficient at telling lies and telling people what they want to hear during my capture, and Megan finally nods as my story grinds to a halt. She seems to reach some internal decision, holds a delicate hand out to me and replies,

"Megan, I mean, my name is Megan. I've lived here for a few years now; my brother lives a few blocks away and he persuaded me to move up here from Kent after our mother died. I work from home mostly, I build websites and freelance for a security firm in the centre of the city, they call me up a few times a week and pay me a fortune to fix any bugs or malware trying to get through their firewalls."

I shake her hand and thank her again sincerely for rushing to help me, because it really does seem that she has just saved my life today, for what it's worth, Christ if only she knew why I was here, I think she may not have been so quick to try and stop me, which also leaves me with a real dilemma. How can I throw this woman to the wolves when she has just selflessly rushed to my aid and, quite probably, saved my life? Even for my mother's sake, even if she is really the White Rabbit, she just proved herself to be one of the good guys. The thought of her being taken by Europa draws a tight knot around my stomach.

Whatever I decide, I have to try and stall for now, I need to think and I need to plan. Somehow, I have to figure out a way of removing the collar, if I can't, I am worried Naru will do something that I won't be able to stop. I don't want to die, 'please Naru, please answer me damn you?' I suddenly feel weak and nauseous but I have to salvage this before Megan leaves, I am sure the company are listening or watching and I need to let them think I am still doing what they want. I do my best to appear perfectly poised, despite my misgivings and say,

"I can tell you are a genuine person Megan, one of the good ones. You didn't owe me a damn thing and you risked your neck to save me back there. Assuming I don't do anything else foolish before I see you again, and believe me when I say, I certainly don't intend to, I swear I've given you the wrong impression about me, I would love it if you would have dinner with me one day soon. I would like to repay your kindness and also it would be great to pick your brain as to some good places to eat and where to go to have some fun around here?"

There is a wealth of emotions flitting across Megan's face as I speak. Happy, sad, slight scepticism, it's hard to tell. I wonder at how lonely she might be, working from home, living in a world of logic gates and binary code, I'm hoping she might like an excuse to have some company and if what Kiko told me is really true, I should be her type, at least in looks and it might be enough to stop her keeping a polite distance from me in future, hoping the crazy lady in apartment twenty three isn't going to start crying and hammering on her door, or do something worse, like throw herself down the lift shaft.

"I am getting the feeling living so close to you is going to be interesting. I can't say that I care to see you planning anymore 'balconing', besides you are only supposed to do that when there is a swimming pool below you. Maybe you should consider taking up a safer past-time, like table tennis or chess?" This last sentence is said with wry humour and a half-lipped smile as she moves to leave and I can't help smiling back. I recall my first thought when I saw her photo just a few days ago, she has a naive way about her, I can't tell if it's a mask or if she really is this decent a human being but she shows it in her bearing, an innocence I lost in myself long ago, a belief in something greater than herself perhaps? Could someone like this really be the White Rabbit? Then again, would she believe me if I told her who I really was and what I was doing here, no, I expect she would call the police and try to get me sectioned.

"So that's a maybe on dinner?" I ask questioningly, getting up to walk her to the door. Megan pauses for a moment, I assume she is weighing up the implications of agreeing to have dinner with me, then finally nods and says, "Ok, how about we meet up Thursday and I can give you some tips about the area?" I nod back enthusiastically and say, "Great, thank you I owe you one, well two now technically. So how about I cook something to say thank you? I make a mean Ramen, it's an old family recipe passed down from my father, goes great with a bottle of sake, what do you say?" At my description her eyes light up, and she shows me what I think is the first genuine smile I have seen in a long time. "Sounds great, shall we say seven o'clock?" I nod and smile back, silently thanking my lucky stars that I have salvaged the situation, "Agreed, see you then. Oai dekiru nowo tanoshima ni shite imasu." She waves goodbye and turns to leave, and I watch her walk up the hallway and head back into her apartment before closing my front door and making sure it's locked. I turn around and press my back up against the door, allowing myself to slowly slide down it until I am slumped on the floor. I feel something start to buzz against my hip and reach into my dress pocket, where I had put my phone after entering the apartment. I swipe the screen and put the phone to my ear, hoping that it's anybody but Kiko on the other end.

"Elizabeth, my my, you do work quickly don't you." It is her, fuck, my heart skips a beat, my breathing quickening with anxiety. "I have to say your little stunt on the balcony did not go down very well with the other board members but your tactics appear to have paid off. I applaud your efforts, first day on the job and I do believe you have made quite the impression. Let us hope your dinner plans go well, I advise you to consider more conventional methods of courtship now that you have her attention. We don't want her thinking you're some kind of crazy person, now do we?"

"No mistress, of course mistress, your will, so I obey."

"So, shall it be, good, continue as planned. You will be hearing from me soon. In the meantime, you are expected at twenty-two Bishopsgate at eight thirty tomorrow morning to pick up your first delivery. I expect you to be on time, no tardiness now Elizabeth, you are on the clock." The phone makes a click and I look at the screen to see she has hung up. No pain in my collar, relief flooding through me. I have bought myself some time, but to do what? I need a plan and fast, but first I need to fix whatever is going wrong in my mind. I feel like I have been split in two, like there are parts of my memory now that are just blanks, as if Naru has become completely separate from me, taking parts of my life with him. I could always feel him there somewhere before but now… now it's like I am truly on my own. And that would be fine, except that I can't anticipate what he might do, and if he's dead set on doing something stupid, I don't know if I can stop him.

CHAPTER 8 –
MIRROR MIRROR
ON THE WALL

I drag my weary body up off the floor, stumble to where I think the bathroom is and swing the door open. I am greeted with a large square mirror, inlaid with silver and gold, over-looking the bathroom sink and I draw myself slowly towards it, staring into my own green eyes, into Naru's eyes, one of the few things that haven't changed about us. Just a few inches away from the mirror and I grip the sink tightly with both hands. There is an old saying that the eyes are the gateway to the soul, my hope is that if I look hard enough, maybe I can find him again, somewhere inside me.

During long months in the cells there were times where I was left in total darkness and solitary confinement for so long that I ended up hallucinating, seeing images in front of me, of old memories like I was watching TV. It's surprising how quickly you can relive your past when you are confined to a four metre by four metre room, with nothing else to do but play the 'what if' game. Still, there were certain memories that I could not recall, pieces of my mind are broken, missing. Whatever part of me that was once Naru has become something other than me and unless I can pull him back to me, I fear that I am doomed to a half-life, of never really being whole.

I don't need to speak, I simply stare intently into my own eyes, our eyes, I send my thoughts spiralling down into the recesses of my mind, looking for the blanks, the places where I should be able to remember but I can't, through half formed memories, fractured dreams and wisps of nightmares, I search for him....

Screams echoing in the dark, our father yelling something to us, he is so angry, desperate, calling for help.... Kiko's terrifying image stalking us in the shadows, slithering, hissing terrible threats, showing us something that we can't bear to see.... We are driving the police Impreza hard and fast, way too fast, sirens blaring, chasing a child killer, knowing we are already too late to save his latest victim....

But HE is still not here, I have to go further back, deeper into our past....

We are ten years old; our father is walking away, not turning back, my mother is crying, sobbing out his name, clutching at me, both of us wondering if we will ever see him again. And I realise I am seeing this from a different perspective, from a reflection in the window, my ten-year-old self turns and sees me there, staring back at him. 'Go away, I hate you.' His words hit me like a hammer blow to the chest, I feel myself torn from the scene, my thoughts scattered to the winds, I am spinning around so fast I feel like I'm going to throw up, I reach out and try to steady myself, try to pull at the frayed parts of my soul, draw myself back into one piece.....

The world is still spinning but more slowly, I can make out shapes, trees, swings, a bench, other children playing on a climbing frame. I realise that of all places, I am on a park roundabout, I used to come here when I was five years old with Mum... As the world goes around and around, I can see her, my mother, sitting on a bench nearby, all alone, so thin, smoking a cigarette, a look of sadness on her face that she only wore whenever she thought no one was watching. Without father she was like half a person too, it was like she couldn't breathe without him at times. Such was her love for him, that her mood, when he left for one of his tours, was one of desolation for weeks afterwards. She could hide it most of the time, for my sake, but I know until he comes home, she will not be right, not by a long shot.

'Get out of my head, I told you to leave me alone.'

'No, I won't, I can't, I'm you, you're me.'

'Baishunpu... you're with them, the bad people, warui hito, you're one of them now.'

'Please, please, I just did what I had to, to survive, it was you that left, that hid, I need you to come back, we have to figure out a way to save her....' I am still staring at my mother, seeing her as she once was, beautiful and oh so fragile and she needed me, needed us now, more than ever.

'If you won't do it for me, do it for her.'

'I don't want to be you anymore, I, we, we're not right, I was a boy, I was a man, you, you're a girl, a liar, I hate you!'

'I am a woman and I love you, I forgive you, for running away, for not wanting to live like this, do you hear me Naru, I forgive you, watashi wa anata o yurusu, please, just come back with me. Together we can fix this, somehow we can I know it, but I can't do it without you, please Naru.'

'You... forgive me?! How dare you! LEAVE ME ALONE.' He's sobbing, curling into a ball, the world is slowing down, the roundabout coming to a halt. But this time I don't leave, I can't, there's nowhere else to go, nowhere else to be but here. I embrace a sobbing, frightened child, and I whisper comfort into his ears, I tell him, I tell myself,

'It's alright, everything's going to be alright, I've got you, I love you, I won't ever stop loving you. Watashi wa, anata o ai-shiteimasu, Naruhito san. Please, I need you, to save her, to beat them.' Somehow, I feel my words reach him this time, there is a change in his bearing and he wipes at his tear stained face, just a frightened boy, reflecting the sorrow of his mother. He looks to her, sees the sadness there, and her form slowly changes in front of us, ageing in mere moments until she resembles the old woman in the photograph, she is more fragile, more in need of us than ever. HE looks at me then, Naruhitto the man, pulls me to him, embracing me.

'Alright, Kanojo no tame ni,' he replies at last.

'For her', I agree, 'for us both.'

CHAPTER 9 –
THE SHORTEST
DISTANCE BETWEEN
TWO POINTS

Having dragged the other half of my soul out from the darkest recesses of my mind, I come back to myself, and there I am, just a pale young woman, with large dark green eyes, staring into a mirror. Only now, I have a ravenous hunger, like nothing I have ever known, and it dawns on me that I haven't eaten a single thing all day. I have been in the real world for less than twelve hours and I am already living off cigarettes and alcohol, just like old times. I spin on my heel and go to the fridge, open the door and begin stuffing my face with whatever I don't need to prepare or cook, which is mainly fresh fruit and raw carrots, not exactly my first choice but I have no patience for anything else right now.

I crack open and swig back the other beer with gusto, what the hell, I nearly died today, might as well celebrate in style. I feel stronger, more myself than I have in a long time.

My hunger sated, I grab a blanket that was draped over the back of one of the chairs and wrap it around my shoulders, then fling myself bodily, lengthwise across the sofa, snatching up all the cushions and stuffing them behind my head and back. The feeling of peace and comfort is almost indescribable just laying here in this moment. For the first time in a long time I feel something like hope awakening within me. Somehow, I am going to figure this out, with Naru's help, we will get out of this mess and save our mother. But how exactly... Come on Elizabeth... think... there must be a way......something they haven't thought of....

A dozen different plans play out in my head as I lay there staring holes into the ceiling. I consider Megan, with her computer skills, maybe she could hack the collar, turn it off somehow, but I have no idea how I would tell her what help I need without giving myself away to the company.... Then there's the kind of tool I would need to cut the collar off. Richard told me it was made of a mixture of titanium and other alloys that allowed it to be shaped so that it could be locked around someone's neck. Which meant it wasn't likely coming off with anything less than industrial cutting equipment. Where the hell was I going to find something like that? .... just think damn it.... I might be able to find something I could use in a hardware store or a chop shop but, the moment I head into one, I suspect the collar would go off or start warning me to leave, the same would likely happen if I go anywhere near a police station.

They will have thought ahead of all the ways I might try to escape and I am sure Kiko will be waiting for me to try something, longing for me to fuck up so she can finally do whatever dark things to me she has been holding in her sadistic reptilian mind. I have a strong feeling she suspects I am not as subdued as I should be, that some part of me never truly bowed to her. Somehow, when I first awoke in that place, my mind fractured, but in doing so it saved a part of me that was still Naru, I did my best to protect HIM, but in doing so I have cut myself in two, and I feel like there are still some things he is keeping from me, memories that I can't quite see yet. I feel him here with me now but we are not exactly one person anymore.

My mother, would have been very interested in whatever has happened to my mind back before she lost hers. As a clinical psychologist, she had always been fascinated with the more extreme mental health conditions. I wonder if she would have diagnosed schizophrenia, or possibly multiple personality disorder? Either way, whatever they have done to me, I don't think any amount of therapy is going to fix me now....

I dose for a time, I have put the TV on in the background, some re-run of an American sitcom, the canned laughter drags me out of of a casual daydream, I had been imagining the seaside where I had grown up, the sound of waves lapping at the pebble strewn beach, half a dozen seagulls hovering in the sky above me, crying out for a taste of my icecream, I was picturing the old pier, reaching far out to sea and in the distance I could make out several huge ships, not much bigger than my hand from so far away, that hardly look to be moving at all, but I know they are, carrying thousands of tons of goods back and forth, up and down the Thames to the city and then back out towards the North sea.

I turn from my reverie to see the gang from Friends on the TV, oh yeah, I remember this one, the one with Chandler in the box. Not so funny anymore, not when you've seen someone tied down inside one, limbs missing, hacked off to stumps, teeth and eyes pulled out, but still alive, being kept as someone's plaything. One of Kiko's little projects, something Naru had blocked from me, to spare me the pain, and the memory hits me with such force that I physically jolt upright. I claw my way out from under the blanket, lurch to my feet and begin pacing the room. Like a caged tiger, I can feel my strength returning but I am still just as powerless as before. There has to be something, some way to get out of this. I just need to apply myself.

The collar is the real problem, there must be some way to short circuit it, cut it off. And then there is the tracker in my arm, not such a big problem if I can get the collar off, all I would need is a sharp knife, a pair of pliers, a hot flame and a shit load of painkillers and wadding afterwards.

I wonder about whether I have anything like that in the

apartment already. The minute I start sniffing around inside the draws and cupboards without an obvious purpose, I suspect my collar will go super nova on me. They have slipped up today with that phone call. Before that, I hadn't known for sure if they would be listening or watching me, or even just waiting for me to call them with news, as and when I had something to tell them. But now, now I know that they are watching and listening.

In all likelihood, the whole apartment is fitted with secret cameras and transmitters so they can watch and listen to my every move. The thought sends a little shiver of unease down my spine. Kuso ttare, of course they will be watching me. So, anything I need, I am going to have to pick up outside the apartment, if I want to avoid rousing their suspicion.

I head back to the bathroom, decide I need to take a shower, I feel clammy and hot and I don't want them wondering what I'm thinking about, pacing the room like this. I strip my clothes off and step under the shower head, turning the tap and letting the frigid water splash over my face before it begins to warm up. Damn that's cold, but it's woken my mind back up, taking my thoughts away from the dark nightmares that threaten to overwhelm my sanity.

Instead, I try to be pragmatic and put my mind back to the task of thinking of a way to get out of this. I recall that Richard said I would be tracked on the bike too. Hottoke, there must be something they haven't thought of already, think Elizabeth, just think....

'The bike, the bike is the key,'

'What.... Naru?'

'What is the shortest distance between two points?'

'A straight line, but what does that have to do with anything?'

'We can do this.'

'You're not making any sense.'

'Do you trust me?'

'You were planning on killing us both earlier today, so forgive me if I am a little sceptical right now.'

'Do you want to get out of that collar or not?'

'Preferably with my head still attached to my body, yes, of course.'

'Then you will just have to trust me, won't you.'

'That is hardly inspiring confidence, Naru, what aren't you telling me?'

'If I tell you, you will just overthink it all.'

'Promise me you are not planning anything crazy.'

'I think anything we try to do at this point to get the collar off, is going to need to be a little crazy if it has a chance of working, it has to be, because otherwise they will have thought of it first.'

'Christ, Naru, ok so just how crazy are we talking here?'

'You already know the answer; I don't need to tell you. Just think about it. Get the tablet and load a map up of London.'

I climb back out of the shower, dry myself hurriedly, wrap the towel around my body and head back to the lounge where I left my things.

I pick up my handbag from the coffee table and pull out the tablet. Within a few seconds I have a bird's eye view of most of London's roads staring back at me. I sit back down on the sofa, tuck my wet hair behind my ear and stare hard at the screen, trying to see whatever it is Naru is getting at. I look for obvious straight lines, my eyes pouring over hundreds of roads, back and forth across the Thames, and then I see it and I suddenly feel goose bumps ripple down my arms...

The Blackwall Tunnel... The sight of it on the map sends my mind tumbling back through time to when I was with the highway interceptor team. Whenever we passed through that tunnel, we always lost satellite navigation and the radio would go haywire. Something to do with the thickness or type of metal it was constructed with and the fact that it went right under the river, combined to stop any signals getting through until you came back out the other side.

And then, I find my mind pulled forward, to my time in the facility, whenever I had to use the lifts. I was always so scared of what was coming next that I never really noticed something very important, something Naru had noticed but hadn't ever shared with me. The collar, it never buzzed, never caused me any pain when I was riding the lifts. I recall Richard once telling me that the construction of the lift shaft had been one of the most time consuming and difficult parts of building the whole facility. In order to keep the whole structure from collapsing in on itself, they had to create concrete walls that were a metre thick, going all the way from the mine to the top of the building.

I had often wondered about how the collar worked, how it received the signals to tell it to cause me pain, anywhere from a little sting of warning to a raging inferno of agony. If I am right, then it must be like a radio signal, which means for it to work, the waves have to be able to travel through walls and ceilings. Even the London Underground had wi-fi running all the way through it, in the stations, and on the trains. But, Blackwall was just a tunnel for traffic to go under the Thames. All radio and satellite signals, like wi-fi signals, were waves and they would struggle to get through both the walls of the tunnel and several metres of water. So… if I can get to the tunnel, I may be able to stop the signal from being able to reach the collar, theoretically at least.

'Ok Naru, so far so good, if we can get to the tunnel, but then there is still the whole problem of getting the damn thing off, not to mention the tracker.'

'The bike, remember, it's a Yamaha, what do they all come with as standard?'

'A health insurance plan?'

'Very funny, but you're way out. What is under the seat?'

'The toolkit?'

'Exactly. Screwdrivers, pliers, just what we need.'

'I fail to see just... wait a minute... you're not thinking what I think you're thinking?'

'You tell me.'

'Aside from the fact that would hurt like hell and could result in us bleeding out before we even pull the damn thing out, there would still be the main problem of the collar.'

'That's where the crazy part comes in.... You might want to save a few of those cigarettes you're getting so fond of. Oh, and be sure to buy yourself a nice strong bottle of sake and don't forget to pack your lighter either.'

It takes a few minutes to figure out just what the other part of me is trying to say and as the realisation dawns on me I feel my mouth go dry and lick my lips nervously.

'Well?'

'You're right it's so crazy that there is no way they will have thought of it. But even if by some miracle, we don't kill ourselves or anyone else doing this, we have no idea how long we would need to wait for it to work.'

'I agree, we would likely only have minutes, before they realise what we are up to.'

'It's a lot to risk for a chance that might not even come off. And, we would still need to get to Mum.'

'If it doesn't work, we can always lie, you have got rather good at it after all.'

'But we would be gambling her too.'

'Do you really think our mother would want us to live like this? She would be devastated to think we were putting up with all this for her sake.'

'You're right, if she knew about this, she would want us to try, if there's even a small chance we can get away and then come for her, before they do. But... there is something else, you remember what was in the box? What these people are capable of if they catch us? And there's more, I know, I can feel it, you still aren't letting me see something.'

'If I did, you would never agree to do this. Why do you think they showed us what they did? To break us, to make us willing to do whatever they want, so that we would be spared the same fate.'

'Naru, how can we trust each other if you keep hiding things from me? Whatever it is I have to know, not just what we are risking for ourselves but what we would be risking for her.'

'I told you that you would just overthink it.'

'Naru! Imaimashi! Just tell me or I refuse to go anywhere near that tunnel.'

'Trust me you don't want this memory, I would spare you that Elizabeth, but if you insist, you can find it, it's your head too after all.'

Now that he has agreed I suddenly get a twisting feeling in the pit of my stomach, it comes with the memory that he is keeping from me. I recall gasping, retching, puking my guts up onto the floor, the terrible stench of death, shit and blood, burning my nostrils and Kiko's sickening, mocking laughter at my reaction to what she had shown me. I had been a police officer for five years and seen my fair share of grim scenes but this, it had been something so horrifying, that I couldn't process it. And suddenly, I know. I know that I don't want to see this memory, that it might just be enough to truly break me. I wrench my mind away, beg Naru to keep it, lock it away and I feel his agreement, and that terrible memory fades from my mind like a mirage in the desert. Only now I have an insight into Naru's soul, it's darker than mine, scarred by things I daren't recall, I can only wonder at what other things he has kept from me.

'Well? Are we going to try this or not?'

'I need some time to think it over, just a little more time Naru. Ok?'

A deafening silence…'Naru? Agreed?'

Then... finally... 'Watashitachiha, akodo o motte imasu.'

CHAPTER 10 – RIDE IT LIKE YOU STOLE IT

I wake to my phone vibrating furiously beside me. I had set the alarm for six am. It's already starting to get light out, I can make out gentle rays of sunlight through the bedroom curtains, tiny motes of dust dancing in the golden beams. The sun, the real sun was just outside my window, it's enough to bring a tear to my eye, so long in the dark, I had begun to dream that I was still there, a prisoner under the mountain. I picture the city starting to wake up all around me in my mind's eye, thousands of other people, dragging themselves up out of bed, preparing for the day ahead. It's Tuesday, just that thought alone sends my mind spinning, how long since the naming of a day meant anything to me at all?

Fortunately, the world hasn't moved on all that much in two years, no flying cars or hoverboards yet, no alien invasion from outer space, just the usual sad tales of tragedy and murder, man killing man. I had stayed up late watching the news channel, trying to get myself up to date with global and local events. It was deeply unsettling to see how little had changed while I myself had been pulled to pieces and made anew. A war was going on somewhere in the middle east, it was unclear whether it was over oil or religion, but the end result was the same, more fighting, more killing. A bad earthquake, seven on the Richter scale, had occurred in Southern Italy, causing a whole bridge to collapse, it's not yet known how many might have been hurt or killed, Then, closer to home, another political scandal,

MP's found setting up tax havens for themselves, in league with rich pop stars and several famous footballers, more corruption, more dishonour. A local school boy was missing, he's not been seen for two days, just a young lad, fifteen years old, he was taking a short cut through the local park on his way home from school, the last time anyone could recall seeing him. It was with a heavy heart that I had finally peeled my eyes away from it all.

So many stories, people were wading in shit all over the world, my own personal hell seemed somewhat insignificant in relation. Still, it's all about perspective I guess, it's time I started planning how to wage my own war on the fuckers who abducted me, who did this to me.

Before I was taken, it always helped when I was stressed or anxious about something, to just jump on my motorbike and get out of the city. There was nothing like that feeling of the open road in front of you, the sound of the engine thrumming like a hungry lion underneath you, leaning into the bends, heart soaring as you pull back the throttle coming into a straight. Just thinking about it was helping to raise my spirits already, that and the glorious sunlight streaming in through my window.

Riding the bike also gave me time to think things over. I had come up with some of my best theories on suspects when I was out riding. I was hoping I might get similar inspiration today, while I was out doing my chores for the company. My best plan I had come up with so far was a little thin, so many things could go wrong and I still wasn't sure just how much I trusted Naru to stick to anything we decided upon.

I take another shower, pull out a dainty matching bra and underwear set from the chest of draws at the end of the bed, that I suspect would have made Richard have dirty thoughts when he picked them. Then I dress in a pair of tight blue jeans and a small black t-shirt taken from the next draw down and take my helmet from on top of the wardrobe and a leather biker jacket from off the back of the bedroom door. There are even some decent fingerless gloves inside the helmet and I pull on and lace up a pair of brown leather boots that I find by the front door.

Once dressed for the day I make myself several rounds of toast and brew a coffee so strong that you could leave the spoon in and it would stay upright in the cup. I don't bother with any more TV for now, I have had my fill of bad news and tragedy, I would rather just be alone with my thoughts. I'm half expecting a phone call from Europa, checking up on me, but they must be satisfied with how things are going so far, as the phone stays dead and silent beside me while I eat my breakfast. Naru is silent too, and for once I am happy with that, his darkness pulls at me like a scab that I can't stop picking at. So much anger and violence is there that it frightens me just what I might be capable of when we are together. I know at some point I will need to draw on that anger, to give me the strength I need for what is coming but for now, I need to plan and think, but mostly, I just need to ride....

I check my watch, seven thirty am. I have time to give the bike a little test ride as I am not due at Bishopsgate for another hour and it's only twenty minutes ride from here. Time to scout the tunnel, maybe... but then I might need to check in with my superiors, make sure they don't mind me getting my riding legs back under me. I decide I need to play things safe for now after my rather wobbly start yesterday. I pick up the black smart phone and scroll down through the numbers in the contact list. Richard's name is on there, Kiko's too, as well as several others that I don't recognise. One says Carlos, the other simply says Q. I presume I will be told as and when I might need to call either of them or what their usefulness might be. Instead, for now, I dial the one number that causes a sharp needle of fear to jab into the back of my neck, and makes my teeth clench momentarily as I fight the impulse to throw the phone across the room and smash it into a thousand tiny pieces.

It only rings three times before she picks up. Her salacious voice almost hissing back at me from who knew how many miles away, but she may as well have been standing right behind me the way my body reacts to it. I feel tight, uncertain of myself, my mouth going dry, my voice ready to crack.

"Speak." A simple command, but I find myself at a sudden loss for words... A sigh, "Come now Elizabeth, I am assuming you didn't call me up to make a prank phone call, are you planning on doing anything other than breathing down the phone at me?"

"I... I was just wondering... er, would you, I mean... would the board mind if I.."

"That's quite a stutter you appear to be developing my dear. Is this about your motorbike? Richard did mention you would be very pleased to get on one again. Frankly I can't see the appeal myself, all that filthy air you will be breathing in, no protection from the elements or other drivers for that matter. And where do you put someone once you have drugged and tied them up?"

It's frightening how easily she can read my mind. Does she know what I am planning already? Unko, why did I even call her? I know why, because I simply couldn't bring myself to call Richard. I swallow, take a deep breath and let it out. I do my best to ignore the sarcastic tone that she always takes with me.

"Yes mistress. I was hoping you would allow me to take the bike for a test drive, it has been a while since I rode afterall."

A short pause, musing on whether I am plotting something? I have no idea, maybe it's just to make me feel more anxious than I do already, and, well, it's working. Then, at last.

"Agreed, just don't be late Elizabeth, or I may just decide to take a city break. Do we understand each other?"

"Yes, thank you mistress, I won't be late, I swear it."

"Was there anything else? You don't want to ask me about how your lover boy is coping without you? Not worried that some other little slut is already sucking on his cock?"

"I'm sure that's none of my business, mistress. My master can do as he pleases."

"Oh Elizabeth, you have nothing to worry about, in actual fact, he is pining for you like a little baby wanting to suckle its mother, poor fellow. You must be very good with that tongue of yours, when you aren't stuttering like a fool." I feel my cheeks flush with embarrassment and shame at her words, reminding me what I have shared with Richard, teasing me that she knows exactly how intimate I have been with him, this is what Naru was prepared to die for rather than live with. I want to end this call now, I don't just want to smash the phone anymore, instead I visualise putting it in the microwave on its highest setting and blowing the damn thing to kingdom come. But, there is something I want to know and rather than put myself through this ridicule again, I will ask now and save my blushes.

"Actually, I was wondering about who Carlos and Q might be?"

"Nicely done Elizabeth, changing the subject like that. Bravo. I will tell Richard how you didn't even bother to ask after him, I'm sure it will comfort him to know how quickly his little pet has forgotten about him, now that she has flown the nest." More mockery, my hatred of her is like a sickness inside me, just get on with it kusobitchi!

"Well… since you asked so politely…. Carlos is the man you are to call once you have confirmation of Miss Archer being the White Rabbit and ideally, a location of the little fucker's safehouse, wherever it is they plan their anarchic little raids from. As for Q, come now, you must have heard of James Bond, no? You are to approach Q if you require any gadgetry that you think might prove useful in extracting the information we require, you know the kind of thing I am talking about, listening devices and micro cameras, or if you want, I am sure he could provide you with something a little more amusing, a garrot wire perhaps, a taser gun, something to aid in torturing your pretty little neighbour if she won't tell you what we want to know."

My mind is doing flip flops at her words. They can't expect

me to...., I will never fucking hurt someone for them...

"I didn't think, I mean, surely if you wished to do that why would you need to send me here in the first place?"

"Dear Elizabeth, are you truly so naive. You will do whatever is necessary, do you understand me?... I don't care if you have to peel the skin off her bones, just get us the information we want. Don't forget, you are still on probation. Until you prove yourself a loyal servant once and for all, you will remain subject to further training and punishment."

"I... understand Mistress."

"Of course, you do, just know that I have high hopes for you Elizabeth, your behaviour reflects well or badly on me, since I was in charge of your training. Best you don't fuck up then hmm?"

"No mistress, your will, so I obey."

"So, shall it be. Oh, and don't call me again, if you hear from me before this is all over the outcome will not be pleasant for you or your mother." The phone clicks dead and I find myself simply staring into the blank screen for a few moments. I feel like I've just been put through a damn blender, Kiko's words cutting at my soul like knives. I have to get out of here, I feel trapped, stifling in this place. No more time to think or second guess. I just need to go, get on the bike and ride...

I get up, dump the empty cup and plate in the sink to wash later, put my jacket on, tuck my phone and a few twenty-pound notes inside my right jeans pocket and pick up my helmet from the table. A quick survey of the room and it looks pretty much how I found it when I walked in yesterday. I swipe the bike keys and the card key for the front door up off the kitchen worktop, where I left them last night. And then I'm heading out the door, shutting it with a click behind me. I aim straight for the stairs, not even bothering to press the button for the lift. Within thirty seconds of leaving the apartment, I am in the stairwell. I take the stairs two at a time, using the opportunity to do a bit of light exercise, get my heart rate up a little.

By the time I reach the basement carpark, I am feeling warm from the walk, which is good, because it feels cool and a little damp down here. I'm starting to get a thrill of anticipation as to what type of Yamaha I am going to find, hoping against hope it's not some one, two, five cc learner bike. I hunt for the number that matches my apartment, see them written on small metal signs at head height all along the car park, each space separated by thin metal pillars, going up from one to fourteen to the left and from fifteen upwards to my right. I turn right and work my way past Audi's, BMW's and Mercedes, some saloons, others SUV's, even a few two-seater sports cars. Finally, I pass a large Jeep Cherokee and come face to face with the Yamaha.

It's a moment of purest joy when I realise the make. It's an XSR seven hundred, just about the coolest looking Yamaha that money can buy, and it's damn quick too, despite the mid-range engine size. It's all gun metal black on the petrol tank and the fairing around the headlight. The engine and parts underneath look like they were hammered together by a half-crazed science fiction fan, the exhaust, flaring up like a blunder buss bolted on the side with an industrial nail gun. In short, it looks like the kind of bike that Batman might have kept in his garage for riding at the weekends. E e fakku! Richard has outdone himself, he literally picked out my dream bike.

Wasting no more time, I put on my gloves and pull the full-face helmet down over my head. I swing my right leg over the saddle, my feet on tiptoes as I straddle the bike, just about reaching the floor on either side of me. I grab the handlebars and twist them straight as I tilt the bike slightly to the right and kick the stand away. I slot the key into the ignition, turn it clockwise a quarter turn and the headlights switch on automatically, lighting up the carpark in front of me. Pulling in the clutch with my left hand, I push the ignition button down with my right and the bike roars into life underneath me, the engine rumbling and purring like a cat stroking a ball of smooth silk. I can feel a heady grin splitting my face behind the helmet. This might just be the best thing to happen to me in a long time. I savour this moment for a few seconds longer before pulling in the clutch once more, stamping the gear lever down with my left foot into first gear, then, giving it a little gas with my right hand on the throttle, I start easing the clutch out and the bike pulls away, the handling feeling as slick and smooth as only a Yamaha can be.

The sound of the engine echoes around the carpark as I aim for the exit and, since there is no one else around, I give it little burst of speed before slowing again as I pull out into the light of the day and past the automatic gate that has opened at my approach. I come to a stop and wait for a gap in the traffic to pull out into. I don't have to wait long, just a few seconds and then I am accelerating, up through the gears, doing thirty miles an hour in just a few seconds. I consider the basic map of London as I recall it in my head. I've still got around forty-five minutes before I need to be at Bishopsgate. Enough time for a recce of the tunnel? I feel Naru's unvoiced assent and start heading towards it, the bike beneath me reacting like a well-trained race horse, the low city speeds feel like its chafing at the bit, desperate to be given its head. Alright my black beauty, let's see what you've got....

I am actually cackling with laughter under my helmet now. I am ducking in and around the busy city traffic with an adrenaline fuelled hyper-alertness, my mind in total focus, at one with the machine beneath me. In my early teens my father had high hopes that I might choose to be a professional racing driver one day, he said I had a knack for it, as well as being fearless back then I had some natural balance of focus and quick reactions giving me an edge that most people have to work for years at. From just about as soon as I was walking upright, he had shared with me his two great loves, Japanese motorbikes and the art of Iaido.

At the age of six, as well as presenting me with my first katana sword he had also bought me a dirt bike, a Yamaha scrambler, fifty cc of pure ridiculous joy when you are charging across an empty field, everything around you blurring because of how fast you are going. I had lived and breathed under his tutelage whenever he was home from a tour, teaching me the ways of our ancestors after school and track racing motorbikes at the weekend with he and my mother cheering me on. I can almost hear his booming laugh in my ears as I pull away from a set of lights, some boy racer beside me in a pimped-up Ford Focus, daring me to race him. In three seconds, he is eating my dust, in ten seconds he is just a speck in my wing mirrors.

A few minutes later and I see the tunnel ahead. It's still early enough that the traffic is fairly light, I ease off the throttle, slow to a legal speed and breathe deeply. After everything that has happened to me over the last two years these few precious moments have given me a joy, I thought I had lost to the darkness. And now, I was heading towards a pivotal moment. I can feel it in my bones, the next few minutes are going to determine which way my life is heading, slave or freeman, prey or predator.

As I speed into the tunnel, the sound of the motorbikes' engine echoes off the walls and it sounds like I am riding on the back of a harrier jump jet, the blood is pounding through my veins, like a drum beat in my ears, thudding to a silent rhythm I can't even fathom. I slow right down to thirty, and lift up my visor. I carefully reach my bare finger towards my collar and touch it experimentally.... nothing, not even a slight buzz. The feeling makes me want to leap off the bike with a fist pump, I can't believe it, I was right. Naru was right... And then, I suddenly get the most foolish notion, again I feel Naru's assent at the thought and I just do it... I pull over to the hard shoulder of the road, right up against the tunnel wall and bring the bike to a complete stop, put it into neutral, and, balance on tip toe for a moment. With both hands free, I feel around the collar until I reach a slight raised bump at the back of my neck. I recall the administrator twisting it to open the open the collar before he placed it around my neck all that time ago. Could it be that simple? Have I been overthinking this all along? With the signal cut from the collar, can I simply just… twist… it… off…

And then I am holding the cursed thing in my hands, staring down at it like it's a live viper, expecting it to suddenly lash or leap at me, but it's just a cold piece of metal in my hands, my mind is completely blank, have I just, did I just?… Naru… We're free….

But then I hear a terrible screeching noise, I turn my head over my shoulder and see my death coming towards me at forty miles an hour in the form of a dark blue Skoda Octavia of all things… a fucking Skoda… Tawagoto no kuso sakuhin, if I didn't have my helmet on I would have spat the thought out in disgust.

CHAPTER 11 - BEST LAID PLANS

I have no time to accelerate, no time to jump out of the way. The best I can manage is throwing myself a few feet up into the air, just as the grill of the Skoda hits the back of my Yamaha. The end result is that I don't end up mowed down under the car's front wheels as it smashes my brand-new dream bike to pieces. Instead, I find myself rolling across the cars' bonnet, then bouncing up and over the windscreen, leaving several human sized dents amongst the cracks I create with my own body along the way and catching only blurred outlines of the two shadowy figures within. Then, for a moment, I am completely weightless, I can't tell which way is up or down. Still spinning, I can't catch my breath, can't work out where to put my hands. I hear a sickening crunch and intense pain follows, across my left shoulder and down my arm. Now I see the pavement coming towards me at terrifying speed, too fast to react, too fast to stop what's about to happen.

If I had taken my helmet off rather than just flipping the visor up when I stopped I know this would have been my death coming to greet me, but the helmet takes the worst of the impact as my head hits the ground with sudden bone cracking finality... then blackness... a tunnel of light... what is that? ......

Fog all around me, I can hear someone calling my name. I glide towards the voice, can't feel my legs, can't feel anything at all in fact... A woman? She sounds concerned. Elizabeth? Who's

Elizabeth...? Is this a dream? Wait.... What? ....

I am eight ears old...... My father is standing before me, dressed in full Iaido fighting regalia. The look of intense disappointment written on his face tells me all I need to know. I am on my knees before him, defeated, again, dressed in novice white. I am exhausted, taking deep gasping breaths, sweat streaming down my brow, my uwagi and hakama are stained with the salt of my efforts. In contrast, my father is as cool as an early spring morning, his breathing deep and even, his stance perfect. He has sheathed his katana, holding it lightly at his side, one hand on the scabbard, keeping it steady while his other rests with disguised readiness on the hilt. My katana lies several feet from me, knocked from my hands by his last strike.

"Fututabi!" He barks at me...

Kiko is marching me deeper into the cells, along a corridor I have only been down once before. Wait... wasn't I just? ... How did I? ....

Each moment is bringing me closer to our destination and the thought of where we are going is drawing fear out of me like poison from a wound. I am counting the steps, jut twenty more before we get there, nineteen, eighteen. Please, I don't want this, not again, I will go mad, I know it, please... seven... six... I am sinking to the floor, cringing under her glare, she is pulling me up, back onto my feet, smiling her serpent smile, three... two... I can see it now, a small hole in the floor, the sounds emanating from it are cries of utter despair, barely recognisable as human anymore. Please no, not the pit... not again...

The phone is ringing, where did I leave the damn thing? I'm coming, I know it's here somewhere... ah... there it is... "Hello?" ... "It's the hospital, we have your mother, she was out wandering in the middle of the night, fell in the road, one of the neighbours found her, just blind luck she didn't die of exposure or get hit by a car. It's called sundowning, part of her dementia, the next stage. It's time she went into residential care, she's not safe to be at home anymore"... "Can I speak to her?" ... "Yes, she's just here... one moment"... "Mum?" ... "I couldn't find him Naru, where is he?" ... "He's gone Mum, remember?" ... "No, it's not true, he said he was coming home"... "Please Mum, look I'll be there soon"... "Tell your father I do not expect to be kept waiting any longer. I won't be stood up again"...

"Look, you hardly know this woman." A man's voice, one I don't recognize, southern accent, clipped and precise. I feel like I have been floating and sinking at the same time, somewhere deep and dark, a void or great lake, the air thick like syrup, was I drowning?

"I have a responsibility now." Is that Megan's voice, almost sounds like an echo? I think so..., what the... where am I? What was I... oh... yeah... oh Kuso!

The sudden recall blows my fogged thoughts away like a swift breeze, as my mind begins to wake from whatever layer of unconsciousness I have been residing in, the realm of the physical is pulling at my senses with utter disregard for my broken and bruised body.

The first and most immediate sensation is pain, like burning, all down my left arm, but mostly in the left side of my head. I can hear and feel my pulse like a drumbeat, pounding against my skull and throbbing its way down my left arm. I try to tell myself, pain is good, it means I'm still alive, for now at least, but it's a hard sell.

I open my eyes a crack, but the light is brilliant white, the kind you can only get from unnatural fluorescent lightbulbs, it intensifies the pain in my head a thousand-fold. Ok, bad idea, keep your eyes shut, just breathe, you can do that at least. Even breathing hurts though, my chest feels like I might have cracked a few ribs. And is it any wonder? How could I have been so stupid. Of course, they would be following me, tracking me closely. It should not surprise me, the kind of ruthlessness in which these people deal with problems. The moment I removed that collar, I became a potential risk to all their dark schemes and plans for me. I wonder how long I have before they send someone to finish me off, wherever I am? How long have I been out, have they already taken Mum? Oh Christ what have I done? Haha wa watashi o yurushite.

I must be making some kind of strangled noise or groaning out my anguish as both my visitors stop talking suddenly. Though my eyes are shut, I can feel that they have turned to look at me. The sudden lack of voices in the room draws a quiet background beeping to my awareness. Along with the light and the echoes, I surmise that I must be in hospital, a side room, as I can't hear any other patients?

The pain is becoming a visceral thing now, I swallow bile building in my throat, bite back against all of it. Getting angry helps, I want to growl, snarl, howl my hurt out to the world. I settle for gritting my teeth and hissing my displeasure at my current predicament. Fuck, shit, bollocks to all of it. I have to get out of here, have to get up. Easy to say, not so easy to do.

It takes everything I have just to drag myself up the bed so that I am sitting up, rather than laying down, no longer facing up at the ceiling, I can bear to open my eyes to slits, my heart beat thundering in my ears.

"Elizabeth?" Megan's voice, asking with genuine concern, somehow, she gives my slave name a musical lilt as she speaks, I hadn't noticed that before. I'm guessing the man with her might be her brother, didn't she say that he lived near to her? What I don't understand is how she is here at all, how would she know to come looking for me, we literally just met after all?

"Where am I?" The words come out husky and little more than a whisper, but Megan hears me all the same. Drawing close to the bed, I feel more than see her take my hand lightly in her own.

"You're in the hospital. Don't worry, you are still all in one piece, but it looks like you've slashed up your left arm pretty badly. The doctor said you had also fractured some of your ribs in the crash and that you had swelling on the brain so they put you in a medically induced coma for a few days while they drained some of the fluid away. They said you would be waking any time now that the danger has passed. Looks like they really know their stuff here." No wonder my head hurts so damn much and her words are hitting me as though I am being pelted with stones, it's like having the worst hangover of my life.

However, despite the company's efforts to eliminate me, somehow, I am still alive, for now at least. I reach up to my neck gingerly, fearing to find the dreaded torture device reattached there. The relief when I feel bruised but bare skin instead, is enough to momentarily silence the pain in my head. Euphoria, just for a fleeting moment, before the pulsing starts anew, reminding me just how mortal I am and how close I just came to losing it all.

I squeeze Megan's hand in my own, my silent thanks for giving enough of a shit to seek me out and be here when I woke. I can't help but find her speech patterns intriguing, this way she has of telling me everything in a great rush, dumping her information on me all at once without pausing for breath, I recall her doing the same back at the apartment. Yet there is an almost musical rhythm to it, a deep intelligence rearing up in the spaces between her words. I suspect she speaks like she types, with eloquence, speed and precision, calculated for maximum efficiency, to give as much information and detail as she can. I bet she is damn good at her job, and maybe somewhere on the autistic spectrum? Either that or she may just have the highest IQ of anyone I have ever met. But she still hasn't told me what I want to know.

"Which hospital?" Again, a hoarse whisper, a little extra pain to my ribs just to gather my breath to speak. I am starting to feel anxiety, nervousness, creeping in on me. Europa have had days, why haven't they simply killed me in my sleep? The only reason I can think of at the moment is that they may want to see me suffer first, for disobeying, for doing the unthinkable. Is there someone here right now, outside the door, ready to fit another collar around my neck and drag me back to that place where all my nightmares began?

"You're in St Barts, name's Graham by the way." It's the man who speaks this time, he seems really pissed at me. Understandable, given what Megan has likely told him about me. I blink, try to clear some of the sleep from my eyes and squint at him under the piercing glare of the hospital lights. He has a hard face, his hair is closely shaved so he appears almost bald, grey stubble and thick brows completing his look. I close my eyes to the harsh light and Megan's brothers scrutiny, try to picture where the hospital is in my head. I think I have come further west from the tunnel, damn it my run of bad luck just keeps going. I figure it would take about two hours to get to Mum's care home in Southend from here, if I was sticking to the speed limit. If I still had the bike, I could be there in less than forty-five minutes. With a fast-enough car, I might just make it in an hour. I have to believe they haven't taken her yet. They would have had no need to, until they are certain I have actually woken from my injuries, plus I still have the tracker in me which shows me as going nowhere fast. Right now they are still holding all the cards, but I mean to do something about that and I need to do it soon while I might still have some element of surprise on my side. But first, I need to warn Megan and her brother. Even if she isn't the White Rabbit, sooner or later they will send someone for her and from what Kiko said on the phone, I suspect they would be just as happy to torture information out of her as to find it out more surreptitiously, like they had originally planned by sending me in the first place.

I clear my throat to speak my piece but the door to the room suddenly opens to my right, a nurse holding it steady, stating matter-of-factly, over her shoulder, "Oh good, yes she is awake, you can see her now..." Then turning to me, "A police-man is here to see you Elizabeth, about the accident, he says it can't wait, would your two friends mind waiting outside a moment?" My heart is in my throat at her words. Before I have a chance to speak, Megan and her brother bustle past her, mum-bling that they will go and get coffee and come back.

I'm still having to squint my eyes to the light but I don't need to see well to recognise the tall, slim frame of the man who walks in. It's not just his gait, I would recognise his aftershave anywhere, I had slept with him pressed up against me enough times after all. What I can't understand is what, of all people, he was doing here.

"Richard?" My voice is still little more than a whisper, but he turns to look directly into my eyes at the sound. He is wear-ing his very concerned expression, reminds me of the time I first met him back in my cell, the look on his face makes me think I must look even worse than I feel. As the door swings shut behind him, he rushes to my side and clasps my hand in his. He leans in and kisses me gently on the forehead and as he pulls away, I can make out a piece of the shining metal collar gleaming under-neath his shirt. "Oh Richard, hontoni moshiwakenai." I can feel Naru's wariness fighting its way past my thoughts of affection for this man. If they have sent him here with a collar on, it means he is their tool now, as much as I was. It would be just like Kiko to make things as painful as possible for both of us. Has she sent him here to kill me then?

"Oh Lizzy, Christ in heaven what have they done to you?" Strangely, I hear no anger in his voice, just worry, and maybe a hint of regret?

"I'm so sorry Richard, I just couldn't.... I mean... I had to try... you know?" My words are stuttered and heartfelt. I can feel myself welling up, tearing up inside as I realise, I have lost, and not only that, I may well have doomed my mother and lover in the process." Naru's anger at my thought is like a bucket of cold water to my face, not just over fear for Mum, he doesn't like my turn of phrase for the man standing before me. What was he then? Jailor, rapist, no, I can see it in every line of his face, this man cares deeply about me, it's why they have sent him, why they have collared him, to cause me more pain, more suffering to know they have done this to him.

Richard draws a chair in close, still holding my hand tightly, not taking his eyes off mine. He reaches into the pocket of the long black coat he is wearing with his free hand and pulls out an exact replica of the cursed device he is wearing around his own neck. My feeling of revulsion at the sight of it is physical, dizziness, nausea, damn I think I am going to be sick.

"They wanted me to tell you, this need not go any further. You can put this on, continue the mission, let this just be a warning. They will leave your mother out of it for now as well." He lays the collar with shaking fingers on my lap while he talks, it takes every bit of control I have left in me not to vomit all over it. I lean back and close my eyes, breathing deeply, ignoring the extra pain this causes to my ribs, I just need to suck in air and clear my head, the world had started to tilt and spin, it feels like someone has their fingers around my throat, slowly crushing my windpipe. I couldn't be more terrified if he had placed a fucking black mamba in my lap.

For some reason, I feel the deepest urge to go to the toilet, my bladder suddenly seems fit to burst. On top of all the other indignities I have suffered, I do not want to add wetting myself to the list. I pluck the collar delicately between my finger and thumb and place it very slowly and carefully on the hospital table by my bedside. I tug at the rail on the side of the bed and lower it down, then ask him gently,
"Help me to the bathroom, would you?"

"Of course, here ... wait ... let me just ..." Richard moves fast as he talks, working his way around the bed. He helps me pull the IV needle from my arm and very slowly and carefully, with a lot of swearing and cursing I find myself sitting at the edge of the bed, a half foot drop to the floor seeming like a jump into a canyon. I grit my teeth; this is not going to be pleasant....

Fuck! Motherfucking bastard... tawagoto to kusoboro! The impact as my feet touch the ground jars up through my body into my arm and head and sears me with agony. Richard has to hold on to me tightly as I nearly sink to the floor in defeat. Leaning my good arm over his shoulder he helps me to slowly wend our way around the bed and the few metres to the bathroom door seem more like miles. I had never wanted painkillers more in my entire life, but right now, I had an even more pressing urge. I am only a few seconds away from crossing my legs, pissing all down myself and crying like a baby by the time I reach the toilet. Richard helps to lower me gently on the seat and steps back mopping a trail of sweat from his brow and turning his back to me, even now he is still trying to act the gentleman.

"You're heavier than you look." He breathes out deeply following this observation, clearly a little out of shape after so many years living underground.

I can't bring myself to reply, the relief I am feeling right now is all that matters as I empty my bladder's contents. But it's not long before my head starts up its regular drumbeat once more...

I can't let it beat me, I have to think, push past the pain, try to come up with a way to win. Naru is pacing around inside my head too, making threats, growling at the man with his back to me. In my weakened state I am not sure what I could do to escape from this situation but Naru is starting to bring dark thoughts to mind, my hands clenching into fists, my teeth bared, he wants to tear Richard's throat out, and there's more.... He would rather die than put that collar back on, and I, well, I second that notion.

Richard clears his throat while I am still finishing wiping myself clean and when I don't answer he half turns to look at me. Whatever he sees in my eyes seems to unnerve him and he takes an almost imperceptible step away from me. How on earth he could be worried what I could do when I need his help just to get up off the toilet I don't know, then again, ... Naru I need you to back off, please. I reason that Richard is many things but he has been the closest thing I had to a friend in that place and the only person who had held or touched me with comfort in mind for nearly two years. He doesn't deserve for me to repay him with violence but I can feel it building within me. If he insists on making us wear that fucking thing, I swear... watashi wa watashi ga motte iru subete to tatakau koto ni narimasu.

I watch Richard with a growing wariness, what are his orders if I don't agree to put the collar on? Can I trust him while he is wearing one himself? I know from experience just how compelling it can be to do as you are told with one of those things around your neck. But before my thoughts start circling down ever darker corridors, Richard suddenly turns and comes towards me in a rush. He leans right past my shoulder and flushes the toilet lever for me. My own body reacting without thought, I barely have time to stop myself from slamming my fist right into his chin. His face is suddenly inches from mine, so close I can smell the mint on his breath, and he pulls back slowly, maintaining intense eye contact, holding out a hand to help me up, doing his best to smile despite the awkwardness.

"Look, I have a plan." His words come out in a hushed whisper and I carefully place my right hand in his, letting him pull me slowly to my feet. I quirk an eyebrow at his statement, not daring to believe anything he might have to say just yet. Having ensured I am standing up, he un-shoulders a satchel from his back and begins pulling out its contents and placing them on the small worktop around the bathroom's sink. All clothes, not the feminine kind, well, everything besides the matching black underwear. Other than that, there is a pair of blue jeans, a small casual grey shirt, a thin black hooded jumper, a beanie hat and a pair of grey plimsoles just like the ones that I had woken up wearing in the Humvee. Before giving me a chance to say more, he also unholsters a gun, a semi-automatic silver and black Beretta, from under his coat and suit jacket, dumping it with a metal clunk next to the clothes. Lastly, he pulls a set of car keys and black wallet from his pockets and puts them down on top of everything else.

"I don't understand," I say, because I am not sure what to make of any of this, except my eyes keep being drawn back to the gun, Naru is thrusting himself forward again inside my head, he wants that gun so badly I am not sure I can stop him if he lunges for it. I can hear my breathing coming faster, my fight or flight responses poised for something to happen. "Wait, there's two more things," at this he pulls out a scalpel and a syringe full of some orange coloured liquid from inside his coat pocket and flourishes them in front of me, placing them down beside the gun.

"Richard, what the fuck is all this?" I can't help the question coming out of my mouth as fast as I think it. "Well I can't say I have missed your foul language Elizabeth, sometimes I forget just how much vulgarity can come out of that pretty mouth of yours."

"Richard please, just tell me what you have in mind before I go for that gun and things get really interesting in here." I see him swallow at my statement, weighing my words and choosing his next carefully. "There's no need for that, I am giving it to you. Look.... wait, I need to go back. It's like this..."

"Richard, my head is pounding like a fucking jackhammer and my arm basically feels like someone plunged it into a volcano, please just tell me what the hell you are planning on doing with that knife and syringe and what exactly all this is?" I wave at all the paraphernalia by the sink as I speak, even this small action causing my arm to burn and sting a little more than it was already.

"It's all for you, to get you out of here, to free you from all this."

"What are you?" ...

"No, wait, please just listen..." He waits for me to nod for him to continue, I do my best to fold my arms, unwilling to feel anything more than sceptical at his optimistic statement, given both our current circumstances, though it hurts like a kuso ttare and leaves me grimacing at him, impatient to hear him out.

"The fact is I knew at some point you would figure out a way to get the collar off. When I heard about who you were before, from that first day I came to find you I could see the intelligence and the steel burning in your eyes. I must admit though; I didn't expect you to succeed so quickly." I open my mouth to speak but Richard holds his hand out a little, bidding me to wait to hear him out.

"You know the company has already fitted wireless signal boxes all through that tunnel now? What you did can never be done again, at least not in London. Anyway, I'm digressing, the point is, I have been trying to work out a way to help get you free since that first day I saw you in the cells, but I knew there was no chance of getting you out of the facility without the consensus of the other board members. I had to persuade them how useful you could be, how I and Kiko had you well trained, willing to do whatever we wanted. Something you very nearly messed up when you stood up to that guard in the servant's quarters. So, they insisted on harder training, they had to make sure they had you truly broken. Gods I am so sorry you had to go through all that Lizzy. For my part, I had been doing all I could to persuade them to give you one last chance, to prove you were prepared to do anything that was asked of you..." Richard takes a brief pause for breath before going on, my own breath is held, waiting on his every word.

"I must admit I thought for one terrible moment that they had actually decided to kill you in that tunnel..." He has to pause again for a moment, the thought of me dead clearly something that brought him genuine hurt. I find my good arm reaching out to him, he is pouring his heart out to me, has been trying to help me from the beginning and my own heart is reaching back, most of it anyway. Naru is still nervously circling around inside me, if he was a cat his hackles would be standing to attention. This conversation is making him feel very uncomfortable indeed, his mind fixed on that gun left on the counter.... 'Ochitsuite kudasai Naru-san, just hear what he has to say, please.' Richard clears his throat once more, clasps my offered hand between his own and continues,

"I also know how Kiko and the rest of those sadists think, anticipated they would want to send me here to be the one to put the collar back around your neck, so I tried to make out it was the last thing I wanted to do and before I knew it they were making all kinds of threats of what they would do to you if I didn't go. So, well, here I am." His explanation has physically stunned me. I don't really know what to say. He has risked everything on a chance that I might prove as clever and unbroken as he hoped, so that I might escape. The fact is, I am far more broken than any of them ever realised. But, despite that, I still got the collar off. However, the great floor in his plan was all too obvious. All he had succeeded in doing was swapping places with me. I unclasp my good hand from his and pluck at the top button of his shirt, revealing the extent of his sacrifice. He stares back at me with a sad smile that brings a tear unbidden, tracking down my cheek.

"Don't be sad for me Lizzy, I don't deserve it from you of all people. Besides, you haven't heard it all yet. I'm going to need you to make it look like you took me by surprise and escaped, that way, when they take me back, I may be able to persuade them I am still on their side in all this."

"You really think they would believe me capable of that? I mean look at me... I can barely stand, let alone fight."

"Well that's what this is for." At his last words, he picks up the syringe. "It's noradrenaline, amongst a few other things you're better off not knowing, I swiped it from one of the labs months ago, there's enough juice in here to give you the stamina of a rhinoceros I should think, at least for a few hours, should help with the pain too." I am shaking my head at his words and reply with a venomous reaction to his proffered wonder drug that surprises me.

"You know I think I hate needles as much as I do lifts, they have brought me nothing but trouble. Just how safe is that thing? How do I know it won't put me in cardiac arrest or knock me out? This could all just be another trick and I will wake up back in a cell with more monsters waiting to hurt me." My words are coming out in a rush, my heartbeat racing, anxiety levels going through the roof, I'm backing away, sudden fear and panic threatening to overwhelm me. But Richard is steadying me, shaking his head, promising me he would never do that to me again, declaring his love for me in a whispered plea for me to listen to him.

It brings me back to myself with a jolt, my breathing has calmed, my mind is suddenly sharp and focussed once more. I was a good cop; I had always had a knack for knowing when someone was telling the truth. Richard's heart felt words cut through my fears and I know that he is genuinely planning to help me. But I don't say it back, I can't, Naru is roaring inside me like an angry lion, his hatred almost too much to bear at hearing those words. It's all I can do not to snarl at Richard as Naru's feelings push hard against my own. The result is that my head starts to throb so badly that I have to turn and collapse over the toilet bowl, no longer able to hold back the vomit that has been trying to boil its way up out of my stomach ever since I woke. I choke and gasp as the hot liquid rushes up out of my mouth and close my eyes, trying not to breathe in the awful smell that follows. I hear Ricard sigh dramatically behind me, I imagine being violently sick is not exactly the reaction someone wants after having openly declared their love.

When I have finished retching and spitting, Richard helps me over to the sink so I can rinse my mouth and swig a few handfuls of cold water to ease the burning and stinging in my throat.

I feel shaky and weak, not sure how on earth I am going to carry off this plan of his. I imagine we don't have much more time before the company send someone else to check up on us and more than that, I need to to get to my Mother. I can feel it like a hardstone building in my stomach, if I don't leave soon, they will get to her first and use her to bend me to their will once more.

I hold out my hand and motion for him to pass me the syringe. This time I will do the plunging myself and pray to whatever gods up there watching over all this that I won't die, that it will give me the strength I need to escape. I feel the cold, smooth glass roll into my palm and close my hand around it. At my questioning look, Richard points directly to my chest, of course, it figures, with a needle half the length of my arm, where else would it need to go? ...

No more time for indecision, no more time for fear. I slam the needle hard into my chest and push down on the plunger with my thumb as quickly as it will allow, then rip it back out of my body and drop it in the sink. The result is instantaneous, I feel a jolt of pure energy blast through me and for a moment I feel like my whole body is going to explode. I am taking great breaths, imagine my eyes have dilated to the size of saucers. The pain in my arm and head have dulled to little more than an itch that I can't scratch, I can't even feel pain in my chest anymore. Naru is mirroring my feelings, he is strong and for the first time in what seems like forever I can feel him smiling. We can do this. We can...

"Better?" Richard's question is said with a hint of mirth as he can obviously see the difference it has made in my bearing. A few moments ago, I was throwing up, barely able to stand, now I am standing tall, and feel like I could run to my mother if I had to.

"What's next?" As I ask the question, my mind starts to catch up with Richard's plan, now the pain has virtually gone, I can think with clarity and my eyes alight on the scalpel, suddenly understanding its purpose. Richard confirms this as he picks it up once more and asks me to turn my right arm towards him. He clasps my upper bicep tightly in his hand and squeezes the flesh until he locates the small lump under the skin. Without waiting for me to argue he acts swiftly, slicing into my arm around the lump and then squeezing underneath it until the small piece of metal that has been tracking my every move for the last two years pops out of my arm and drops with a gentle plink on the white floor tiles at my feet.

As blood begins to pour freely down my arm, I watch, fascinated, barely registering it as pain, or something I should be worried about. Richard pulls out a bandage from his satchel and after first ripping and holding a piece of it tightly against my arm for a few moments to soak up the blood, he then starts binding it tightly round and round my arm. I am smiling down at him as he does this, feeling a little lightheaded but otherwise strong and ready for anything.

Minutes later, Ricard has finished his work and I waste no time in tugging at the hospital gown's loops at my back and then pulling it off me with more force than was really necessary. I am standing in the bathroom completely naked in front of Richard and he can't help drawing in his breath sharply at seeing me suddenly standing before him in all my glory, having had no time to politely turn his back. I can't be letting him get distracted though and so turn to the worktop and begin plucking clothes one by one off of it and dressing hurriedly.

I am soon fully dressed in jeans and hoody, a beanie hat pulled on tight to cover my bandages, then tugging on my shoes, while Richard has bent down and picked the tracker up off the floor, twisting it in his fingers doing his best not to watch me changing in front of him.

Lastly, I pick the gun up off the counter, its weight is very reassuring in my hands and this makes me feel nearly as good as when the first rush of adrenaline flushed into my blood stream. I automatically check the safety, pull back the action and sight down the barrel. Then I unclip the magazine, happy to see it is fully loaded, slap it back into place and tuck it into the back of my jeans, extremely grateful for the cold steel pressing into my back.

Richard places the tracker carefully down next to the sink and before I have a chance to stop him, he pulls the collar meant for me out of his coat pocket and clasps it around his neck above the other. He must have picked it up off the table when he was helping me to stand.

"Holy fuck! I can't believe you just did that. Anata wa naniwoshita." I am staring at him open mouthed.

"I believe it may be the most foolish thing I have ever done." The crazy bastard is actually grinning as he says this.

"No shit Sherlock. You had better hope they never set both of those things off at once. Christ Richard!"

"I think that's enough blaspheming for one day Elizabeth. Besides, it should buy you some time as they will think you are back under their control once more. Now, I need you to get on and knock me out. But before you do there are just a few more things I have to tell you. Firstly, the car, it's a BMW M series, midnight blue, it's parked in car park C, over in the left-hand corner on the second floor. There is a tracker magnetically attached under the rear driver's side wheel hub, I suggest you pull it off and stick it to another car before you go. Secondly, and most importantly, the name of the mountain is An Teallach."

"This is so fucked up Richard, I can't believe you want me to do this. And what do you mean by the mountain, why are you telling me?"

"Come now Lizzy, the same reason I picked you in the first place. Of everyone who has ever been brought under the mountain, you had the highest chance of escaping and, I hope, of liberating those still being held there. Oh, which reminds me, you shouldn't go to the police, even if you get to your mother in time. The company has taken the time to give Elizabeth Shaw the back story of a paranoid schizophrenic with violent delusions, and a nice long rap sheet full of offences. If you turn up at a police-station they are more likely to arrest you and throw you in a mental asylum than listen to what you have to say."

"You are just full of joyful news today." I am still buzzing like crazy from the gargantuan cocktail of drugs rushing through my body. It all feels like everything is happening too quickly, like I should have more time to speak to Richard before I leave, after all he has just sacrificed so much for me already, but now, now he wants me to truly hurt him. Watashi wa sore o okonau koto ga dekiru to wa omoimasen. And even more, the thought of deliberately going back to the mountain where I was broken, seems completely insane at this moment. Fuck that, I want to get as far and fast from there as I can.

.. 'I can do it'.... 'Naru?' .... 'Let me come forward'...' What do you mean? ... NO ... wait... just wait'...

I reach out and clasp at Richard tightly, staring into his light-blue eyes, trying to pluck up the courage for what comes next. I press my forehead to his and kiss him gently on the lips just once.

"Arigatogozaimashita Richard-san." At my heartfelt thankyou he gives me a quirk lipped smile and with a theatrical flourish he pulls off his long coat and holds it out for me to shrug into.

"They said it's going to be unusually cold tonight. Hmm... It suits you." I blush under his gaze, thank him again and before I can think of any more excuses to back out, I finally let Naru through my mental walls...

CHAPTER 12 - NO MORE I LOVE YOU'S

There is a strange pressure that fills my head and I am pulled backwards, deeper inside myself somehow, now only able to watch as an observer, rather than participate in whatever comes next.

Naru wastes no time and slams our knee hard between Richard's legs. The air leaves his body and he folds-in on himself, clutching at his groin while making a terrible noise, like an animal with its foot caught in a trap. We step forward, shove him hard and he stumbles and crashes against the bathroom wall, slipping down it into a heap on the floor. Finally, we turn towards the toilet basin and before I realise what Naru is doing, it's too late to stop him. We pull the ceramic cistern lid off the toilet and swing it, with speed, at Richard's head. He has no time to defend himself, his arm only half raised as he sees what's coming. The lid hits him with a bone-chilling crunch and he drops like a stone, unconscious or dead I can't be sure, a great pool of blood spreading across the bathroom floor from the back of his head. What have we done? Have we killed him? Watashi no yujin watashi o yurushite.

I can feel a great sense of satisfaction emanating from Naru and, his task complete, he seems happy to let me retake control of our body. I immediately kneel down and press my fingers against Richard's throat, praying for a pulse, for a few moments my heart is in my mouth, then, yes, it's faint but it's there. I am so angry at Naru right now I can't even begin to explain the depth of betrayal I am feeling. How could he do this after every-thing Richard has just done to help us escape.

...'He wanted us to do this, it had to look realistic'... 'Fuck you'... 'It needed to be done, and you know you wouldn't and couldn't do it, you are too weak'... 'You nearly fucking killed him Naru! ... Naru! ... Naru? ... You fuck'....

I guess he's ignoring me again. Fine, two can play at that game. 'You hear me Naru, you can stay away from now on, how the hell can I trust you? You're a psychopath, just like those bas-tards that took us'....

I can't just leave Richard to bleed out on the floor and so reach for the emergency cord hanging from the ceiling and yank on it hard. I snatch up the last few things from around the sink, put them in the satchel and draw it over my shoulder. Sparing one last glance at Richard's still form, I turn on my heels and burst out of the bathroom door.

I don't know how long I have before the company realise what has happened, before they go after Mum but I have no more time to waste. I bustle out of the side room, turning my head left and right, looking for the exit. I see some double doors to the left that look like they lead to another corridor and so begin heading that way, keeping my eyes down, looking at the floor, passing a few nurses and other hospital employees talking in the corridor outside another side room. One of them pauses and tries to say something to me but I ignore them and speed up my pace. It won't be long before the alarm is raised and they find Richard's prone form on the bathroom floor.

As I step through the double doors I pause and check left and right again. A longer, wider corridor heads off in both direc-tions, an exit sign to the right, so I start to jog in that direction, my worry and anxiety about everything building up in me and forcing me to move faster. I am about to start an all-out run, when I hear Megan calling my name. She and her brother have just walked in through a side door I hadn't noticed in my panic to get away. I slow down and wave them over to me, not stopping, still walking hurriedly towards the exit.

"Elizabeth? Where are you going? Isn't that the coat the policeman was wearing?" I don't have time for the third degree, or a real explanation, but at least I have the chance to warn them both. I shake my head and keep aiming for the main doors.

"Look, Megan, I don't know how you knew to find me here but you need to know that you and your brother are both in very real danger." I wait for them both to share a silent look between them and continue as we walk.

"There are people, well a company technically, called Europa. Among other things, including human trafficking and enslavement, they are currently working for the British government under a black budget. Unfortunately for you, they seem to think that you might be a terrorist, part of some anarchic cell called Wonderland, that you are hell bent on bringing down the government and the current status quo. I was sent to London to find out more about you and, if it turned out you were the one they were after, they wanted me to join your team, then betray your location once I had you all in one room. However, I had no intention of helping them and as soon as I got the chance I tried to leave and, well, they ran me down like a dog in the street....

Quite frankly I couldn't care less if you are a terrorist or not, I have problems of my own to deal with right now but since you have shown me real kindness, I feel I owe you this much. You both should run, get out of the city, fuck it, out of the country if you can, lay low and never stop looking over your shoulders, these fuckers are ruthless, sadistic bastards, believe me when I say they will not hesitate to torture or kill you and your loved ones." At my words both brother and sister have gone silent, the weight of what I have said likely stunning them, for a moment, into disbelief. I can almost see the gears whirring inside Megan's head as I catch her gaze out of the corner of my eye. There, is fear there but something more, determination, anger. It's all I need to know to confirm what Europa suspected all along, I am almost certain she is the White Rabbit after all.

Her brother has a look of thunder on his face too. Whether that's directed at me or not, I am past caring. With a fully loaded hand gun tucked into my jeans and the synthetic adrenaline pumping around my system I am not planning on taking any more shit today. In fact, the way I am feeling at the moment, I almost want him to start something, just to release some of the pent up, nervous energy flooding my senses. But, before Graham has taken a step closer, Megan speaks with calm measured words as though we were just discussing the weather.

"I thank you for the information and the advice Elizabeth, but there is something you should know about me. I am an Archer, we don't run, my brother and I are hunters, we are not prey. We will turn the tables here I can assure you. We have been anticipating something like this, it was only a matter of time before someone started connecting the dots, we have contingencies in place, people we can count on when we need them." Her brother nods grimly at her heartfelt speech and in that moment I name him Grim in my head, since I doubt the grumpy bastard has ever smiled in his whole life. I also wonder if the gang call him the Cheshire Cat, like Little John in Robin Hood, the irony in the name would suit him. As for Megan, her bearing has completely changed. Where before, she came across as a caring and intelligent, yet naive introvert, she was now pacing along beside me with a warrior's gait and grace, her head held high, her eyes watchful and focussed. I did not doubt her words, or sincerity in that moment, and a part of me rejoiced to think that I might just have given Wonderland their next target for the gang's special kind of anarchic fuckery.

"And so, where do you go now in such a hurry Elizabeth, and what happened to the Policeman whose coat you are now wearing?" As she finishes the question, we both push open our sides of the large double doors at the end of the corridor, back out into daylight, from the height and direction of the sun in in the sky I make a rough estimate that it's around four or five o'clock in the afternoon. I spot the sign for the carpark that

Richard told me to head for and start upping my pace again, almost turning my fast walk into a jog.

"That was no policeman, he was a friend, sort of, well, it's complicated, but thanks to him I stand a chance of getting to my mother before they do."

"Your mother?" Her words come with compassion laced in them. I nod once, my face turned to stone. I glance across at Grim, I imagine we look rather alike right now. We are all storming across the hospital grounds, fortunately it's one of the few places where people moving in a hurry is not likely to be arousing much suspicion. While we talk, I am constantly surveying the different people we pass, looking for any sign of recognition or potential threat.

"They threatened to do things to her, awful things, to both of us, if I didn't do what they wanted. As soon as they realise I have gotten away from them, they will send people for her, I have to make sure I get there first, get her to safety."

"I will come with you, help you, Graham too." This woman keeps on amazing me every moment I speak with her. Any normal person would be running for the hills, or screaming to have me sectioned by now, but to volunteer herself and her brother without even a moment of doubt. Kuso, I can see her now as she truly is, a leader, a fighter. Her brother too has again nodded at her word, his stoic silent agreement like an army sergeant ready to follow his commander into battle. But I am shaking my head, even before she has finished speaking.

"I can't ask you to do that, either of you. You don't owe me anything. This is my mother, my problem." I feel Megan's hand gently take hold of my wrist and we come to a stop, me preparing to make my goodbyes. I'm still scanning people's faces and bodies for potential violence lying behind their eyes, or in their movements. We are next to the car park entrance now, I can see the door to the stairs off to my right. I really need to go before the police, or worse, Europa agents arrive. I can't help the sudden surge of guilt at the thought of Richard's body bleeding out on the floor of the bathroom, kuso, I am so sorry Richard.

"I have said I will help you and I mean to. It seems to me you have a real knack for getting yourself into trouble, while my brother and I happen to be specialists in causing it. Consider yourself under the care of Wonderland." At this she lets go of my arm and holds out her hand to shake on her offer. I don't know what to say, I am literally speechless. All I can manage is a grateful nod of my head and then clasp her hand tightly in return. I don't have the time or the inclination to argue about this anymore and in all honesty the idea that I might have some help after everything I have been through is almost enough to break me, it's been so long since I felt that kind of camaraderie, since I have been part of a team....

CHAPTER 13 – FAST AND FUCKING FURIOUS

We are all jogging through the carpark, I can see the one car ahead that I want, exactly where Richard said it would be, a brand-new BMW M series five door saloon, it's a beautiful piece of German engineering and I am almost salivating at the thought of driving it. I briefly explain about the tracking device under the rear wheel arch as we draw closer, so Grim runs ahead and ducks his head under the car to search for it. In a matter of seconds, he has pulled out a small silver box from under the car with a flashing L.E.D light on the top. With a calm aloofness that gives the impression he does this kind of thing all the time, Grim strolls over to a silver Toyota nearby, and sticks the tracker in place underneath it's front wheel-arch, out of sight. He flashes me the first smile I have seen him make and I almost laugh out loud at the sight. I turn my head away, trying not to grin back at him, this is no time for fucking around after all.

I unlock the car with the key fob in my coat pocket, and climb into the driver's seat. I quickly readjust the seat and the mirrors while Megan slips into the passenger seat next to me and Grim gets in behind her in the back. I push down the clutch and press the push button ignition switch behind the steering wheel. The engine purrs to life, so I stick the M series into reverse, marvelling at the smooth gear shift, and swing the car out of the space with ease.

I can feel my brain hardwiring, bringing my focus into a pinpoint, my heart is beating fast but steady, the adrenaline appears to have worn off a little but, whatever else was in the drug Richard gave me, is keeping my pain at bay and my mind sharp, for now at least. I click my seatbelt in place and warn the others to do the same. With calm precision I accelerate to a safe speed, keeping the car moving under ten miles an hour and weave my way out of the huge car park, not wishing to draw any attention. I am desperate to put my foot down but I need to get out of the hospital grounds first as I don't want to risk running any pedestrians down or causing anyone to recall us leaving. I can feel the gun digging into my back, so reach behind me, pull it out and slide it into the driver's door shelf.

"Is that what I think it is?" A slightly raised eyebrow the only sign of potential alarm on Megan's face as she glances meaningfully at the shelf where I just put the gun.

"If you think it's a fully loaded semi-automatic Beretta nine millimetre, then yes, it is exactly what you think it is." I am trying to be sassy with my reply but I am not sure why, I think I must be trying to impress these two. I feel the need for them to know I am just as capable at certain skills as they are, that they don't need to babysit me.

"Another gift from your friend?"

I swallow bile at Megan's words, recalling the moment that the ceramic toilet lid hit Richard's head, the sickening crunch I had heard. I shake my own head to clear the memory and grit my teeth against the overwhelming guilt that I suspect will continue to haunt me until I can learn if he survived what I did, no, what we did. In the end I just nod at Megan's question, not wishing to discuss it any further. Now is not the time for distraction, I have a job to do. I push the bad thoughts down deep, let Naru deal with them for a while instead.

As I finally pull out onto the main road, I put my racing head on and ease my foot down on the accelerator. The BMW responds like a thoroughbred racehorse charging out of the gates at the start of the grand national. I feel myself pulled back hard against my seat, hear Megan and Grim's collective gasps of terror at the sudden speed we are going. All the anger boiling away under the surface of my thoughts is threatening to bubble over, but I grasp hold of it somehow and twist it inside me, like I did in the interview room, let it become ice, cold and hard. I imagine wrapping steel around my heart for what is to come. If they have hurt her, if they have taken her... I'm coming Mum... I'm coming....

The world is passing by in a blur of colours and sounds that I barely register. All my concentration is on the space ahead of me, on the gaps I can slip the magnificent blue beast I am riding into. I am driving aggressively, using the horn like a call to war and revving the engine so hard, I'm red-lining the needle between gear shifts, the BMW responding like a roaring lion snapping at the heels of some hapless gazelle on the plains of Africa. The other cars ahead clear a path for me, desperate to get away from the teeth gnashing behind them. Megan and Grim have remained deathly silent for the last twenty minutes, no doubt wondering what the hell they were thinking getting into the car with me in the first place, maybe having visions of their lives flashing before their eyes. I glance down at Megan's hand and can see she is holding onto the side of her seat with pale fingers, yet there is a very slight curve to her lips which suggests she may well be enjoying herself despite the fear. I check the interior mirror, adjust it slightly until I can see Grim's face, no change there, he looks just as angry as the first moment I saw him. I scan the road ahead, check my speed. We're doing ninety-five and have finally got some clear road ahead now we are outside of London. I crack my neck and allow myself to relax just a little. So far so good, no police in sight and I estimate that we should be at my mother's care home within thirty minutes at this pace. I take a breath, long and slow. It's time I gave them both a better explanation of what we are up against, of the people who will be coming for them, for me...

They listen intently as I begin my tale. Little more than a raised eyebrow from either of them when I tell them I used to be a detective, like maybe they had guessed that already. An awful scowl begins developing on Grim's face as I tell them what was done to me after I started investigating Darren Winters, of the facility where I was taken, the underground hell of my nightmares. As I describe the collar and how it was used to control me, Megan's face pales as white as her hand. I can see her clenching and unclenching her jaw, a single tear spilling down her cheek at my recollection of events as they unfold before my mind's eye.

For my own part, I manage to keep my voice free of the anger and emotion that has threatened to overwhelm me in the past, focussing on driving the car is a welcome distraction, and I can still feel that cold steel that I have drawn around my heart keeping me steady inside. I can't feel Naru at all, I wonder if I have somehow sealed him off from me, since he was all fierce anger and rage. I haven't told the others about him, I am not sure how to explain what has happened to my mind, that sometimes I am me, sometimes us, sometimes him. Whatever has happened to me it's not like any personality disorder that I have heard of, or my mother ever told me about. I wonder how many people out there can have full blown arguments and conversations with their own mind or soul or whatever the hell we were. The thing that frightens me most about it is that I couldn't stop him acting when he wanted. He would have killed us if not for Megan's swift intervention, I am sure of that now, and I know he wanted to kill Richard, that he didn't care how I felt about it one bit.

For her part, Megan comes clean with me that she actually broke into my apartment that first day we met, since she interprets from my tale that I really had been intending to throw myself off the balcony. For a hacker of her skills, it was no problem for her to crack my lock code and break in to save me. She also explains how she learned what had happened to me after I was knocked off my bike. When I didn't answer the door to her for our dinner date, she had become concerned, asked around and learned that no one had seen me since the Tuesday morning when I had left for work. She had then hacked into the NHS computer system and run a check of my name and description at all the local hospitals, finding me almost immediately.

I haven't told them much about Richard either, I am loath to think too hard about our relationship and what it might have meant, but I brush over the finer details, merely explaining how he was the architect responsible for building the underground facility, that he was tricked and then kept there against his will, that the two of us had formed a bond in there and that the company had collared and sent him to put a new collar around my neck or shoot me dead if I refused, thinking that it would be more painful for us both that way. But they had underestimated what he was prepared to sacrifice to see that I got away. I didn't tell them what I did to him, only that he gave me the means to make my escape, the adrenaline and painkillers, the gun, the car and the clothes. Not only that but I now knew the location of the facility, I keep this to myself for now too. I suspect Megan and her brother might well take the fight to Europa but I am not ready for that yet, right now I just need to get to my mother and take her somewhere she will be safe, thinking beyond that is only giving me a headache...

CHAPTER 14 – A SHOWDOWN AT APPLETREE LODGE

We are so close to her, I know every turn, every round-about, as I navigate the streets of my home town. I had grown up here for eighteen years before moving to London to join the Met. It's a weird sense of nostalgia and homesickness that is filling me up inside now. I have slowed to legal speeds since coming off the last A road into town, it's a busy, built up area, close to the seaside and the weather is fine, so there is more traffic than usual and I don't want to risk any innocent blood being on my hands, if I can help it, by driving too recklessly around here. We have come to a more comfortable silence now, both Megan and her brother seeming to sense that I needed the peace to focus and keep going. I am beginning to feel pain blossoming in my head and chest and a tingling starting in my arm. Just a little further, I keep telling myself, please, I am not one for prayer but I am asking now, if anyone is up there please let her be safe…

Appletree Lodge is coming up on our right. I drive slowly past the main entrance and park in the side road around the back of the home. I couldn't see anyone waiting or sitting in their cars in the car park. I'm hoping that's a good sign. I drive up to the curb and pull on the handbrake, leave the engine running. "This is it, would one of you mind keeping the car running and be ready to get us out of here quickly?" I ask it generally to the air while I take the gun from the door shelf and pull the action back, locking a bullet into the chamber, before tucking it back into my jeans out of sight behind me. "I'm coming in with you, Graham, you take the wheel." Megan's voice is firm and commanding, brooking no argument from either of one of us. I simply nod, Grim grunts his assent and we all get out of the car at once. Grim jumps back in to the driver's seat and shuts the door, giving me a wink and a thumbs up before reaching for the stereo and turning the radio on.

As Megan and I walk warily towards the main entrance, I can hear him tapping away at the steering wheel while a Killers song plays in the background. I can't recall the name of the track but it reminds me it is the first bit of music that I have heard in a long time, besides the posh classical bollocks that Richard liked to listen to in his apartment back at the facility. Inwardly, I can't help feeling that something by Rage Against the Machine would have been more appropriate, the way I am feeling at the moment, so I start playing the first few bars of 'Wake Up' in my head to help build up my courage for what might be coming next.

Beside me, Megan is moving with that warrior's grace again, her face showing no sign of fear or anger. The two of us scan the car park and entrance as we walk, no one around, apart from an old lady moving slowly up the path towards us with her zimmer frame, likely heading to the bench nearby to sit and have a cigarette, since there are a number of half smoked butts dotted all around it and not much else out here besides a worn hedge and a large apple tree offering a little shade from the late afternoon summer sunshine.

We pass the woman with a kind smile and a how do you do and she responds with a sour face and a mind your own business back at us. Megan and I share a look and continue on to the main door. The home had been rotating the same three codes for several years before I was abducted so, on a hunch, I try them all out, figuring if anyone from Europa was already inside, it would be better not to go ringing the doorbell. On the last attempt, I type in 1066 and the little green light flickers on next to the keypad, unlocking the door and letting us straight into the main lobby.

As we walk in and turn the corner, I can see that the home has changed little since I was last here. The same worn carpet and wallpaper decorate the corridor, but there are no bad stains marking the carpet and the general smell is one of fresh lemon and soap, suggesting the place is well tended despite the shabby appearance. I step up to a reception desk a few metres to the right of the main corridor and advise I am a relative come to visit Mrs Yamamoto, Naru's cousin, and that Megan was just a friend who has driven me here. The lady on reception is a thin middle-aged redhead, with a sharp face but wrinkles and crow's feet around her eyes, suggesting a lifetime of smiling and laughter. I know she is called Janet but she clearly doesn't recognise me anymore as she also passes on her condolences for Naru's death, which feels extremely uncomfortable since I also know he is listening to all this somewhere inside me. Janet advises us that all the residents are in the lounge, having just had their dinner, and offers to show us through. I explain it's fine I know the way, ask if anyone else has visited her today but Janet advises she has only just started her shift. I thank her by her own name, to help put her at ease and turn left towards the main lounge, Megan following closely on my heels.

My heart is beating fast and hard, I have one hand reaching behind my back, taking hold of the handle of the gun, partly for reassurance, partly just in case there are any sadistic Europa employees lying in wait for us. I can see Megan has also tucked one of her hands into her coat pocket, I can make out the vague outline of a blocky shape that she is holding onto inside it.

"Is that what I think it is?" I ask the question with a half-smile on my face as we draw near to the lounge doors.

"If you think it's a series four Durham rape alarm with a two-thousand-volt electric stun attachment, then yes, it is exactly what you think it is." I guess I deserved that, but it's good to know she isn't without her own weapon if things go south. I push one of the lounges' double doors open and scan the room before heading inside. Nothing appears amiss, just a group of old people sitting around in armchairs, a few are sitting around a table doing a jigsaw puzzle, some sort of landscape scene by the look of it. A few of the staff are making rounds, handing out medicines or just sitting with the residents speaking quietly. I spot my mother, over in the corner, almost exactly as she looked in the photo that Kiko had shown me. She is sitting on her own, staring out into the garden, looking a little out of place since she is so much younger than most of the other residents here. She looks to be dozing, taking in the last of the days sunshine and I can't help the lump that forms in my throat at the sight of her sitting there, without a care in the world, seemingly safe and sound.

I stomp across the room straight towards her, still wary, still hyperalert, glad that Megan is watching my back. Within moments I am by her side, down on one knee, asking to speak with her. She turns her kind but confused countenance towards me and at that exact moment I see the red dot that has alighted on her forehead...

Half the people in the room are screaming, I am pulling my mother down to the floor beside me as all hell breaks loose, glass shattering above and all around us, my mother's chair suddenly covered in bullet holes where only moments ago she had been sitting in contemplative silence. Feathers and other pieces of the chair are floating about above our heads, I have the Beretta out in my right hand, edging along the floor towards the hole where the window used to be. Meanwhile, Megan has crawled over to my mother and is helping pull her back further into the room to temporary safety.

I ease up against the pillar next to the window, my plimsoles crunching on broken glass, trying to calm my breathing, thinking about the angles and the carnage in the room. The only place with any cover in the garden would be the willow tree, likely the same place that the photo had been taken from. I try to recall it to my mind, and I can picture roughly where I think the shooter would be. I take a deep breath and launch myself around the pillar, the Beretta held out in front of me in both hands, I sight down the barrel and point the gun into the heart of the tree where I am fairly certain the shooter was aiming from, dashing sideways across his line of sight. I don't hesitate to try and pick him out, I just fire off four rounds at speed in a roughly two metre area around the centre of the tree before throwing myself to the other side of the window next to the wall.

After a few moments of tense silence, I hear the crackling of branches and then, a full sized human body dressed in camouflaged combat fatigues and wearing a balaclava, falls lifeless from the middle of the willow tree and hits the ground in a boneless heap, the silenced Smith and Wesson rifle with laser sighting attached that had just shot up the care home, still held in one hand. The smell of smoke and cordite is filling the air and I can taste the tang of copper in my mouth where I have bitten my lip and caused it to bleed.

There is no telling whether there are other Europa agents around but since the shooter was watching the back garden, I consider this is now likely to be our safest exit route from the home. I motion to Megan that the shooter is down with a hand across my throat and point that we should go out through the hole where the window used to be. She helps my mother to her feet and as the buzzing and ringing clears from my hearing, something I have only just become aware of, I can hear the sound of sobbing and crying all around me. One of the care staff suddenly climbs to her feet and aims a small pistol she must have had hidden in her boot right at my mother. Before I have a chance to react, she jerks her arm to the side, begins shaking uncontrollably and falls trembling to the floor, like she is in the grip of an epileptic seizure. After a few moments of convulsions, she becomes still, knocked unconscious by the electric volts that Megan just shot into her. The Durham two thousand clearly works and I silently thank Megan with a look and a nod.

With no time for sentiment, or worrying about anyone else I rush to embrace my mother and check her over. She seems just as confused and bewildered by the turn of events as when I had taken her out for ice cream along the seafront on my last visit. I clasp her head in my hands and press my forehead against hers. "Thank God, thank God your safe, that we got here in time. Would you like to go for a walk Maria?" I whisper the words and clutch her hand with my own.

"I'm scared, I want to see my Daddy." Her childlike statement cuts me to the core, her mind has regressed so much since I last saw her. I nod to her, and then again to Megan, tell her to come with me to find her Dad and together we head outside into the garden.

"Oh look, how lovely, I think it's a blue jay." My mother is smiling and pointing to a bird table near to the tree, a little blue bird has just alighted and started bathing itself, oblivious to the dead body a few metres away in the grass. At least she hasn't noticed the dead man lying still on the lawn and I motion to Megan to grab the rifle as we pass, and pat down the body. She sets too it, while I distract my mother by aiming us towards the back gate and admiring the passion fruit that is climbing up the fence panels all along the back of the garden.

I keep the Beretta out and by my side, trying to listen and look for anything suspicious, and keep checking behind us. Megan wastes no time, I see her sling the rifle over one shoulder by the strap and she also appears to have found some extra ammo from inside the dead assassin's pockets. Satisfied with her plunder, Megan jogs over to me at the gate. This time she goes ahead, reloading the rifle and holding it out before her like she knows how to use it. I watch our rear and direct my mother out of the gate, telling her we are playing sleeping lions and we must be quiet to make sure we don't wake any of them. She giggles at the idea and goes along with us as we sneak outside, me looking in all directions before closing the gate quietly behind us.

Grim will be waiting in the BMW just around the corner and I follow closely behind Megan as she edges up to the corner of the fence and leans carefully around the side to see if the coast is clear. She suddenly makes an audible hiss and holds out her left arm for us both to stop and wait, I swallow nervously and lick my swollen lip. I put a finger to it and warn my mother to be very quiet and she smiles and nods, still believing this to be some child's game, mirroring my action back at me she places a finger to her own lips and whispers ,"Shush, shush", to me as if I needed reminding myself. I close in on Megan's tense form and wait for her order.

"There's two of them by the car, a third on the floor, not moving. One has a gun trained on Graham, he's got him pinned up against the car, the other is looking towards the main entrance to the home. They both look like they are carrying Glocks. Fuck, you weren't kidding about these guys, were you?" Her voice sounds truly nervous for the first time, but I imagine it's more the fear for her brother than herself.

"What do you want to do?" I am deferring to Megan in this since it's her brother in the firing line, her call.

"Just how good a shot are you Elizabeth?"

"With a rifle? I was one of the best in my unit but that was two years ago."

"I need to know, no time for maybes right now, really, how good are you?"

I try to recall my time training in fire arms but it's blurred, out of focus and only half formed. I have been largely acting on instinct so far but with a burst of insight I realise why I can't form this memory.... 'NARU!' I call for him inside my mind, I have never truly demanded his presence before but I do it now. I need his memories, his ruthlessness. I feel a strange surge inside me, anger and resentment boiling up, making me feel queasy. Without warning, he pushes me back and I am no longer in charge of my own body. He moves us quickly forward with a kind of liquid grace, motions for Megan to pass us the rifle and keep an eye on our mother. There must be something in the way we are looking at Megan, as she passes the rifle to us without further argument, taking the Beretta from us and covering our rear, while holding onto Mum's hand.

We sight through the rifle's scope and tuck the stock into our shoulder, inching forward, lowering ourselves to a kneeling position for better balance, before leaning just enough to see around the corner where the two remaining agents are waiting to take us all out. With the scope's zoom, I can see Grim's expression up close and if it's possible, he looks even more pissed off than usual. I can see that his knuckles are skinned and bloody and there is blood running down the right side of his head.

Naru tracks the cross-hairs away from Grim up and along the arm of the agent pointing the gun at his head, until they are directly in the middle of his greasy shining forehead. For a moment we are completely still, just breathing, waiting, then Naru moves the sight over to the other agent, who is standing a few metres to the left of the car and watching the care home entrance intensely, his lanky frame all angles and lines, likely anticipating we will try to head out the front of the building with the back garden being covered by their sniper. With both positions marked, Naru moves the rifle back to the man covering Grim and lines the sight back on him. He has no need to use the laser sight, with the scope on its target we take a deep steadying breath and hold it...

Naru pulls the trigger once, moves the gun a few inches up and to the left before firing again. In less than a second, two more men are lying dead on the pavement. Unable to turn away, I had watched through Naru's eyes as both men's heads had exploded like ripe melons dropped onto rocks. My feelings of unease with how casually Naru had dispatched two people, are warring with his own sense of satisfaction at two more Europa agent's dead. I can't help but wonder if they had any more choice in what they were doing here than I did when I was wearing the collar. I have little time for such thoughts though, as with Naru still in control, we stand up and sweep forward towards the car, holding the rifle out before us, scanning the road in all directions while motioning Megan to follow us. At sight of me and then Megan with my mother, Grim actually cracks a relieved smile and gets back into the car, starting it up and pulling it forward to meet us.

WE climb into the back of the car with our mother and Megan jogs round to the front passenger door, after helping Maria inside and jumps in next to her brother, pausing for a brief moment to hug him tightly. A flash of nervous smiles all round, then, from Megan,

"Drive, go, go." Her voice is tight and strained but still commanding. No one else speaks, Grim floors the gas and the BMW takes off at speed down the small residential street and away from the death and carnage behind us. Grim weaves the car through mazes of back streets eventually arriving on the main seafront road that leads back out of the town. Naru, who has been watching out the back window intently the whole time since making our escape, turns and simply stares at our mother for some time. We take hold of her hand, then we are telling her how beautiful she is and how much we love her. I can feel Naru's emotions finally merging with my own, the tears tracking down our face at the relief and love we are feeling. There is an unspoken agreement between us and, finally, his presence fades back into the shadows of our mind and I can once again control my body.

I lean forward and pat both brother and sister on the shoulders, thanking them for their help and directing them off the main road and into the heart of the small town I had once called home. I have a destination in mind, my father's old lockup. With any luck, his old Suzuki Grand Vitara is still there and we can ditch the BMW, since I suspect we will have both Europa agents and the police looking for it now....

CHAPTER 15 – SEEKING SHELTER

"Turn left here, ... Yes, that's it, then a right, that's it just under that arch and through the alley... this is it." The tension has been building inside the car with every minute since the shoot-out at the care home. Several times we have heard police and ambulance sirens coming closer, then moving away, never actually seeing them up close and I imagine that they are all heading to Appletree Lodge to deal with the mess we have left behind us. But, finally, we are off the road and have pulled in an area full of lock-ups, round the back of a row of shops where there is not a soul in sight, just a few locked up garages with faded white numbers painted on the corrugated metal shutters. I direct Grim to pull us up next to number six, my father's, and for the first time since I learned he died, I allow myself to be glad that I couldn't bring myself to come and deal with this before now. It just might save all our lives today.

I turn to my mother and give her hand a gentle rub and smile at her, scarcely believing this moment. She smiles back at me beatifically, not a care in the world it seems and with her other hand strokes my cheek gently, "So pretty, a lovely girl, just lovely," she has no idea how much her words hurt both me and my darker half lurking in the shadows of my mind. Before I start sobbing my sorrow out to the world, I quickly turn away from her and climb back out of the car.

Wiping away a tear and sniffing some unwanted mucus back up my nose, I walk towards the huge padlock that has been keeping the garage secure for all these years. It's a toughened steel, six-digit combination padlock with a million possible combinations and has clearly stood the test of time. I don't have to think about the number, it's my own birthday after all, my father having chosen it so he would never forget it. I kneel down and flick the different numbers back and forth until it reads 040394. With a satisfying click, the lock opens with ease and in a matter of moments I have pulled up the shutter and let the evening light into the small garage.

Amongst the dust motes floating in the air, the Suzuki is still there in all its glory, carefully covered with a special see-through sheet that was supposed to wick away unwanted moisture from the chassis and prevent rust. I pull off the cover, throw it into the corner of the garage, then take the keys from a hook screwed into the wall and unlock the driver's door. I pull the catch that releases the bonnet then lift it up and lock it into place with a small metal lever designed for the job, just behind the cars' gleaming engine. This car had been my father's pride and joy, no matter what adventures he took us on in it and how dirty or filthy it ended up, he always lovingly cleaned and waxed it before putting it away again. There is only one thing I have to do before we can drive it. I walk over to a small work bench at the back of the garage and pick up the large car battery that has been placed there. By disconnecting it, it should have ensured that there has been no drain. I carry it back to the front of the car and reconnect it. Before I lock the bonnet back down, I quickly jump back into the cab and turn the key in the ignition. It only takes three tries and a little gas before the engine rumbles into life and I realise I have been holding my breath for nearly a minute and have caused my lip to start bleeding again, due to biting it anxiously.

I jump back out of the car and slam the bonnet down, give the others waiting in the BMW a big thumbs up, then get back in and pull the Suzuki out into the waning light of the day. Grim and Megan help me to persuade my mother to change cars, her mood becoming sullener and angrier as she is beginning to tire from the afternoon's events. Grim parks the BMW inside the now empty garage at my direction, I pull the shutter back down and lock it up once he is back outside and as I stand up from locking the padlock back in place, he gives me a hearty clap on my good arm and grins at me fiercely.

"Not bad for someone who was lying on their death bed a few hours ago." I feel my cheeks reddening at the way he is looking at me and avert my eyes from the intensity in his gaze.

"I can't thank you both enough for helping me, for risking yourselves so readily. And now... well now we are all in fukai tawagoto I'm thinking." My words come out in a rush and at Grim's confused expression I realise I have sworn in Japanese again.

"She means we're all in deep shit Graham." Megan's words come from over my shoulder and we both turn to see her smiling and offering me a lit cigarette as she leans casually against the Suzuki's sturdy frame. I smile gratefully back at her, recalling that she had never asked me what I had said back at the apartment when we made our goodbyes and so, now I realise, that she can actually speak Japanese, at least the trashy hybrid version I speak when I am stressed out.

"Arigato Megan san." I bow politely as I accept her gift and Grim shakes his head at our sudden brevity considering the seriousness of the situation.

"So, what now? Did you have somewhere in mind to take your mother?" Megan speaks with her usual frank and honest tone, her head cocked towards me awaiting my answer and I have a strong desire to tuck her blowing hair back behind her ear as the wind brushes a few stray strands across her face. I nod and take a few well-deserved drags of the cigarette she gave me, watch the smoke swirl out of my mouth and dissipate up into the air above me.

I do have somewhere to go in fact. My father's closest friend from the army lives up in Norfolk, about three hours' drive away. It's an area that is largely off the grid and he owns several acres of land with a lake and woodland on his property. I recall going for fishing and hunting trips and hikes into the dense woodland with Jack and my father years before, when I was a teenager, and had always had fond memories of those days. Jack himself had been honourably discharged back to the UK due to being diagnosed with PTSD after my father was killed on their last tour. He had come to my father's funeral and told me that if I ever needed his help that he would do what he could. He said he owed me a blood debt because of something my father had done. Though he never told me exactly what happened, I suspected that my father had sacrificed his own life to save Jack's and some of the other soldiers in their unit.

I wasn't usually someone that liked to call in favours, especially ones that I hadn't earned myself. But, in this case, I had no real other option that wasn't likely to result in my recapture or, worse, my mother being targeted or killed. Jack had good instincts and being an army veteran meant he might have weaponry I could use as well. There was something in particular I had recalled as the plan to go there was forming in my mind. Jack had a blacksmith's skills, after learning the trade from his own father before he joined the army. He had been repairing the strap on the hilt of my katana as a favour, before they got called away for their fateful tour where Dad never returned.

I had forgotten all about the sword in my grief but during my incarceration under the mountain I had thought of it often. What I would have given to have held that blade in my hands that first day when Kiko came for me. As time had gone by, there were moments when I could almost feel her calling out to me to be taken up again and used to fight back against the darkness consuming me. I cannot deny that I hungered to hold her, to wield her against those kuso yaro! I can feel Naru's agreement with this deep inside too and wonder for a moment if it's his hunger truly, rather than mine.

In short, there were a lot of good reasons to head to Jack's place. Not only would it be somewhere safe to keep Mum, while I worked out what to do, it would also provide me with some much-needed respite from the constant hypervigilance I have been living with for the last two years.

However, I had not planned to turn up with anyone other than myself and my mother. I wasn't sure how Jack would react if I turned up on his doorstep with a whole gang of fugitives. Megan seemed able to pre-empt my thoughts and was already smiling and nodding back at me before I can word a reply.

"I can see that you do, that's good, I think it best we all lie low for a while. Graham and I need to get back to London and warn the others. We have measures in place to disappear when we need to. Here, let me just...." Megan is digging in her pockets while she is speaking and pulls out a light pink lipstick from inside her coat. She is already pulling up my sleeve while she talks and then starts writing a series of numbers across the skin of my bare arm, the feeling is sending little bumps right up to my elbow and, this close, I can smell her perfume, or it could be the shampoo she uses in her hair, I can't be sure, a most pleasant scent of lavender and roses all the same.

"When you are ready to take the fight back to them, get a cheap pay-as-you-go phone and call this number. Let it ring three times, hang up, then call again so I know it's you. Be ready with what you want to say, I won't stay on the phone for more than sixty seconds. After we have spoken, shut down the phone, destroy the sim and throw the handset away."

She really means to fight them; I can hear the conviction in her voice and she has no idea how much this means to me to think I am truly not alone in all this anymore. I glance over to Grim and catch him staring right back at me with an intense kind of weighing up look in his eyes. Was he wondering if I ever would call them back, if I really had it in me to keep fighting now my mother was safe? I recall that these two have done their fair share of dangerous missions and they are masters of causing chaos, it's why the authorities want them so badly to be erased.

The professional way in which Megan gives out her instructions is a real reminder that they were no amateurs, they had proved themselves to me, as much as I had to them today.

Before Megan can pull away, I wrap an arm around her and hug her to me, careful not to press her too hard against my fragile ribs and shoulder. The drugs are wearing off fast and I still have a way to go before I can consider us safe yet.

"Thank you, thank you both for today. Arigato fukaku. I owe you my life and my mother's." I whisper the words close to her ear, manage to get it all out without choking or sobbing. Naru is sending up his gratitude too and it feels good when we are both in sync like this. She pats my back, smiles her not quite perfect white teeth at me and pulls away, then starts walking back out of the alley, waving Grim to follow.

"You don't want a lift to the train station?" I offer it freely, gladly, but both Megan and her brother shake their heads. Grim waves his goodbye and keeps going. Megan stops, turns and says,

"They will be looking out for us all together. Graham and I will jump on a few buses, get one of our friends to meet us, don't worry about us. Just get your mother somewhere safe and call me when you're healed, when you're ready." She salutes me with a peace sign, turns on her heel and jogs off up the alleyway to catch up with her brother.

I turn back to the car and climb in to the driver's seat. My mother has fallen asleep in the passenger seat, snoring softly, with her head resting against the window. At the sound of me shutting the door, she wakes with a start and looks around in confusion. I can feel my heart bleeding for her, at the constant fear and disorientation she must live in everyday now. I smile at her encouragingly, tell her, "It's alright Maria, we are going to see an old friend who loves you very much." She calms at my reassurance and pats my leg, peering at me with a vague look in her eyes, before smiling suddenly and nodding.

"Oh yes, that would be wonderful, just wonderful. Oh, how exciting, such a lovely girl." I smile back at her, inwardly cringing at her words. If only she knew, oh Mum, I need you so badly right now. I fight back the tears that threaten to blur my vision, pull on my seatbelt and concentrate on driving the car back out to the road. The smell and feel of the car is inwardly calming my jangled nerves, I can picture my father sitting in this very seat, smiling across at me as we headed off on our next adventure together. I needed to stay strong, just a little longer, he would want me to take care of my mother, make sure she is ok, before I see to myself. I make an internal promise to him that I will. I will get her to his friend and then I will sleep for a week....

CHAPTER 16 – LOST AND FOUND

If someone asked me how I found my way to Jack's property that day, I swear I could not entirely recall. I drove in near silence for hours, keeping exactly to the speed limit, always staring ahead into the dark endless motorways that seemed to go on forever in front of me, driving my father's car like I was sitting my driving test, constantly checking my mirrors for any sign of pursuit, my body tense and a thumping pain running through my head, beating in time with my heart. My mother had been periodically falling asleep beside me, then waking up scared and constantly needing my reassurance that everything was ok. Every now and then I had to wind the window down and blast in some cool evening air, constantly rubbing at my eyes, fighting to stay awake.

In a strange way, the pain helped. As the drugs began to completely wear off, it came back with a vengeance. My left arm was practically useless and for the first time since he bought it, I was truly glad my father had insisted on getting an automatic. Every deep breath I took would give a sharp little spike of pain in my chest, so whenever I started to feel drowsy, I inhaled deeply and soon found myself jerking forward in my seat and blinking through the pain. It must have been close to ten o'clock at night as we pulled up the long gravel drive that led to Jack's house. The huge dark elm trees pushing in on either side brought a sense of relief and comfort to me that I could not fully describe.

We made it…. we're really here….

I ease the car up alongside a dirty silver Land Rover Defender, switch off the lights and turn off the ignition. The sudden silence in the car is deafening, my mother is twitching in her sleep, softly mumbling words that make no sense to anyone but her. Then I start to hear the bark of a dog, not quite believing my ears and my eyes as I see what looks like a huge orange fox charging up the path towards the car. He would have to be nearly thirteen years old by now but there was Gunner, as exuberant as ever, running at full speed to greet us. Half Alsatian, half Greyhound, Jack had named him after his favourite football team. Gunner had always been a friendly beast but he also had a boundless energy. His favourite past-time was playing fetch with bigger and bigger sticks, well whole tree branches sometimes in all honesty. He could run back and forth for hours and never tire as long as you were prepared to throw a stick for him. He always looked like he was smiling with his tongue hanging out one side of his mouth. When I had been here as a teenager, he had barely left my side, finding me to be more fun than Jack I suppose, he had seen me more as a friend or pack mate than a human that would order him around.

As I stumble out of the car, I fall to one knee. In seconds I am bowled over by a huge ball of orange fur. It hurts my ribs like hell but I don't care. For a moment I am simply lying in the dirt, laughing and hugging an old friend, probably the only creature in the world who could recognise me, despite my transformation. Like all dogs the world over, his breath stinks, and he is licking my face between exited barks of greeting. I pat him on the back hard with my good arm and push my forehead against his cheek, just resting against his heaving, panting form for a few precious moments, his wagging tail thumping rhythmically against my leg, before I claw my way back up off the ground, having to lean against the car for support.

Jack's voice calls out from the house, quickly followed by

a beam of torchlight and his footsteps crunching on the gravel towards us. Gunner's ears prick up at the sound and he tears off back across the driveway, answering his master's call, barking his excitement all the while. I turn and check on my mother, she has woken from her doze and is staring out into the dark, her perpetual puzzled expression written on every line of her face, and my heart breaks for her all over again. This is a good place, among friends, where we were always welcome and safe, yet because of Mum's condition it's just another scary new experience that she doesn't know how to process.

I turn back towards the house and blink into the beam of light suddenly shining at my face. I hold my hand up to shade my eyes as Jack's commanding voice booms out from just a few metres away.

"Where the hell did you get that car? Who the fuck are you?" I swallow at the violence implied in his tone and can make out the outline of what looks like a shotgun in his hands, currently pointing at the ground but it wouldn't take much time to swing it up at my body, faster than I would be able to pull the Beretta out from behind my back. I take an almost imperceptible step back and bump up hard against the bonnet of the Suzuki. I hold both my hands out high and wide, my palms flat.

"Please Jack, just hear me out, I came here for your help." I keep my voice calm, speak slowly, though inwardly my heart is beating fast and hard against my chest. I am so exhausted I could collapse any moment but I need to show Jack just who I am.

"How the hell do you know my name? Who's that in the car with you?" The menacing tone in his voice has not diminished and I am suddenly very afraid. Jack is an ex-marine and he seems really pissed that I just rocked up on his drive in his dead friend's car.

"It's Maria Yamamoto." My voice seems to have raised a few octaves and it takes a lot of effort not to stutter the words out like a gibbering idiot. There a dark spots forming around my vision, I can feel the world shrinking around me until all I can see is Jack's silhouette and the gun in his hands. Gunner has gone silent by his side, then suddenly lets out a soft whine as he obviously senses the potential violence in the air but can't understand why.

"Maria?" ... He takes a few steps nearer, his curiosity getting the better of him, then turns the powerful torchlight towards the car windscreen, lighting up my mother inside, who blinks back at him vacantly.

"Jesus Christ, it really is her. I thought she was ... well ... that she ...?" Now it's Jack's turn to seem uncertain.

"And that's Hiro's car, isn't it? No... I'm sure of it." I nod, clear my throat. I have to tell him, Naru is stirring inside me, he doesn't want Jack to know, there is great shame in what has been done to us but he has to know the truth before I pass out or faint. If he calls the police, all this will have been for nothing.

"Yes, it's Hiro's car. Yes, that's his wife sitting inside. Please Jack.... You don't recognise me but you do know me." I am imploring him, holding my hands out placatingly, desperate for him to understand.

"Fine I'll hear you out. Enlighten me young lady, just who the hell are you and what are you doing here with a dead man's car and his broken wife?" Jack lowers the gun a little and turns the torch back on me.

"Four and a half years ago you stood beside me over my father's grave and told me that you owed me a blood debt because of what my father did, that if I ever needed your help, to come to you and you would do everything you could to help me. Do you remember that Jack?" I nearly choke on the words as I recall that moment in my mind. Everything had felt grey and numb that day, like all the light and life had been sucked out of the world. But I could recall almost every second of it in minutest detail, and I suspected Jack could too. You didn't forget a thing like what he said, at least that's what I was counting on. No one else had been within ear shot when he said it, it had just been him and me standing over Dad's coffin before it was to be buried, everyone else had started to leave the graveyard, even my mother, who had been lead back to a waiting car by one of her carers.

"Naru? … It can't be, Naru is dead too. How do you even know about that?" Jack is shaking his head; the gun is raising back up. I have to do something fast as I can see he doesn't believe me, that I have just made him more wary and confused. I sink back down to the ground, the pain and weariness is draining me, part of me wants him to just point the damn thing at me and pull the trigger, get this over with, but I have one last trick up my sleeve. I pat at my leg and call Gunner to me. He barks back in response and bounds across to me in a few quick strides of his powerful legs, licks my face once more and lets me pat him and wrap my good arm around him. I know Jack trained him to be a guard dog. If I was a stranger he should have been growling and baring his teeth at me, not jumping around me like a four-year-old child that just got shown an ice cream cone.

"Jesus fucking Christ." He is shining the light directly in my eyes and I am blinking back at him, ready to surrender to the moment now. I don't know what else I can do to convince him, but I can see that I don't have to. The gun has lowered to the ground and he is stomping towards me across the gravel. I smile up at him, my strength all but gone now. I close my eyes in relief, feel the darkness pulling me under, everything is fading first grey, then black….

CHAPTER 17 – THE LEGEND OF IDOSHI YAMAMOTO

The last true samurai in our family, Idoshi Yamamoto, served under Daimyo Mitsurugi, on the ouskirts of Edo before the fall of the last Shogunate towards the end of the nineteenth century, in what was called the Tokugowa era, named after the Shogun himself. Idoshi was both a skilled swordsman and master swordsmith and he could often be found working metallurgy alongside the local craftsman of the town, or teaching students, including his young son Haru, the sacred arts of Iaido at his dojo. Well-liked and respected, he kept order in his allocated Han for many years and all who served under him enjoyed peace and prosperity throughout his tenure.

The legend of Idoshi truly began, however, when the newly appointed Daimyo, Mitsurugi, the spoilt son of the previous Daimyo, and, so it was whispered, quite possibly, the man responsible for the death of said Daimyo, visited Idoshi at his home, met his beautiful wife, Aiko and fell madly in love with her. Mitsurugi left that night, obsessed with Aiko and jealous of his loyal samurai, and with no honourable way to take her for his own he elected to use the way of shadows to dispose of his rival.

The story goes that Mitsurugi sent a Shinobi assassin to Idoshi's house the very next night with the sole intention of killing Idoshi in his sleep. Unfortunately, as with all such tragic tales, the Shinobi sent to assassinate Idoshi mistakenly killed Aiko, who had been meditating in the bedroom wearing her husband's kimono, as she liked to do. From the back, both Aiko's and Idoshi's long black hair looked much the same when tied into a warrior's tail, so it was not until her body slumped dead to the ground beside him that the Shinobi realised his terrible mistake. Fearing for his own life after making such a disastrous error of judgement, he fled Edo never to be seen again.

As for Idoshi himself, one can only imagine the feeling of horror and loss he went through discovering his beloved Aiko lying dead on the bedroom floor, as he returned from his vigil by the side of their sweet young son Haru. For it seems, Haru had routinely suffered from dark nightmares since the age of four and could not fall asleep without either his mother or father by his side. Perhaps his dreams were more prophetic than anybody realised, for at finding his wife slain, Idoshi became filled with a terrible rage he could not control. Already suspicious of the Daimyo's lecherous glances the night before and the way he had kissed Aiko's hand goodnight, then finding his wife dead, dressed in his own clothes, it did not take him long to realise what had happened.

There are various stories about what happened next, but the tale I was told is likely the closest to the truth since it was passed down from father to son at their naming day, when they turned sixteen, along with the sword 'Naitoben', the very same sword that he took up that fateful day, the finest blade he had ever crafted, due to be given to the Shogun himself as a wedding gift in a few months time. The Shogun would never receive the sword, however, since Idoshi Yamamoto, took it for himself, put on his full battle armour, tied Naitoben to his waist and set off on foot for the Daimyo's palace.

Clad in his red and blue armour and screaming out the Daimyo's name, most sensible townsfolk fled before Idoshi and locked their doors behind them. As he came upon the palace, a few well-paid Ronin, loyal to Mitsurugi, sought to stop him from entering, having been pre-warned by all the commotion running ahead of him through the town.

Idoshi carved through the first three Ronin with such speed and skill that the last two fled rather than join their comrades in the bloody dirt. Idoshi didn't even need to open the palace gates. Witnessing his skill and due to word of what had happened spreading ahead of him, the men inside the palace, still loyal to the previous Daimyo and well aware of the reputation of both Mitsurugi and Idoshi, settled for opening the doors wide for the samurai warrior and allowing him to stalk, unchallenged, straight into the heart of the palace.

With no one willing to put their lives before his, Daimyo Mitsurugi was forced to face his rival or risk forever having his honour besmirched. And so, they met in the Courtyard of his own palace, two great warriors dressed as though heading to war. However, this was to be no epic drawn out fight where the two men traded blows and danced with death while onlookers watched in awe. Idoshi simply came at Mitsurugi, no words were exchanged, no clever trading of insults or philosophical musings were uttered. Idoshi moved with sudden speed, running at Mitsurugi, his sword still sheathed. When Mitsurugi sought to swing his katana into Idoshi's side hoping to stop him in his tracks, the lithe warrior suddenly ducked and rolled under the blade's deadly swing and leapt up behind Mitsurugi, drawing Naitoben and spinning his whole body around in a great arc.

Naitoben sliced through the Daimyo's armour and his body like they were made of vapour and sprayed Mitsurugi's life blood in all directions, his corpse falling to the ground in two separate bloody pieces.

Victorious, Idoshi wasted no time in sentiment, did not honour the body with any fine words. Instead, he stalked from the palace, returned to his home, buried his wife in the garden under her favourite cherry blossom tree, gathered clothes, horses and supplies and left with his son Haru the very same night, never to return to Edo. He left his estate to the townspeople to do with as they would.

As I understand it from what my father told me, Idoshi fled to Ryukyu and became Ronin, a masterless mercenary for hire. He made a good living as a bodyguard on the long dangerous caravan and shipping routes, helping merchants protect their wares from thieves and bandits that haunted the seas, forests and mountain paths, always insisting on bringing his son with him wherever he went and making the boy into a hardened warrior even more feared than him.

And so, on his sixteenth birthday, Haru Yamamoto, the son of a humble Ronin bodyguard, was handed one of the finest katana blades ever made. As Idoshi passed it into his son's waiting hands, he whispered the blades name into his ear and its purpose…. Her name and her purpose were one and the same, she was called 'Night's bane'.

CHAPTER 18 – DIGGING DEEP

Something inside me fights back against the gathering darkness pulling me down into unconsciousness. My father's tale of my great great grandfather, told to me on my sixteenth birthday, when he handed over the legendary katana into my own hands, flashes through my mind, reminding me of the warrior blood I have inherited that still flows through my veins. It's almost as though I can feel Naitoben, she is close, calling out to me to get up, to keep going, and something deep inside my being refuses to give in. I tell myself I have come too far to pass out here on Jack's driveway. I gather the ebbing light to me, clutch at it, take another breath, then another, grit my teeth against the pain and exhaustion and slowly, somehow, I pull myself back up off the ground and climb to my feet.

Jack comes forward to help me but I wave him away, ask him to help Mum. I wait and watch as he helps her out of the car and leads her back towards the house, his gruff voice doing its best to sound calm and reassuring. I wait a few moments, drawing what little strength I have left to me and then, step by step, I begin to follow along behind them. Gunner is a constant presence at my side, whining softly to himself, clearly anxious at my unsteady gait. I lean into him slightly as I walk, rest my hand on his back, feeling our old bond of friendship returning with each moment by his side. It's barely ten metres from the car to Jack's front porch but by the time I reach the door to the house I am panting heavily, sweat dripping from my forehead and shivering all over as though I am coming down with a fever.

I stagger inside to warmth and light, stumble over to a comfy looking armchair beside a crackling log fire and practically fall into the chair. Gunner pushes his head gently against my leg and lays down beside me and, for a time, we both just stare into the hypnotic orange, yellow and blue flames of the fire. The heat is doing wonders to draw out the shivers and the cold that has wormed its way down to my bones. I close my eyes, breathe in deeply, stretch my legs out closer towards the fire and, finally, allow my mind and body to rest, after what feels like the longest day of my entire life.

I am dozing in front of the fire by the time Jack returns from helping my mother to bed. He draws a chair over from his dining table nearby and sits close enough that he can reach across and place his hand reassuringly on my arm.

"Maria was shattered, she practically fell asleep as soon as she got in bed. You look even worse than she did." He nods to another door on the other side of the room as he speaks. "You can use your father's old room; I don't think anyone's slept in it since you two last came for a visit. But first, I need to know, should I be expecting any trouble to follow in your wake tonight?" I rouse from the dreamy state I had been in at his words. I try to think back through the day. Was it possible I might still have a tracker somewhere on, or in me? Could they have access to CCTV and traffic cameras, find out what car I had driven to get here? Both were unlikely but that didn't mean it was impossible. I shake my head slightly, "I don't think so, but.... Well, I can't be entirely sure about it, but if trouble is coming, it won't be far behind me." Jack is nodding to himself at my words and pats my arm as he stands. "I figured that might be the case. Listen, get what sleep you can, and know this. I will keep watch over you and Maria tonight. If trouble comes looking for you here, it's going to find itself staring down both barrels of my shotgun and Gunner's stinking canines!" At mention of his name, Gunner sits up and barks happily, his tail wagging. I find it hard to imagine him attacking anyone, but perhaps he could slobber them to death? But Jack, well he was a different story. Standing there, towering over me, he had a grim determination on his face, he was strong and commanding, like his old self before he had come back that last time without Dad. His chance to fulfil the promise he had made to my father, that he would look out for me, seems to have given him new strength and purpose. I can't imagine how he must have felt at hearing of my death and what he must have gone through these last few years. I thank him gratefully for his reassuring words and feel an overwhelming relief filling me. "Now, let me help you get to bed before you fall asleep out here."

I allow Jack to pull off my shoes and haul me carefully back to my feet. The fire has done a lot to make me feel better but it has also drained the last of my strength. He keeps tight hold of me and steers me into the larger of the spare bedrooms. Once inside the room, Jack helps me carefully out of my coat, then pulls the covers aside on the double bed. It's colder in here, and I slump exhausted onto the bed, pulling the covers back over me with my good arm, shivering a little at the sudden change in temperature. Gunner slinks into the room behind his master, climbs up onto the other side of the bed and lays down right beside me. It brings back good memories of him sleeping by my side when we used to camp out in the woods all those years ago, his body heat would also be very welcome tonight.

"Christ... If I had any doubts, I can't believe it's you in there Naru, but he knows you that's for damn sure. Alright old man, you stay here and watch over your friend. Sleep Naru, we'll talk about all this in the morning, ok?" I agree and give my thanks once more, lift my arm and rest it on Gunner's warm flank, close my eyes and fall asleep so quickly I don't even hear Jack shut the door behind him as he leaves the room.

CHAPTER 19 – A MAN OF HIS WORD

That night, while I slept like the dead, despite years of suffering terrible nightmares, PTSD and survivors guilt at his best friend's great sacrifice and my untimely death in a house fire, Jack sat wide awake on his porch all through the unseasonably cold summer night, shotgun loaded and resting in his lap, listening intently for the sound of any oncoming vehicles, scanning the dark for any sign of trouble. Several times he had slipped stealthily through the shadows around the outside of the house, checking for any signs of movement in the woods and fields to the rear of his house, but he had seen and heard nothing other than a startled deer and the neighbour's cat.

For the last two years Jack had shut himself away from the world, angry and bitter at yet another loss that he had been unable to see coming. He had sometimes wondered about the fire that had supposedly killed me, if there was something more sinister to it, but the official police report had stated it was a gas leak that had caused a small explosion underneath the building, just bad luck really. He recalled standing over yet another grave of a Yamamoto, beside poor Maria, though she had no real notion of why she was there, she had still wept rivers of tears, some part of her deep-down understanding it was someone she should have known, should have cared about.

Jack had taken to drinking heavily most nights after that. Whiskey, brandy, anything strong enough to take away the pain for a few hours. He admitted most of this to me the following morning when I discovered more than a few empty and half-full bottles of the stuff left lying around the house and we had begun to tell our respective stories to each other over breakfast.

As dawn broke and the sun finally began to rise above the horizon, his long vigil complete, I imagine Jack breathed a huge sigh of relief and perhaps rose a little taller that morning, a piece of himself broken for so long having finally repaired itself. No trouble had come calling after me but Jack had kept his word, just as he promised all those years ago. It seemed for now that I had truly escaped from the clutches of Europa and, thanks to Jack, both my mother and I had somewhere we could rest and where I could begin to figure this whole mess out.

CHAPTER 20 – A SAMURAI'S HEART

I wake the next morning with a great weight lifted from my heart. No one had come in the night, Gunner had woken me as he leapt off the bed, then began scratching and whining to get out of the room, clearly as in need to alleviate his bladder as I was. I drag my aching body out from under the covers, pleased to feel that the pain has lessened in both my head and my arm. Still fully dressed from the night before, I stumble over to the door and let poor Gunner out of the room, then do my best to recall which way the bathroom is. A few moments to orientate myself to the old surroundings, then I set off to the left in search of it. It doesn't take long to find, just down the hall, past the kitchen. After a long and relieving few minutes on the toilet I decide I might as well wash while I'm at it. The sun is still low in the sky through the bathroom window, so I estimate it must be around six or seven in the morning.

I carefully peel my clothes off one by one, wincing at every little sting. It only takes a few minutes but I am breathing heavily and perspiring a little by the time I am down to my birthday suit. Though I don't like to look at myself naked, I decide I need to examine the damage and glance down at the places on my body that hurt the most. My left shoulder and bicep are bruised black and blue, reminding me of a mottled stilton cheese. Further down, my left arm is lacerated in a number of places, and has been taped up with butterfly stitching. It must have happened when I hit the windscreen of the car that ran me down. I stare at the mobile number written in pink lipstick along the underside of my right arm and take a mental note of it, stirring goose bumps and heady feelings as I recall the woman who put them there,

I head to the mirror over the sink and lift my dark fringe to reveal the gauze and dressing taped to the side of my head. It's dark brown with dried blood in places but as I press gently against it doesn't feel too badly swollen, which is a mercy given the whack my head took when I face planted the ground only a few days before. I take a few experimental deep breaths, I can still feel a sharp pain in my chest when I breathe deeply and it's something I'm going to have to live with for a while, since ribs notoriously take longer to heal than most other bones due to the fact that they are constantly moving with each breath you take. I make another mental note to ask Jack if I can raid his medicine cabinet for painkillers after breakfast.

All in all, I'm looking and feeling pretty damn beat-up. It will take me a few weeks before I'm back to anything like my old self. The trouble is I doubt I have weeks. The whole time I stay here in hiding, Europa's agents, maybe even Kiko and the other board members, are going to be hunting for me. I wonder how long I have before they link me to this place, maybe never, maybe tomorrow? There's no way to know but I have to assume I don't have long...

I stay under the shower just long enough to scrub myself down and rinse off. I step back out after a few minutes, dry off with one of the towels from the laundry cupboard and pull out the spare clothes that Richard had packed in the satchel he brought to the hospital. It would not be my first choice, but the thought of putting my rather aromatic and slept in clothes from the day before back on is enough to make up my mind. As well as a lacy black matching bra and underwear set, there is a thin, sleeveless, navy blue summer dress that fits a little too snuggly around my breasts and waist for my liking but has a looser flow to it as it falls to just below my knees. Dressed once more, I put my worn clothes into the laundry basket, tie my hair back in a warrior's tail, pause for a moment on my way out and stare at my reflection in the mirror.

The woman looking back at me seems harder somehow than when I last saw her. The thought suddenly flashes through my mind that I killed three people yesterday, possibly four if you count Richard... 'No time for self-pity though', that thought comes from Naru, as clearly as if he was standing beside me, whispering into my ear. His words are harsh but pragmatic, but he's right, we did what we had to do to save Mum, to get away from them, they gave us no real choice in the end. Richard though, I still swallow back the lump in my throat at what Naru did to him. At the very least I suspect he would have some brain damage from the blow he took. Naru's anger is building again, no good can come from thinking about this. I close my heart to such weak thoughts of worry and guilt. I need to become hard, steel myself for what lies ahead. For I can sense the idea of a plan forming in my mind inspired by the memory of my warrior heritage.

The way of Bushido demands retribution for the dishonour that has been done to me and countless others at the hands of Europa and its council of sadistic sociopaths. I have to bring the fight to them, it was the only way to stop them from hunting me down, or spending the rest of my life looking over my shoulder. Then there was my mother, her advanced dementia made her ill-suited for a life on the run, she would be a constant burden and worry to me, making blending in and disappearing more than a little difficult or next to impossible. In the end there was only one path that I could realistically take from here, if I wanted some semblance of a normal life back for myself and my mother...

A true samurai, a follower of bushido, would not waver in the face of overwhelming odds, they would turn to face it and smile, knowing that this was the way and the will of the world. There would always be suffering, it was as much a part of life as breathing, and in the end we all must face the great unknown from whence we came, it's just a matter of how and when. Most people don't get the chance to choose it but a samurai, they have to exist in the moment, always ready to accept that the next breath could prove to be their last. Such thoughts help to pull the world around you into sharper focus, giving you an edge as sharp as your blade. As my thoughts begin to take shape, there is a growing itch that I need to scratch, for no true samurai can be without their sword.

Naitoben is here, somewhere in this house, I can almost feel her calling to me, demanding to be taken up once more. And in truth, I long to hold her again, to feel the connection to my ancestor spirits, especially my father. But first, I have duties which cannot wait any longer. I need to check on Mum, take her through her new morning routine, make sure she gets settled in and then I need to sit down with Jack and explain my whole sorry tale to him. Then, then I will come for her ...

CHAPTER 21 – BEFORE THE FALL

My mother is still asleep when I open her door a crack and peer inside the little bedroom where I had spent many happy nights myself as a child. At the sound of the door creaking, she opens her eyes to slits and begins to stir awake. I do my best to make my voice cheerful as I imagine the carers would have, in the hope it will help her feel at ease in her new surroundings.

"Good morning Maria, oh what a wonderful day it is outside. I hope you had a good night's sleep?" I cringe inwardly at the sickly-sweet tone I am using with her but having witnessed her regression and innocent remarks the day before I figure that she may well believe herself to be a little girl now. I recall that the carers at her home had advised me that sometimes, the best thing you can do for someone with dementia, is to go into their world a little, rather than insist on forcing them to confront the reality of their condition over and over again.

"Oh yes thank you, I had such exciting dreams…. And do you hear the birds this morning? There are so many of them. I'm so sorry but I can't remember your name for the life of me." I smile back at her and come into the room, ease myself next to her on the bed and take her hand gently in mine.

"I'm Elizabeth, I'm the one who brought you here, for a little holiday and to see an old friend." My mother pats my hand and beams back at me. "Elizabeth, such a pretty name, oh thank you Elizabeth, I love my room, it's so cosy and quiet here, but I do rather need to go to the toilet something fierce."

"I'm glad you like the room Maria. Come on, let me show you to the bathroom ok?" My mother is nodding back at me, giggling and smiling, and I can't help but feel my heart melt a little at such simple pleasures making her so happy...

I show Mum to the bathroom, help her to use the toilet and then to get the shower going and wait until the temperature is 'exactly, just right' as she demands it of me, before she agrees to undress and get under it. I tell her to call me if she needs anything after passing her the soap and pulling the shower curtain closed. I use the time while I wait to quickly clean my teeth over the sink and then head to Dad's car to check the boot for supplies. My hope was that he had left both his and my mother's rucksacks in the back with a few days' worth of clean clothes, ready for an impromptu adventure. Thankfully, he has done his usual boy scout prep and I am able to provide Mum with a fresh set of clothes, perfect for the woods. There are also some good hiking boots and a set of camping clothes of my father's that, though a little on the large size for me, will be more preferable to a summer dress as my only spare set of clothes. I pull Dad's old dark green army jumper out of the bag and hold it up to myself. A little on the baggy side but it will cover up the more conspicuous parts of the dress nicely. I pull it over my head and can't help feeling some small comfort in it.

The pleasure on my mother's face when I show her the new clothes that I have purloined from the car, is priceless, and after I have helped her dry herself and get into them, I feel a strange sense of accomplishment and satisfaction. Her wide eyed wonder and curiosity at every small detail in the bathroom, down to the blue fish on the tiles and the little rubber duck on the edge of the bathtub, is enough to bring a foolish grin to my face. I know this because I spot my reflection in the bathroom mirror and laugh out loud at the sight. Mum laughs along with me too, my good cheer at her happiness becoming infectious. Before we leave, I put some toothpaste on her travel toothbrush that was packed in the front of her bag that I got from the car, and pass it to her, encouraging her to give her teeth a good scrub before we return to the main room…

Jack is just filling the kettle and putting some toast on as we arrive. I study him more closely in the morning light, where once he kept his hair short and always had a clean shaved face, he was now sporting thick grey and black peppered hair, almost down to his shoulders as well as a thick darker beard that gave him a real woodsman's appearance. Gunner is sitting expectantly by his side, his tail pounding on the floor as he waits for Jack to open a can of dog food and empty the contents into his bowl by the fridge. As soon as it touches the floor, he buries his face in the bowl and chomps his way through the whole lot before the toast has even popped back up. Though he looks like he has stayed up all night, Jack has a lazy smile and seems relaxed and cheerful this morning, though he does raise a questioning eyebrow at me as he takes in my choice of outfit. I shake my head, not sure where to even begin a conversation like that. Instead, I settle for thanking him for taking us in last night and for watching over us, Gunner too, but Jack waves my gushing thanks aside, bids us both sit down and brings over a steaming cup of tea for Mum and a strong black coffee for me, as well as two thick slices of browned toast, each with lashings of butter all over them.

I savour the moment as best I can, watching Mum tuck into the toast and then daintily lift the cup of tea to her lips and blow on it before taking careful little sips one at a time, trying to hold out her little pinkie all the while, until my growling stomach begins to protest at me to stop ignoring it. I take a hearty swig of the coffee, both smelling and getting an almost instant caffeine hit, that wakes me up like a smack to my face. Damn Jack that is strong coffee. I wolf the first slice of toast down before Jack has even sat down at the table with us, then try my hardest to eat the second slice with more care and respect for our host. I raise my coffee cup and cheers Jack, clinking our mugs together and toasting absent friends....

We keep the conversation simple and cheerful in front of Mum, speaking of the weather and some local village gossip. While we talk, she keeps looking at Jack out of the corner of her eye, between sips of her tea, until suddenly she points at him and says, "Jack, you're Jack." He and I share a look of surprise and for a moment the only sound in the room is Gunner's soft snoring coming from the kitchen. I lick my lips, clear my throat and say hopefully, "That's right Maria, so you remember Jack?" She nods enthusiastically at my question and smiles back at me and Jack in turn.

I find my heart doing backflips in my chest, hoping that she may recall more than I gave her credit. But then she dashes my hopes with her next exclamation. "You're Daddy's friend Jack. Is he here? Is he coming to pick me up? I think I should wait for him out there." She is pointing to the old wooden bench on the front porch. "I expect he is ever so worried." As quickly as it had soared my heart sinks once again at her skewed perspective of the situation. Somehow, I think she still remembers my father but those last few years before his fateful tour, he was doing more and more for her as her mind and memory were deteriorating and now, I realise, it has left the impression in her head that he was her father, not her husband.

Despite the sorrow filling me, I keep my voice light and cheerful, unwilling to sour her happy mood and seeing a good chance to have a private conversation with Jack. "I'm sure he is Maria, why don't you sit out there for a bit? It will be nice and warm in the sunshine on that bench and you can keep a lookout for your Papa, OK?" More smiles and nods from Mum. She thanks Jack for her breakfast and asks if she can please be excused from the table. Jack goes along with the game and says, "Of course Maria." We both watch her quietly as she slips out of the house and takes a seat on the bench just outside the front door, humming softly to herself and swinging her legs back and forth like a small child. Jack turns to me with real sympathy on his face,

144

and says, "So, what happened?" I wipe away an idle tear from the corner of my eye and cast my mind back to how this all began two years ago, to the day of the raid on the brothel, back before the fall...

CHAPTER 22 – THE WOMAN, THE DOG AND THE SWORD

By the time I finish telling Jack my story, at least those parts I am willing to share with him in order for him to know enough as to why I ended up on his doorstep, he has given up any pretence of sobriety and washed his breakfast down with several large glasses of cheap Scotch whiskey. He tells me a little of his own tale, explaining the booze away and I don't blame him for it in the least. He looks pale and worn, last nights lack of sleep starting to catch up with him. More than that though, I can sense the anger boiling within him. Like my father and myself, Jack had devoted his life to his country, to safeguarding others, to fighting for something he believed in. He had trusted in the right of what he was doing, believing that he served a government that shared those views. To learn that same government was also secretly helping to fund a human trafficking organization to carry out assassination and torture and that they were complicit in what had been done to me and to who knew how many others, well, it was enough to tip someone right over the edge who might already be teetering on the precipice, and I should know after all.

I don't remember how it happened but we are embracing each other tightly. Jack's huge frame is enveloping me, his body shuddering with sobs, letting out years of pent up guilt, frustration and anger. I sense he is desperate to comfort me somehow but I find that I am comforting him, telling him I'm ok, I'm still here and thanks to him, Mum and I are safe for now.

Since my resolution in the bathroom this morning I am feeling stronger inside, just having this peaceful morning, witnessing my mother's tender and innocent joy in the world around her, feeling a friends' genuine concern and compassion for me, even the simple love of a dog sharing his body heat to keep me warm through the night, has invigorated my spirit once more. It also means I have something to lose as well as to fight for, which leads me inevitably to pull away from Jack's concerned arms, look him hard in the eye and say, "My father once told me an old phrase of our people that has pierced my soul today. He told me, when we are at our wit's end or facing impossible odds, to fight until your sword breaks and you run out of arrows, katana-ore ya-tsuriki made! Do you still have her Jack?" Jack's eyes widen at my impassioned words and he draws himself up, back straightening, standing a little taller than before, a grave nod of his head is all I need to know. He places a strong hand on my shoulder and says, "Yes, of course, wait right here, I will bring her to you."

Jack heads off to the back of the house and I hear his footsteps recede down the hall and then up the stairs onto the floor above. I turn my attention back to Mum, tug my plimsoles back onto my bare feet and walk outside the house and into the sunshine. Gunner slips out beside me and together, we join my mother on the porch. For a few minutes I feel truly at peace, just sitting on the little wooden bench, holding my mother's hand and listening to her exclaim in wonder at a lone leaf blowing in small circles in the soft morning breeze then pointing excitedly at a small flock of birds taking flight above us. By the time Jack finds me, I have already thrown a stick for a third time for Gunner, who had steadfastly charged off in pursuit as though he hasn't aged a day and is now plodding happily back with the tattered piece of bark hanging out of his drooling jaws. My mood becomes solemn at Jack's approach, and I feel Naru draw himself forward inside me at the sight of what Jack is holding before him…

"Naitoben." I whisper the name reverently as Jack passes her into my waiting hands. Her scabbard is obsidian black, so dark it's like a living shadow, and her hilt is newly wrapped in fine black leather, a testament to Jack's blacksmith skills. She is perfectly balanced, almost weightless, I lift her up to the light of the morning and bow my head in obeisance and contemplation to her craftmanship and purpose. Though beautiful, she is still a tool of death and dismemberment and I would be a fool to forget this. I sense Naru and I twining around each other, our broken soul seeking to find a way back together until, somehow, we are no longer he and I, not even us… just … me…

I take a deep cleansing breath and close my eyes, lower Naitoben to my side. I cannot explain the calm that has come over me. There is also a yearning for release, to pull Naitoben out from the shadows and let her gaze upon the light once more. Jack seems to know exactly what I am thinking. He sits down beside Mum and points off into the woods to the East of the property. "You remember where your Dad and I built that swing for you back when you stayed here for a whole summer?" I nod, smiling at the memory, I can picture it like it was yesterday in fact. "I have cleared the woods back around the willow tree over the last few winters, planning on building a hut out that way, somewhere I can store all my fishing gear so it's closer to the lake. Why don't you go with Gunner and take a look, have some time to yourself, I'll stay here and keep an eye on Maria."

I don't need to think about Jack's offer, I am nodding and grinning wolfishly at his words. I sling Naitoben across my shoulder with the makeshift baldric my father had fashioned for her, give Jack a big thankyou hug, kiss Mum goodbye and call Gunner to my side.

Within moments I am stepping into thick woodland, the

outside world and all its troubles receding from my mind. As always, the ancient trees feel sacred and aware of my clumsy intrusion so I do my best to walk with due reverence and care, trying not to tread too deep a path, instead twisting and bending around each obstacle, this also helps to prevent tearing the dress I am wearing on every thorn bush and creeping vine that I pass along the way.

As I walk, I listen to the songs of the birds serenading each other under the beautiful blue summer sky and the soft breeze rustling and whispering it's secrets as it passes through the high branches of the large oak and ash trees surrounding me. Every now and then I hear the crunching of leaves and twigs somewhere in the undergrowth and imagine I have disturbed some squirrel or fox from its daily routine, likely scurrying up a tree or down into a burrow until I am out of their sight once more. Gunner scouts all around me as I continue heading east, his tongue lolling out of his mouth just like when he was a carefree pup, only now he has a more lazy, casual trot to his gait than I remember, and keeps stopping every now and then to snuff the ground or cock his leg to mark his territory.

After about twenty minutes of strolling blissfully between the trees, I suddenly find myself in a large clearing that never existed when I was here before. Gunner, sensing we have reached our destination, finds a spot in the shade and settles himself down, watching me expectantly.

The old willow tree is still there, with a rotted rope long passed the time when it would be safe to swing on, still attached to one of its lower branches. I walk right up to the willow and gaze up into its dense hanging branches, trying to recall a time when I was a just a boy wondering how high I could climb and if I made it to the top, whether I would be able to see the whole of the county. There is a hanging branch that I hook Naitoben's baldric over and allow her to swing gently beneath the great tree for a moment, while I stand a few paces away and begin a slow, gentle kata, easing my aching muscles into the exercise in order to stretch and get my blood flowing properly. Each kata is something I had performed countless times growing up, first under my father's tutelage, then eventually, practicing them as a daily routine myself for years. I don't have to think as my body performs these actions, almost with a will of its own.

My breathing has become calm and even, my mind simply in the here and now, my awareness expanding out all around me. At some point a decision is made, and I walk back to Naitoben, grasp her hilt with one hand and, with sudden speed, draw her at last from her years of slumber. The ring of steel and the whoosh of the very air being cut in two announces her to the clearing. For a moment I am completely still, holding Naitoben above my head in both hands in the pose of 'Eagle preparing to strike', letting the light of the sun warm us both, the sun's rays glistening off her gleaming steel. And then, as one, we begin to dance...

I am moving swiftly on the balls of my feet, and with a lightness of being I haven't known in years I circle the clearing, following in Naitoben's wake as she slices the air ahead of and all around me. We dance an ancient pattern of sequences together, a series of killing strikes and defensive postures, passed down from Shidoshi to student over hundreds of years, each new wielder of the blade adding an extra move, strike or posture to aid the next in battle. There is pain blossoming with each movement and each sudden pause as I lead into the next sweep of the blade, but there is no suffering. As we dance together, I become aware of the world around me in a more visceral way than ever before. Every sound, every movement within thirty feet of me, is examined and weighed for potential threats by this heightened awareness and then dismissed when found to be nothing more than some small woodland creature, or the very trees themselves swaying and creaking in the breeze. Despite the pain and weakness from my injuries, I endure the dance far longer than should have been possible.

When I finally stop to catch my breath, wipe the sweat from my brow and slowly lower Naitoben to my side, the sun is high above the trees and I estimate I have been gone for close to an hour. But during that time there has been a sea change within me. Whole again within myself, I have access to all my memories once more, some so dark and terrible, that I know if it weren't for my grip on Naitoben my hands would be trembling. Instead there is a fierce joy bubbling within me for I have found my purpose here in this place, on this day. I am a warrior, like my father before me, his blood is pumping through me, calling me to arms and I intend to answer. I draw Naitoben up close to my chest and slice the palm of my left hand with her, squeezing my fingers in tight to form a fist, watching intently as my bright red blood drips into the lush yellow and green grass at my feet. At the same time, I swear an oath to myself, to dedicate my life from this moment to hunt down all the agents of Europa and their monstrous masters and become their shikei shikko hito. I swear I will fight them until my last breath, so shall it be...

PART 2

CHAPTER 1 – PREPARING FOR WAR

I emerge from the woods remade, every step I take is now filled with purpose, taking me closer to my goal. I went into the woods an escaped slave; I have returned as Ronin. Gunner has kept pace beside me, but I can see that his age is finally starting to show as he is panting heavily in the midday heat. As we close in on the house, he trots over to the porch and quietly lays down under the shade of the bench, dunking his face in a silver bowl that Jack has filled with water for him. As for me, I still feel tired and in pain but my mind has risen above it for now, the pain just means I am still alive and I can catch up on sleep when I'm dead and buried. Naitoben is a reassuring weight across my back, her dark promise concealed for the time being.

I can hear Jack and my mother talking quietly at the side of the house, so follow their voices around the corner of the porch to a small allotment that Maria is helping Jack to tend. She is radiating happiness at this simple task of tilling the earth and pulling up a few weeds from between the rows of vegetables growing out of the dark, healthy soil. The smell of herbs hits my nostrils as I draw close, mint, rosemary and thyme to name a few, and it makes me want to take long, slow breaths, to pick up each distinctive scent in the air. There is a real sense of peace to this place, so different to my old life in the city where everything was always so fast paced and frantic and a million miles from my terrifying indenture under the mountain.

For a brief moment a part of me balks at the vow I just

made in the woods, I wonder if I could have this, if all three of us could be at peace here and help to heal one another... But then I push the thought back down as I reason that, if I don't do something to stop Winters and his sadistic corporation, they will continue to cause misery and suffering to many others and sooner or later, they will come to take back what they believe to be their property. No, I can't have this for myself, but maybe, just maybe, I can ensure that Jack and my mother can.

I clear my throat and greet my mother first, who embraces me warmly and starts pointing and exclaiming at all the lovely things she can see before her with a child's fascinated delight. I turn to Jack as my mother lowers herself back onto her knees and becomes absorbed in the task of digging and pulling at the weeds.

"I have another favour to ask." Jack raises an eyebrow at my request but keeps his tongue for now. I move closer to him and raise my chin, look him straight in the eye. Whatever he sees on my face, the smile leaves his own and I can see he has understood and is waiting with more gravity at the seriousness I am pervading. "I need to do something and I don't know how long it will take me, or even if I will ever come back. Jack I'm so sorry to ask this of you when you have already done so much for me.... Jack would you look after her for me, keep her here, keep her safe, until I return?"

He reaches out to me, clamps his strong hands on my shoulders, returns my look and says, "You don't need to ask this of me Naru, consider it done, I swear to you I will watch over her until you are ready to come back... But I beg you, wait a few more days before you go, you need time to rest, to heal."

I can feel a single tear roll down my left cheek at his sincerity and heartfelt words, I embrace Jack and whisper my thanks, barely able to speak at the sudden depth of emotion I am feeling. As I pull away, I am shaking my head, the decision has already been made, there is no turning back from the path that is set before me. Though I see the wisdom in his words,

I can't help thinking about the others like me still being held under the mountain, desperately hoping for salvation. I may not be able to save them, but I intend to try. With the help of Megan and her team we may stand a chance, and with Naitoben in my hands, a chance is all I need…

Determined to waste no more time, I spend the rest of the day making preparations for my departure. My stolen clothes washed and dried, a few hastily made sandwiches and a flask of Jack's extra strong coffee still piping hot from the kettle, all get packed into Dad's old rucksack along with his spare clothes and a roll of twenties that I find in the front pocket, which I tuck into the inside pocket of my trench coat. I turn my attention to the Beretta Richard gave me and the silenced rifle Megan had taken from the dead Europa sniper. I cast my mind back to my fire arms training and carefully take both guns to pieces on Jack's kitchen table, cleaning and checking all the moving parts, before piecing them both back together.

Jack disappears out to his huge barn that doubles as his workshop and returns a few minutes later with several boxes of forty-five calibre bullets, a side holster and a wicked looking hunting knife that he insists on giving to me as his own parting gifts. I have exactly fifty-six bullets left for the rifle, thanks to the extra magazines Megan took when she searched the dead body under the tree, and close to a hundred bullets for the Beretta, by the time I have finished packing.

I turn my attention to my mother, who is having a mid-afternoon nap in the armchair by the fire. Gunner is curled up by her feet and I take a mental picture of them both to help keep my determination strong for what lies ahead. I kneel down beside Gunner and give him a farewell pat and a hug, a lick of my face and few wags of his tail and he curls back up, his old bones needing their rest after the mornings adventure. I want to wake my mother to say goodbye but I don't want to distress her and I imagine she will likely forget I was even here when she wakes.

My smile is a bitter sweet one as I return to the table, draw the now fully loaded Beretta up, check the safety and tuck it into the holster on my left side. Jack checks over the rifle for me, sights down the barrel and gives a grunt of approval at the weapon before handing it over to me. I take everything out to Dad's car but Jack stops me with a word and hands the keys to his Land rover to me. "I'm thinking the Suzuki has no MOT or tax and probably not a good idea to be getting pulled over with all that gear on you."

I know it makes sense to swap and I am extremely grateful at Jack's insight, something I hadn't even thought of, but I can't help feeling a little wrench in my stomach at the idea of giving up another part of my past, of my father. Reading the distress on my face, Jack goes on quickly,

"Don't worry I will take good care of them both, we will all be here waiting when you come home." Such a simple statement but the words imparted mean more than he can ever know. I nod gravely, not trusting myself to say anything more, steel myself to my path and march over to the silver Rover, dumping most of the gear in the back, but keeping Naitoben close.

With one last hug farewell to Jack, I pull my long coat on, climb aboard the old beast and start her up. With a reassuring rumble the engine bursts into life giving a bone rattling shake as it starts to warm up. I drag the clumsy long gear lever into something that looks like it should be first gear and start to pull away. As I reach the end of the drive, I take one last glimpse in the mirrors at the house that could one day be my home, if I survive what comes next. Thank you, Jack, watashi no tame ni kanojo no anzen o mamorimasu.

CHAPTER 2 – THE LAST HEIR OF NAITOBEN

After driving the BMW and the Yamaha, Jack's Land rover feels like the equivalent of riding a stubborn old mule across the desert, frequently turning around to nip at its rider or stopping to piss in the only watering hole for miles around. In short, the journey north towards Scotland is painfully long, loud and expensive. The old Rover rattles and shakes so much my headache has come back with a vengeance and the frequent stops I have to make to refuel, are a welcome relief from sitting inside the tortuous metal box I have readily swapped for my father's comfortable automatic.

With no working radio to drown out the sound of the engine, after five hours on the road, I am cursing Jack's name, after three more, I am puking my guts up at the side of the motorway, my headache finally having got so bad the pressure needs some form of release so that I had to pull over and stumble away from the car to avoid making the journey even more onerous by throwing up all over my lap.

At the next motorway service station, I finally give in to my protesting body and stop the car dead. I manage a few hours of fitful sleep, waking up at the sound of a large lorry blaring its horn, the driver waving to someone across the car park, on his way once more to who knew where. Awake again, I feel the urge to empty my bladder so decide to stretch my legs and make my way into the main services, a huge building divided into all kinds of shops and restaurants full of other milling road users gawking or grumbling at the high prices of everything on sale but still queing up to pay for them. A part of me wants to shout to them that they have no idea how lucky they are to have the freedom to be here at all, but another part of me can't help nodding at the high prices and making the same face as those around me. The problem is, its the only place for miles around, a shitty kind of oasis to be sure, but when needs must.

I follow the signs to the toilet, then have to check myself as I realise, I am heading to the men's, fucking Darren Winters, kuso yaro. I change direction and head further down an outside corridor to the women's loos instead. Once inside, I lock myself into a cubicle and sit down with my feet pushed up against the door and my gun held in my lap. It might just be paranoia but I can't help feeling vulnerable, especially when I am reminded at times like this of all that I had and all that I've lost.

A few minutes later, and I am just another lost looking motorist stumbling around the services, doing my best to appear casual but feeling my heart rate pounding through me and having to ignore several interested smiles from random men that I pass by. If only they knew, I suspect those smiles would quickly turn to scowls or worse. I aim for a newsagent since I need to get a decent road map of Scotland, motorway signs can only get you so far after all. I manage to get a fairly detailed map as well as several basic mobile phones that should only cost around ten pounds each but end up costing me another fifty pounds all in. If it wasn't for my father's rolled up bills that I had found in his rucksack and the few hundred pounds that were in the wallet Richard had given me at the hospital, I would be struggling to get across the border into Scotland at this rate. I hand over the cash to the bored looking shop assistant, doing my best to appear nonchalant about it and asking for ten pounds worth of minutes and texts to be put on both phones.

As I leave the shop, I spot a pharmacy and decide it's time to finally do something about the pain lancing into my head. I stock up on a box of ibuprofen, taking two right there and then with a bottle of water and on a whim I buy an out of date cheese sandwich on offer that looks like it was made by a blind man with most of his fingers missing and doesn't taste much better either, adding another few pounds to my ever growing bill and doing little to sate my appetite. I figure if I stay much longer, I am going to need to get a job here to fund the rest of my journey, so start walking quickly back to the car.

As I walk, I keep my eyes alert for trouble and ensure that my hand is always just covering my face or that I am turning away as I pass any CCTV cameras pointing in my general direction, it doesn't hurt to be cautious either.

Back in the 'old bone shaker', the nickname I have affectionately given to Jack's Defender, I breath a heavy sigh of relief as I lean back in the cab, crowded places are not helping my anxiety any more than the car has been helping my headache. I try to find that feeling of inner peace that had come upon me in the clearing. It remains elusive for now but helps when I reach back and place my hand over Naitoben's hilt. I have stashed the sword behind the driver's seat out of sight from casual inspection, the Beretta is nestled comfortably in its holster by my side, under my coat once more. I pass one last wary eye around the car park looking for anybody suspicious or out of place...

After a few moments of holding my breath and clutching Naitoben for reassurance, I finally allow myself to breathe easy. I start the bone shaker up and pull her out of the carpark, back onto the motorway. I keep my speed at fifty, any faster and the steering wheel begins to shake as much as the rest of the car. I am constantly checking my mirrors to see if any cars are following me, several times pulling off the motorway, taking a few smaller A and B roads and then re-joining the motorway further north. I use the map to plot a winding course that eventually takes me just a few miles south from Hadrian's Wall, where I

Robert. P. Martin

pull over and make the phone call that I hope will change everything...

After three rings I hang up. When I re-dial she answers the
phone on the first one, "Elizabeth? I wasn't expecting to hear
from you so soon. So, what can I do for you?" I have sat thinking about what I wanted to say, remembering what Megan said
about the possibility of being traced, to make the conversation
as quick and concise as I can, but I still find myself catching my
breath a little as I hear her voice again,

"The facility where they held me was in Scotland, underneath An Teallach. I am almost at the border now, near Hadrian's Wall. Mum is safe with a friend for the time being. Will
you come?" I try not to betray my worry that she will say no, or
that this is all too soon to expect her help but Megan doesn't dis-
appoint when she replies,

"Scotland huh? ...OK, listen close, go to the Firth of Forth,
there's an old navy base on the coast where a friend of the cause
works as the caretaker. The place is deserted at the weekends,
as it's a bank holiday it should be a good safe house to stay for a
few days while we work on a plan of infiltration. Tell Steve that I
sent you and he will look after you, just bear in mind he's a little
bit... eccentric, likely on account of how much time he spends
on his own up there. The rest of us should be there by Sunday.
Stay safe, stay lucky." She hangs up before I have a chance to
ask any questions but, in all honesty, she has exceeded my ex-
pectations, even offered me somewhere to stay when I had been
planning to sleep in the back of the Defender for a few days at
least. I close my eyes, lean back and stretch in the cab, then, remembering Megan's instructions, I pull the phone apart on my
lap, take out the sim and snap it in two. I climb out of the car
and throw the various pieces of the phone into the bushes by
the side of the road, then pause for a moment to just take in the
view. A beautiful forest of conifer trees lies to the north east for
as far as I can see. It leaves me with with a feeling of being very

small, with no other souls in sight, I could be the last human being left alive out here.

There is a forest in Japan near Mount Fuji, that has a dark reputation for people seeking to bring an end to their story. Many are drawn there out of morbid curiosity, some have the urge to seek out and speak with the spirits of the dead, others go with the intention of never coming back out. I can't help feel a similar kind of pull, to simply walk into the forest ahead of me now and lose myself under those trees. Even if I survive what's coming, Europa has ensured that the future I had always dreamed of can never come to be. I will never be able to father children of my own. For the first time it really hits me, I realise that I am the last true heir of Naitoben, the last of the Yamamoto line that had survived the dark days of feudal Japan, two world wars and a dangerous ocean crossing to England. I would have no one to pass on the stories of my ancestors too, no legacy but a river of blood laid out before me.

I am clenching my hands into fists, the icy rage that Naru had helped to keep at bay is starting to melt and bubble back to the surface. To know such hate, such despair, should pull me to my knees, but I have learned to channel it now. Like an arrow released from a bow I am heading relentlessly towards my target, there is no going back, no diverting from this path. I owe it to every Yamamoto that has come before me to fight back against the ones who did this to me. I may have lost my future but if I can, I will ensure that Europa doesn't destroy any more lives.

I drag my eyes away from the forest, stare down at my closed hands, breathe it all in, breathe it all out. Time to go. From the height of the sun in the sky, there looks to still be a few hours of daylight left, so I should be able to get to the base before sundown. I get the map out of the car, rest it across the bonnet and look for the best route to the Firth of Forth... I figure it's about two more hours' drive from where I have pulled over, if I don't make any more stops I might just make it before dark. I spare one last glance into the trees, the ghost of a thought sending a shiver down my spine, then resolutely turn my back, square my shoulders and get back in the car...

CHAPTER 3 – THE CARETAKER

The Royal Navy Reserves base in Dunfermline looks run down and completely abandoned, reminding me of some apocalyptic scene from a disaster movie. Not the most reassuring of sights but better than sleeping in the back of the car. The last of the days' light is beginning to fade, the sun having just disappeared below the horizon, leaving a hazy reddish hue in the sky. I pull the bone shaker up to a huge gated fence and stop next to a solid metal intercom box sticking straight up out of the ground. It's a simple piece of rusted steel that looks like it was built back in the 1960's. I wind down the car window, lean out and press the faded red button to call through to the man who, I am hoping, will let me in to finally get some rest. After a few minutes of waiting and no answer from the intercom, I try the button again and hold it down a little longer than before. I wait a few more minutes and am just about to press the button a last time when the box suddenly crackles to life and a male voice with a thick Scottish accent angrily shouts out at me,

"Don't yeh dare press that button again or I am authorised to use lethal force. Now get yeh gone this is no place for a lady." I very much doubt the validity of his statement but I can't help being taken aback. I was hoping for a warmer welcome, but then again, Megan did say Steve was eccentric, assuming I've got the right base and the right man. I spy the mounted camera on top of one of the outbuildings that has turned to point right at me, he must be watching me from some security room within the complex.

"Am I speaking to Steve?" I ask warily back to the old metal box. If I have got the wrong base, it's going to be hard going driving around in the dark when I am already exhausted from the long drive here.. "Ay and what's it too yeh then lass?" I sigh with relief and keep my fingers crossed that this man is actually going to open the gates for me once I mention the woman who sent me here. I lick my lips and say hopefully, "Megan Archer sent me, she said you were a fellow member of the cause, she and the others are on their way here too."

"Megan? ... Ach why didn't yeh say so in the first place. Pull that old jalopy over to the mess hall and I will come and find yeh." Without waiting for a reply, the gates make a sudden, loud buzzing noise. Then, with much screeching and squealing, the decades old gates slide apart allowing me entry into the base. I pull forward slowly, craning my neck left and right, trying to determine which building he was referring too, since they all look the same, faded with cracked white paint on the walls. In the end I make a guess, turn the Defender to the left and head towards the closest building within sight. As I draw closer there is an old rusted sign pointing the way to the mess hall and by pure luck, I see that I have guessed correctly. I pull to a complete stop outside the building and switch off the engine.

The sudden calm and silence is like music to my ears. I climb out of the car, stretching my legs and back. As I wait for the caretaker to find me, I tug my coat tight around me and hug my arms around myself, noticing for the first time just how much colder it is this far north now that the sun has gone down. Before long, I see a short but well-built man with the bushiest, blackest beard I have ever seen, strolling towards me with the kind of gait that looked like it belonged at sea. Wearing a tattered tweed blazer and a brown flat cap to complete his look, Steve stomps right up to me and grins broadly, at least I think he's grinning, it's hard to tell with all the face fuzz covering his mouth and lips. He holds out a hand in greeting and I take it, regretting it almost immediately, as he has the strongest grip of anyone I have ever met and pumps my hand up and down with more enthusiasm than our meeting warrants. I do my best to mask the pain of my crushed fingers and introduce myself,

"Elizabeth Shaw, pleasure to meet you Steve." I smile politely as I speak, Steve's dark eyes are like an old gunslinger as he stares back at me, I can almost count the crow's feet on his weather-beaten face and guess his age at somewhere in his eighties. He continues to stare right back at me, still holding my hand, still crushing my fingers beyond politeness. I get the feeling he is trying to weigh me up, and wonder if he does this to everyone he meets for the first time. Eventually, he releases my hand and nods once before saying,

"Well met lass. I can see you've a warrior's look to yeh, and I can see why she likes yeh. Megan's always had good taste in women, aye, and if you don't mind my saying so, you are just the sight to see for my sore old eyes on a lonely summer's eve." This close, I can see Steve's discoloured teeth grinning back at me out of his dark mass of facial hair. I can smell tobacco smoke on him too. From the strength of it, I imagine he either smokes a pipe or strong rolling tobacco. The thought sends a little thrill to my nicotine starved brain, it's been over twenty-four hours since I smoked the cigarette Megan had passed to me, after we had escaped with my mother, after all. I do my best to ignore the implication of what this stocky old sea dog just said and instead nod past him to the mess hall.

"Arigatto Steve san, I don't suppose you have anything left to eat in there? I've been practically living on nothing but bread, water and coffee for the last few days." It's no exaggeration to say that my stomach has been trying to hold a conversation with me for the last ten miles of my journey. At my words, the caretaker doffs his cap and offers me an arm like an old English country gent.

"Aye where are my manners not offering you repast upen your arrival? Right you are lass, walk this way." I hold out a hand to bid him wait, reach back into the car and pull Naitoben out, lifting the baldric over my head and resting it lightly across my left shoulder. I am loathe to take Steve's arm like some fair lady being asked to dance but I don't want to offend my host so I grit my teeth and link arms with him, ignoring the questioning look in his eyes at my earlier actions, before allowing him to practically drag me by the arm towards the mess hall.

"You look like you had a long journey Miss Shaw." I smile grimly at his words and reply,

"Is that a polite way of saying I look like shit?" Steve shakes his head and smiles back at me warmly, before saying,

"Ah well, you like like yer need a good rest is all, but first, something to fill yer belly aye?" I heartily agree as we make our way inside the large old building and as soon as we cross the threshold, I can smell must, sweat and, very faintly, a tang of vinegar in the air. The inside of the mess hall is like a huge old barn with a ceiling about thirty feet above my head at its apex. Dozens of long wooden tables and benches line the room, our footsteps echoing off the dark, polished floor as we make our way across the room, leaving me with a sense of smallness at the shear cavernous size of the place. The kitchen and serving station lie over in the far-right hand corner of the room and it's here that Steve directs us. After insisting that I put my feet up and wait for him, Steve disappears into the kitchen and comes back about ten minutes later with a steaming full English breakfast, a Scottish twist of black pudding added to it, as well as a large ceramic mug which, I am hoping, contains something a little more exciting than water.

To my intense relief and satisfaction, the mug is hiding a cold draught pale ale, which I take a mighty swig of the moment it touches my parched lips. I clunk the half-filled mug down on the thick oak table shortly afterwards and wipe the foam from my face before tucking into the hearty meal that has been put before me. Steve holds his tongue, disappears back into the kitchen and returns a few moments later with a mug for himself and offers me a cheers before drinking a few mouthfuls, his merry countenance a sharp contrast from first meeting him in the yard outside. In just a few minutes I have polished off the entire plateful of food, I lean back and rub my stomach in gratitude. I raise my mug and Steve joins me in a clink and another cheers, this time I sup the beer more carefully, savouring every mouthful.

Eventually, Steve clears his throat and says, "It's customary in me country to repay a hosts meal with a worthy tale, to help us get through the long lonely nights o' winter. I appreciate it's summer and winter's a way off yet but would yeh humour an old fool Miss Shaw and tell me a grand tale of the southlands or mayhap yeh ancestors' homeland, since I am guessing there is quite a story attached to that old weapon upen yeh back?" It was a story, centuries old in the making in fact, but I reply sincerely,

"I would tell you my tale if you have the will to hear it through, or any that I know of my ancestors that you might wish to hear, since I have little else to repay you with for your kindness but first I would ask, just how do you know Megan?" Steve slaps the table, relishing the chance to spin me a yarn it seems,

"So yeh be wanting a meal and a tale too? Alright, yer lucky I like the sound of me own voice so much Miss Shaw and I can never say no to a beautiful lady. Aye spare yer blushes for a younger man; I am well past my sell by date but it doesn't mean I can't appreciate the finer things in life. I may be old but I am not blind, at least not yet." I suspect I am indeed blushing at his words as I can feel my cheeks becoming warm, this might just be because I have wolfed down a hot meal and drunk half a pint of ale in just a few minutes. The craving for a cigarette has not left me either and I can't help myself from asking,

"Also, and I realise I am pushing my luck and my manners here, but would you have any spare cigarettes, there is only one thing I know that is finer than a cold pint of ale and that's having a smoke of finely rolled tobacco along with it."

"Damn if I were fifty years younger, you just might be my dream woman. Here, take it with me compliments lass." Steve takes out a gold cigarette box from his inner blazer pocket, pulls one of the cigarettes out theatrically and hands it over to me, before patting himself down and pulling a lighter out of one of his trouser pockets. I feel bad about his harmless flirting but I can't quite bring myself to gainsay him just yet. I promise myself, I will tell him all of it before the night is through, before Megan and the others get here. I would not want Steve to make a fool of himself in front of them as he has shown me nothing but good will and kindness since my arrival.However, first things first.

I reach out and take the proffered cigarette, then lean into Steve's outstretched hands as he holds out a small orange flame burning brightly from his lighter for me to use. A few seconds later and I am basking in the heady nicotine rush, breathing out a great plume of smoke and watching it dissipate into the air above me. Seeing my satisfaction, Steve pulls another out for himself and for a moment we simply sit and smoke in companionable silence...

I draw the last toke right down to the butt, nearly burning my lips with the heat from the cigarette's cherry. Steve has made another swift exit to the kitchen while I smoked and provided us both with an old bronze ashtray that already had half a dozen butts or more stubbed out in it and is now resting on the table between us.

"So yeh wanted a tale and so I will give yeh one. The fact is I have known Megan since she was a babe in arms. The reason for this is because her great grandpappy and me have a history going back to the war. And don't say what war, I'm talking about The War, aye the one with the b'stard Nazis in it. Megan's great grandfather, like millions of other poor souls, was drafted at eighteen and spent the best years of his life fighting and living in trenches in a country that weren't his own, being shot at and seeing damn near all of his friends killed by the end of it." Steve pauses for a moment in his story, adding a little dramatic effect to his words,

"Now I'm no soldier lass, a fisherman and a damn fine sailor if you don't mind me saying so meself, but I don't know one end of a rifle from the other. Truth is, I was still a wee nipper when we got word that they needed boats to get our boys 'ome. Every fisherman and sailor worth his salt for a hundred miles took to their boats at the call, I managed to persuade a few of me mates to come along and took me Da's fishing boat, on account of the fact that he was there somewhere fighting too and I figured I could go rescue 'im. Ha, it's crazy when I think back, I was barely eleven years old at the time. Aye and well, we were told to turn back by many o' the grownups but we ignored their warnings until they finally gave up shouting...

So, it were a whole armada of us what sailed down the North Sea coast to aid our brothers in arms fighting and dying across the English Channel. I won't lie to yeh lass, I have never been so scared or so proud of what we did that day at Dunkirk. With bullets and bombs coming at us from all directions I have no idea how or why we didn't get blown out of the water a dozen times over and ended up in a watery grave at the bottom of the sea, but somehow, we the lucky few, made it to that dreaded beach and pulled as many soldiers as we could back into the boat, then turned tail and fled like the hounds of hell were chasing us. What I saw on that beach will haunt me till me dying day, which ain't none too far off I'm thinking. I never did see me Da, nor never heard from him after that day, but, well, among the few dozen souls we managed to get aboard the boat I was piloting, one Henry Archer was among them.

Aye and he never let me forget the day I saved his life, insisted we become lifelong friends despite years, class and hundreds of miles, separating where we grew up and how we lived. Over the years, after the war was over, we kept in touch through letters as best we could and every summer, he would come all the way up here and bring his whole damned family along with him. It always brings a tear to me eye thinking about it, how he would drag his children and, later, his grandchildren here, just to introduce em to me. He would say that they all owed me their lives in a way and I s'pose that's true, but I would never have asked it of 'em.

Anyhow, you wanted to know about Megan, aye, when I saw her for the first time, she was barely six months old, but I thought, here is a soul that has been on this earth before. I am telling you lass, she had an intelligence to 'er eyes, never seen the likes of it before or since and over the years she is the only one of them what come after, that still insists on coming to visit me every year, dragging that quiet brother of 'ers along with 'er."

I have sat in respectful silence listening to Steve's tale, of his pride in what he did at such a young age and feeling some of the horror in what he went through too. My father had never liked to speak about what happened on his tours and I figured there were things he had seen and done, he simply felt he could not share because of the trauma of reliving it in the retelling of it. I can see that Steve has become very emotional having spilled out his tale and drawn his mind back to a time when the world was on fire, when he and all his friends must have wondered if they would ever see their home again.

"How about another ale?" I suggest. "Aye and another ciggy too I'm reck'ning." He agrees with a wink, then draws himself slowly to his feet, stomps off to the kitchens and returns with another smooth pint of ale for both of us. A few minutes later and I have another strong cigarette lit, billowing smoke and hanging lazily from my lips, as well as a belly full to bursting. I'm starting to feel a little light headed from the beer and dog tired from the long journey here but I promised Steve my tale in return for his kindness and I aim to get it done. If he calls me lass one more time, I am going to be blushing with embarrassment for the rest of the time I am here. I clear my throat, place my mug down carefully on the table, take a long slow drag of my cigarette and blow it out, then I begin my tale...

CHAPTER 4 – ENTRY INTO WONDERLAND

My throat is all dried out, every one of Steve's cigarettes are burned to ashes. The old man in front of me, who kept his cool through his own tale of the terror of war and losing his father to the Nazis, is openly weeping at hearing mine. He has patted my shoulder and rubbed my back more times than I can count. I don't doubt his heartfelt sincerity but for myself, I have become numb to the telling. Maybe it's because I am so tired, or simply because I could draw on the strength from having Naitoben resting against my leg. Either way, I am able to tell Steve the whole thing with a kind of cold detachment, like it had happened to someone else. He is also now well aware that some very bad people are gunning for Megan and the others, and who knew what Europa would do to them if they were ever captured?

"And so, you figure to take the fight to 'em then?" Steve asks me, rubbing his eyes with the back of his hand and clearing his throat trying mightily to pull himself back together. I nod, lift Naitoben into my lap, stare hard into the inky depths of her obsidian cloak,
"I mean to bring the whole fucking place down on their heads or die in the trying." I state my purpose with conviction, recalling my oath in the clearing just a few days ago.

"Then yeh have my blessing, for what its worth and what small protection I can offer yeh here in the meantime. Come, let's find yeh somewhere to sleep for the night a'fore yeh fall down."

I thank the old caretaker with a nod and rise carefully to my feet, using Naitoben as a temporary balancing aid, the few ales that I have drunk leaving me feeling somewhat unsteady. Steve directs us back out of the mess hall, across the deserted yard and into a smaller tin building of similar design, reminding me of a large, worn corrugated garden shed. Inside the old steel building, there are rows of bunk beds, enough for at least two dozen people or more. Steve waves his hand in a gesture that encompasses the whole room and tells me to take my pick of the beds, then shows me where to find the bathroom and toilet if I need or want to use either. His tasks complete, the caretaker bids me goodnight and advises me to meet him back in the mess hall in the morning for breakfast.

I choose the closest bed to the door, reasoning that I can hear better if anyone or anything is moving about outside. I tuck the Beretta under my pillow and keep tight hold of Naitoben as I finally lay my head down to rest. Exhaustion washes over me as soon as I lie flat and, despite my wariness, I fall into a deep sleep within mere moments of closing my eyes...

The nightmares find me eventually, as they always do. I don't know how I got here but I am back in my cell. I can literally feel Kiko breathing on my neck, whispering the nameless horrors that she wants to visit upon me, just inches from my ear. She reminds me that I am hers, that I am weak, demanding I obey, to speak the affirmation as I have been taught. In the dream I try to defy her but an invisible weight pushes me down onto my knees, no matter how much I want to stand up and fight her. I find, instead, I am begging forgiveness, naming her as my master once more. I am crying with shame, desperate, why can't I fight her, where is Naitoben, where is my sword? And then I see her, cast aside, lying broken in hundreds of shattered pieces. At the sight of my broken blade, I scream in anguish and wake suddenly, a cold sweat tickling down my spine, my knuckles bone white from clutching Naitoben in a death grip, my teeth gritted and bared in a tight snarl. For a moment my heart is beating like I have just run a race, my darkest fears had been playing out in front of me, but as the dream fades, I realise Naitoben is still whole, held tightly in my hands and Kiko is not here.

It takes me a moment to become fully aware of my surroundings, my sleep addled mind recalling where I am and why I am here. Like most mornings since my forced transformation, I carefully reach down between my legs, hoping to find something which my mind knows to be long gone. I suppose it is the kind of hope born of desperation, that it's all been a bad dream, that the monstrous thing that was done to me could not really be true. But, like a hundred times before, my hand finds the empty space that I already knew to be there. I wipe a lonely tear from my cheek, pull my hand away from the void between my legs and sit up. I listen intently for a few minutes, sitting completely still, my body once again kicking into its now usual hyperalertness, straining my senses for anything untoward... Nothing.

I let out a breath I hadn't even realised I had been holding, pick up my rucksack, take Naitoben and my gun and make my way to the bathroom. I give myself a fast wash in the shower, deliberately keeping it cold to fully wake me up, before changing into my father's old cargo trousers and the hooded jumper Richard had given to me at the hospital, zipping it up to conceal the Beretta, tucked snugly into my side once more in its holster. I tie my still wet hair back into a warrior's tail, sling Naitoben over my shoulder, her weight at once familiar and reassuring. Ready to face the day, I start to make my way back over to the mess hall, depositing my rucksack back in the Land rover on the way past. As I go to lock the door, I hear the noise of a car drawing up to the gates, and carefully edge myself along the back of the car to check it's not someone I need to start shooting at.

To my intense relief, I recognise Grim in the driver's seat of a dusty black Audi saloon. I cast my eye to the right and feel my heart surge when I see through the glare of the sun, that his sister is sitting right beside him. Forgetting my hungry belly for the moment, I find myself striding towards the gates as they begin their screeching slow slide to the left.

By the time I have neared them, Grim has already pulled the car inside the compound and cut the engine. The metal gate is slowly closing again. As Grim and Megan climb out of the car, the back doors open too and a very thin pasty white man, looking like he hasn't bothered to shave or maybe even wash in several days, wearing a black leather biker jacket, baggy black-grey t-shirt and ripped blue jeans, and black boots with a roll-up tucked behind his ear, gets out of the side behind Grim. On the other side of the car a tall, dark-skinned Hispanic woman, with short, spikey hair and wearing tight black trousers, a blue shirt and a green army jacket, gets out behind Megan. The two siblings come forward to greet me warmly and we share a brief three-way hug before Megan turns the killer smile she was directing my way on to their two companions and bids them to introduce themselves.

"Elizabeth, this is Cole," Megan advises me indicating the woman first, "She's our sniper, specialises in weapons and tactics." Cole steps forward and we share a brief handshake, "Selina Cole," she says and I detect a similar accent to my own, suspecting she must have grown up somewhere near London. "Elizabeth Shaw," I offer in return feeling a genuine warmth coming from Cole as we greet each other. "Elizabeth is one of the fastest drivers I have ever seen and she's a damn fine shot too." Grim announces to the group. I find myself half smiling at him for his compliments, despite that familiar sallow look on his face. It's the kind of camaraderie I guess you can only feel when you've been through something like we had just a few days before.

The thin man has held back, smoking the roll-up from behind his ear and watching the three of us with a sour look on his face, like he just sucked on a lemon. As our eyes meet, he smirks at me like he thinks I'm not what he was hoping for, then coughs from deep in his chest, turns to the left and spits a wad of greenish brown phlegm onto the dusty gravel by his feet. Wiping a greasy palm against his jeans before holding it out to me, he says, "Lister McCreedy, It's Macca to me mates. You can call me Mr McCreedy. You want something unlocked or blown up, you call me. You want to see what's under me shirt, well, that will cost most folks a little extra but in your case I'm willin' to make an exception." The overly sordid wink he sends my way leaves little to the imagination as to what he's getting at. I find I have an almost instant disliking for this man, his accent is maybe Northern Irish and he is looking at me with something like disdain or maybe something more suggestive, it's hard to tell since he is squinting in the light of the late morning sun. I get the feeling he's the sort of person who would see bullying as harmless banter. I have met plenty of arseholes like him my whole life, both in college and even at work in the police over the years. He wants a reaction from me, maybe he's just testing my metal but whatever he's hoping I might say, I don't get the chance to reply as Cole turns to him, slaps the roll-up out of his mouth with a fast flick of her wrist and says, "Why are you always such a cunt Lister?"

It's the kind of thing only friends can get away with saying to one another as McCreedy flushes red in the cheeks but doesn't gainsay the tall woman glaring at him with a look like a mother scalding her recalcitrant child, and instead of reacting to her hot glare, McCreedy reaches down to pick up his crumpled cigarette off the ground, flicks some of the dirt from the end and takes several quick drags before lifting his eyes back to mine, a look of mild apology and perhaps embarrassment playing across his face this time.

I raise an eyebrow at the strange exchange between the two, before stepping forward to offer my hand in greeting. Whether this man was an arsehole or not, his skills could come in very useful for what I had in mind, so I put my most polite smile on my face and say. "Arigato Misuta McCreedy. Anata no enjo wa dai kangeidesu." McCreedy grinds the last of his roll-up out underneath his boot heel and clasps hands with me. He nods once, releases my hand then turns to Cole whispering, "Feck she just say to me? Should I bow or some fecking shit?" Cole shrugs back at him with a total lack of caring and heads to the boot of the saloon to start unpacking, clearly deciding she was not going to bail him out with regards to his terrible lack of manners. "The Japanese bow to one another as a term of respect Mr McCreedy. I simply offered my sincere thanks for you coming here." I reply to his question, though he hadn't directed it at me. I can see my cool demeanour has left the man bemused as he was likely hoping to create a little more drama between us, rather than making a poor first impression. He scratches the back of his head, looks down at the floor and mumbles, "Aye well, my services don't come fer free. You can thank the boss fer that and save yer thanks fer when the jobs done." I nod in agreement and thank Megan for bringing the team here at all. She offers me an apologetic smile before dispersing the tension with a shrug of her own and directing us all to the mess hall to eat and discuss just what we were going to do about Europa and the facility beneath An Teallach. She draws alongside me as we all turn towards the huge old building where I had spent most of the previous evening with the caretaker and whispers, "Nicely done", pats my back in friendship and eyes the hilt of Naitoben sticking up over my shoulder with undisguised interest. "Is that what I think it is?", she asks me, a smile breaking out across her face. I can't help myself and grin back at her question before replying, "If you think it's a two century old named katana sword, crafted by one of the finest swordsmiths in all Japan, handed down from father to son for five generations, then yes, it's exactly what you think it is." We both laugh at my description. "A weapon worthy of your talents for getting into trouble then." Megan replies and as our gazes meet, I can't help feeling a little tingle at what I see in her brown eyes...

CHAPTER 5 – A PLAN COMES TOGETHER

Steve greets us all by the doors to the mess hall and he, Megan and Grim share a warm embrace and some whispered words of good greeting before he turns his attention to the rest of us. "Come on yeh bunch o' vagabonds, let's be getting some grub down yeh." He waves us all inside and stomps off to the kitchens, leaving the rest of us to set down at one of the long benches close to where I had sat the night before. McCreedy and Cole place several large duffel bags down on the table beside us and at Megan's nod of command they set too, emptying the contents out onto the table. There is a reasonable sized armoury inside one of the bags, including several shotguns, three handguns and two police issue, semi-automatic rifles, as well as numerous boxes of ammo of all kinds.

McCreedy empties the other bag next to the first, which appears to be mostly sizeable bricks of plastique, plus all kinds of wires and circuit boards as well as a lock picking kit that wouldn't have looked out of place in a hospital surgery. Finally, he pulls out a handful of special issue black ops night vision goggles, enough for each one of us and several old fashioned looking army walkie talkies for clandestine communicating.

Satisfied with their haul all accounted for, Megan pulls a silver laptop from the satchel at her side and opens it up to show us all several detailed maps of An Teallach that she has been examining on the way here. She zooms in on different points of interest, explaining all the while and pointing out the places she wants to draw our attention to, "It's a good four-hour drive from here to Dundonnell village. This village is the closest one to the mountain's summit and the only thing there appears to be a youth hostel and a farm so I'm thinking either one or both might hold the key to getting into the mountain's underbelly. I pulled some paper maps from an archive in the Edinburgh city library on the way here and the old mine Elizabeth described, appears to be situated roughly in the middle of the hostel and the farm, When you zoom in it looks likely it's this area here, it's all boarded up but that may well be just for show." Megan pauses from her briefing to zoom in more closely on the map on her laptop, showing us the area, she is referring to, before going on,

"The real problem we have, is that this place is in the middle of nowhere. I mean there is no cover besides the peaks and ridges of the other mountains for miles all around. They don't call it the great wilderness for nothing I suppose. The closest thing I can see that we could use as a place to scout from, is some private woodland to the northeast of the village. So, here's what I'm thinking, we wait until it's close to sundown before we leave, make sure it's full dark by the time we get to those woods, kill the lights when we get close to anything that might resemble signs of humanity, then go in with night vision. With some care, we can secure the woods, then wait until the morning before we sidle up to the village and do a little recce of sorts before anyone starts waking up.

We have to assume anyone we come across is a potential threat and complicit with what's going on, since there is literally nothing else nearby and I can't see how anyone local would not know about what's going on right underneath them.

As a further observation, it's worth noting when we were at the library, Graham came across an old newspaper article that reported a number of earthquakes in the area around ten years ago, which matches with when the place was likely under construction. He also found a number of other more recent articles warning of the danger of climbing the mountain itself, including a few horror stories of climbers going missing or being found dead from falling off the mountainside. It all adds up to a very good way of keeping people from wanting to go there and it's isolated enough that I think this is the perfect place for keeping their dark deeds hidden from the eyes of the curious." Megan has gained my full and undivided attention. Her calculating mind has stunned me and I agree with her assessment and her reasoning. She has had barely a full day since I called her and she has already formulated a plan worthy of a marine commando or police superintendent, though I suspect telling her so was more likely to insult her than compliment her.

But there was still the matter of what we would do if we even managed to find the entrance. For that, my new companions are going to need me to provide a detailed description of everything I know and can remember about the layout of the facility and what Richard had told me about some of its secrets. Well, we have all day before we are looking to leave, plenty time enough for me to educate them about the finer points of what had been my underground prison and my home for the last two years of my life...

After a decent hot breakfast courtesy of Steve and the royal navy yearly food budget, I find myself standing over one of the long tables of the mess hall, having drawn the closest thing I can to represent how I recall the interior of the facility on a huge piece of paper that Steve pulled from an easel he found in the officer's quarters. The drawing looks a little like a pyramid, starting from the largest level, the cell blocks at the bottom of the mountain, moving up through the servant's quarters, then the boardroom and laboratories, before reaching the individual executive suites.

At Megan's urging I also explain about the collars that they use for control and punishment and how I figured out how to get mine off. Megan surprises me again by advising she had put the problem to McCreedy almost as soon as she and Grim had left me at my father's lock-up. Lister smiles his sour smile, runs his hand through his mass of curly, tangled hair and produces a small black cylinder from his jacket pocket and waves it around in front of us like a magician trying to show off their empty sleeves. "I have here a prototype mini electromagnetic pulse I have named McCreedy's MEMP..." Lister takes a brief pause for effect but while the rest of us are waiting for a little more explanation, I hear Cole whisper, "Prick," under her breath just loud enough to ensure everyone in the room heard her.

McCreedy clears his throat, doing his best to appear unfazed by Cole's taunt and goes on with his speech. "It should have enough juice to help knock out any power inside the collars. Reckon there's enough battery in this little beauty to knock out around five or six of them before it would need a recharge. Because of its size, it will need to be held within a few inches of a collar to short out its power. I have a bag full of them in the car, made enough for one each, since, from what Megan said, it seemed that there couldn't be more than around ten to fifteen people being trained and tortured down there at any one time." I step closer and ask to have a better look at McCreedy's cunning little gadget, hardly able to believe that this man could have come up with something like this at such short notice, it is a real work of genius. Like Megan, he seems able to put a persona out to the world that belies the true soul underneath. Before McCreedy has a chance to make another caustic comment I simply look him in the eye and bow my head a few inches, keeping eye contact the whole time. McCreedy flushes red in response, scratches the back of his head and tries to look anywhere else but at me. "Ah well it was no bother really; I just used some parts I had left over from a larger version I was building to make something that could shut down a time-lock safe. Hey, we have to fund this piece of shit outfit somehow, right?"

I realize I might have misjudged Lister McCreedy on first meeting him. I now think that maybe he uses his caustic humour to hide his own lack of confidence, or maybe he is just awkward with social skills, maybe too much time pulling locks apart or sitting too long in dark rooms thinking of ways to blow things up? Regardless, I decide, since Megan has faith in his abilities, I will do my best to keep civil with him, but I imagine it's going to be hard going, especially if he keeps looking at me the way he's been doing when he thinks I am not paying attention.

Perhaps sensing my unease, or realizing we have reached a natural conclusion to our meeting, Megan calls us all to order and bids us sit around one of the tables once more.

"Now that business is out of the way, I think it's time we officially initiated Elizabeth. Besides, she will need to have a codename when we are on comms. So… Elizabeth, I would like to introduce you and welcome you to Wonderland. You already know my codename is White Rabbit, as for Graham, he is Gryphon, Selina is Caterpillar and Lister is Hatter. I selected our code names based on certain attributes or idiosyncrasies that help define us, easier to remember that way.

I am the White Rabbit because there is no dirt that gets buried that I can't dig back up. Graham has always been my protector while I'm busy with my nose buried in the ground, he is my eyes and ears and no matter what kicking he's got over the years looking out for me he has always gotten back up. Selina used to be a chain smoker when she first joined us." Megan pauses and gestures to Selina who huffs loudly before she pulls her sleeve up to reveal a nicotine patch, it also begins to explain just why she seems so tetchy and why she was so pissed off with McCreedy when they first arrived, since it was likely he was taunting her as much as me when he lit up his roll-up and blew the smoke all over her. "As for Lister, well he's a crazy bastard, obviously, since his favourite past time is blowing things up… Now we come to our newest member. Elizabeth, let me ask you something, just what is it you plan on doing with that sword?"

At her question I have to seriously take stock of why I still have my katana sword strapped to my shoulder. When I made my vow in the clearing, it had felt right but what we were planning here was no noble charge at the enemy where I could challenge Kiko to a duel for honour, as my ancestor would have done. No, what we were doing would be dark, bloody work. I had titled myself Shikei shikko hito, there was no turning back. I would be their executioner, I turn to Megan to explain my purpose but she holds out her hand and says, "You don't need to tell me after all, it's written all over your face... Ladies and gents, we have our Kingsleigh."

At the confused look that passes across the rest of us Megan sighs and whispers, "Why am I surrounded by Philistines?" Speaking more loudly she explains, "Kingsleigh is the last name of Alice. She wielded the Vorpal sword and used it to slay the Jabberwock... And before you ask, the Jabberwock was the name of the dragon that the Red Queen used to maintain her tyrannical rule over Wonderland." At her words I can't help thinking of a certain reptilian smile and, in truth, it is Kiko's head, above all the others in that facility, that I plan to remove, that I feel Naitoben is calling for. Megan has read me as well as an open book and perhaps, after all, I long to slay the dragon of my nightmares, and if I am to truly put them to rest, I have to confront her, or bury her under the mountain, I will be satisfied with nothing less.

CHAPTER 6 – A QUIET WORD WITH THE GAFFER

McCreedy, Grim and Cole have bunked down for some sleep after the long drive getting here. We are due to leave in just a few hours' time for the dreaded mountain that haunts my dreams. I am so keyed up there is no way I will be getting any more rest before we leave. Megan has stayed behind with me in the mess hall, pouring over the maps and asking me all sorts of questions about the different levels within the facility, the likely guard and camera positions, what types of weapons the guards use, any potential booby traps that could lie in wait for us. It has forced me to draw my mind back to those dark days with more clarity than I would like.

After interrogating me for what seems like hours, Megan finally relents, seeing the pained expression on my face at recalling the pit and what it was used for, trying my best to describe it without crumbling to the floor in front of her. She places a hand gently on my shoulder and looks me in the eye before apologising sincerely. I do my best to shake off the bad memory of that time, and still wonder whether I will be able to go there of my own volition without freezing up or running in the opposite direction. It helps that Megan is now looking at me so closely, turning my mind toward more pleasant thoughts. My body is reacting to her closeness, sending tiny shivers where she is touching me, making my breath come a little faster. There is a chemistry building between us and I know she feels it too, her hand is lingering a little longer than necessary on my shoulder, her eyes, burning with intelligence and something undefinable, staring deeply into mine and I realise that all I want to do right now is pull her too me and kiss her...

Except I can't bring myself to do it, and as the moment passes, I read something like disappointment on her face. She removes her hand, takes a step back, perches herself gingerly on the edge of one of the tables and folds her arms across her chest. I feel my cheeks flushing a little, embarrassed by my feelings and this sudden awkwardness between us. I try to cleanse the building tension by changing the subject and say, "Your brother is quite the silent type, isn't he?" She quirks an eyebrow at my words but smiles and nods after a moment, clearly thinking about him and replies, "We had a rough childhood, our father was a real piece of work. He was a very angry man, hated his job, liked to hit the liquor when he got home, then take his anger out on Mum by hitting her too. As Graham got older, he started try-ing to put himself between her and our father's fists and, well, I'm sure I don't need to tell you what happened. Graham never cried though, never complained, and he kept doing it too. I would get hysterical, scream and shout for my father to stop but he could shut me up with a look, because I knew he would do the same to me if I interfered.

It got really bad for a while after I turned thirteen, when our loving father started taking a little too much interest in me." She pauses briefly, clearly caught short with the sudden emotion flowing through her as she dredges up old memories best left in the past. "One-time Graham saw what he was doing, he was only fifteen, he had never fought my father back despite all the times he had taken his blows or the lash of his belt, but when he saw him putting his hands on me something in him just snapped. He attacked our father, I mean he went at him with a rage, like he had stored it all up for that one moment. That

Robert. P. Martin

day, Graham beat our father bloody, until he crawled away from us a broken, weeping, cretin of a man. The same day he packed what few belongings he had and up and left us. We never saw him again. It was a tough few years after that, Mum hadn't ever worked and Graham had to get two jobs just to stop us losing our home. But he still never complained, not once. All my life he has been looking out for me, if it wasn't for him, well I don't dare think what my life might have been like. And, yeah, it took it's toll on him, forcing him to grow up so early like that. I don't think Mum ever truly forgave him for what he did to Dad but I made sure to thank him every day, in whatever small way I could. It made us closer than most siblings would be I suppose, since we learned we could only truly rely on each other as both our parents let us down in their own way."

Megan has poured her heart out to me and I have moved to sit beside her, but unsure of what I should do, I have simply listened and made no judgements. I feel sad that such good people were raised by a tyrant, but pleased that they were able to fight through it together and that they still have such a strong bond. It also goes a long way to explaining Graham's constant grim expression that he wore like a favourite coat.

As Megan's tale draws to a close, I find that I have pressed up against her almost without thinking, and I look down to see that our fingers have become entwined. "The thought of letting you down, of letting any of you down, it terrifies me." I whisper the words to the empty air in front of me and suddenly feel Megan's hand on my chin, turning me to face her, only now there are mere inches between us, our heads so close I can smell the coffee on her breath and the gentle fragrance of her lavender perfume. She doesn't let go but instead, slides her palm up and round, stroking my warm cheek before tucking a few stray hairs I have missed back behind my ear. I couldn't lean back or pull away if I wanted too, I let the gentle pressure she is putting on the back of my head draw us ever closer...

The kiss is long and soft and tastes so sweet I can't help thinking about the first time I ate strawberries. I can't recall ever being kissed so well in my whole life but, eventually, Megan pulls away and for a timeless moment she just stares deeply into my eyes. Just when I think it's all over, she reaches across my shoulder, lifts Naitoben up and off me, resting her carefully on the table behind us. She pulls me in close to her, sliding her other hand into my side, sending a tremor of anticipation through me. I start to unzip my hoodie, to give her better purchase and she aids me with it, pulling the jumper down over my arms, still leaning in, seeking my lips as I seek hers in return.

Suddenly, she pulls away from me, stepping back a few feet, the Beretta held tightly in her hand, pointed straight at my chest. "I don't understand, I thought, I mean, why Megan?" I gasp out the words, the hurt too raw to conceal at this sudden betrayal. She is looking at me sadly, like she really didn't want to do this, but the safety is off and the hammer is pulled back. I don't dare try to move; she could kill me with one little twitch of her finger. I can feel my heart hammering inside me, nanfakku?

"There is a fine line between bravery and recklessness Elizabeth. I'm sorry but I just can't take the chance you won't do something that could get us all killed. Believe me, I want you on the crew but you aren't ready for this, I told you to take time to recover but you came rushing up here barely a day after you got out of the hospital. Just talking about what it was like for you in that place has you shaking in your boots. Besides, I know you want to help those other people but we don't have the time or the resources to pull that off. We will do the next best thing for them, give them a quick death, like you once planned to do to yourself. If we get the chance, we will save who we can but the real mission here is to blow that place to hell and all those fucked up sadists down there along with it. Then maybe they will think twice about messing with my family next time, or anyone else for that matter."

There is something in Megan's voice I haven't heard before, a kind of ruthlessness born of fanaticism and I realise I should have seen it sooner. She and her friends have an agenda I'm not even sure I agree with and now it's too late, I have told them all they need to know and they will take my chance to fight back, to save the others, to save Richard, if he's still alive, and instead they're going to use McCreedy's plastique to cave the whole mountain in on the heads of everyone inside. I start to beg, sink down to my knees before her, "Please Megan, don't, we can save them, just give me a chance to do this please?" But she is already shaking her head, about to tell me no, only a strange noise in the distance brings us both to a sudden halt. I tilt my head this way and that, trying to work out what it is, where it's coming from... What is that? Is that what I think it is? Oh no... Oh fuck no... It's them, they've found us!

CHAPTER 7 – TERROR FROM ABOVE

Megan's eyes have gone huge and rounded into a kind of 'oh fuck' look of startlement. I imagine I look much the same to her too. The sound is becoming clearer now, two helicopters coming from the north west, from the very direction that we were supposed to be heading to, An Teallach. My most immediate thought is how, how could they possibly know we are here? Then a very real sinking feeling sets my head spinning, it has to be me, they have tracked me somehow, the thought sends an icy chill of dread down my spine. If they tracked me here, then it's likely that they know about Jack and Mum too. I have to warn them, if it's not already too late. I recall that I have another phone in my coat, sitting on the passenger seat of the Land rover. I also feel a terrible sense of responsibility, my masters had ordered me to get the Wonderland crew together, all in one place, so they could take them out in one fail swoop, and I have led them right to them, just like they wanted.

They must have implanted another tracker in me, it's the only thing I can think of that makes any sense. My mind begins to work furiously, where, how? Then I find my eyes alighting on McCreedy's bag of MEMP's. I have a flash of insight and surge to my feet. Megan lurches back at my sudden movement and for a moment I am certain she is going to simply shoot me and be done with it, but her bright mind must have made some alternative calculation as she has a change of heart, pushes the hammer back in and passes the gun back to me, pistol grip first. "GO!"

She shouts at me, already turning to the weaponry laid out on the other table across the hall, "Save yourself, if you can." She runs to her walkie talkie standing upright on the table next to the armoury of guns and plastique, snatches it up and holds the button down, speaking with command and decisiveness despite the sudden mess we were in, "Mayday, mayday, this is an abort. Take evasive manoeuvres. Gryphon? Gryphon get your arse over here. We are Alpha, Charlie, Foxtrot, do you hear me? This is not a drill."

While Megan radios the others, I take Naitoben back up off the table, hang her across my shoulder where she belongs and lunge over to the bag of MEMP's. Taking one out and turning it on I run it up, down and across my body, letting it seek out what I know to be there somewhere. As I draw it down past my belly button the slow clicking noise it is making suddenly changes in frequency and becomes rapid, like a Geiger counter that has found serious radioactivity. Cold certainty sinks into my bones. Fuck, those fucking motherfucking kyuntos. It's the exact place where the chip inside me was placed, that was responsible for sexual stimulation, it could trick my mind into believing I had working female parts down there, when I shouldn't be able to feel a damn thing after the butchery they performed, at least that's what they told me it was for.

Without further thought I turn the MEMP on and a strange pulse, like a small electric shock, jumps through my body and leaves me feeling weak and lightheaded for a few precious seconds when I need all my strength. I hope what I have done has been enough to at least stop them from zeroing in on us. The navy base was a huge complex, nearly a half a mile across all told. I hope I have bought us all a fighting chance of getting out of here alive... I hope...

I am running, sprinting in fact, every fibre of my being is alive with one simple thought. I have to get to the car. I need that phone, and I need the rifle on the back seat if I'm going to do any good here today. Plus, the feeling of responsibility for the Wonderland crew is weighing heavily upon me. I need to lure at least one of the helicopters away, both if I can, but I doubt I will be that lucky given my recent track record. I have already passed the others, running to gear up alongside their leader, preparing to fight and flee as only they know how. A part of me wants to stand beside them, to be part of the team once more, but after what just happened between Megan and me, the urge to flee as far away from them all as possible is stronger.

I am panting for breath by the time I reach the Rover. I jump in and crank the engine into life, slamming my foot down on the gas pedal as I punch it into first gear. The wheels spin in the gravel before they can find purchase, then the car suddenly lunges forward as though it has been kicked up the backside. I glance in the wing mirror, tilting it so it's pointing up into the sky and I feel my heart lurch up into my throat at the sight. A sleek black helicopter is bearing down upon me with shocking speed. The noise of the helicopters' blades are almost deafening, but then the sound of something even louder starts blasting from the sky towards me, a hail of bullets ricocheting in every direction, bouncing off the roof and spraying across the bonnet of the car. I can't accelerate any faster, so instead I change course, zigzagging across the compound, desperately trying to dodge the storm of death raining down upon me, before spying a lookout tower that might just be the key to my salvation.

I wrench the steering wheel to the left and aim straight for the tower. A dozen more bullets rip through the car and I have to fight the urge to cower under the dashboard. I speed past the tower and slam on the brakes, spinning the car behind it and out of sight from the gun barrels seeking to end my life. With only a few precious seconds to spare, I grab my coat and rifle, shove the driver's door open with all my strength, leap from the car and start running for the tower door, shooting at the lock with the Beretta and shoulder barging into it so that I practically fall through the door, just as the helicopter circles round to get me back in its sights.

I scramble back to my feet as hundreds of bullets rip into the side of the building and across the door where I had fallen through mere moments before. With nowhere else to go, I make for the spiral staircase that leads right to the top of the tower. Just twenty seconds after I begin my ascent, a huge thunderous roar hits the side of the building and knocks me down to my knees. For a terrible moment the tower seems to sway, creaking and groaning like some metal beast that has just taken a mortal blow. I look down and can see that the stairs have been blasted out of existence about ten feet from the ground floor and there is a huge hole where the door used to be. Thick black smoke is billowing up from where the building was hit, so I pull my hood over my head, hold my coat up to my mouth to try to filter out the fumes that are seeking to choke the air from my lungs and continue my climb.

The smoke is getting thinner as I climb ever higher, so I take the phone out, tuck it into my trouser pocket and drop my coat on the stairs behind me. The tower is still swaying slightly and I wonder if it would survive another strike like the last. I can hear the helicopter circling around for another pass, the brief respite from the rain of bullets is going to be coming to an end any second. I dig deep, try to find my resolve, call on the darker half of my personality that has been lying dormant ever since I took Naitoben from Jack's hands. I growl out a savage snarl of vitriol at the malevolent forces hell bent on turning my life into a living nightmare. If I'm going to die here, it will not be as some cowering, frightened creature clinging to the stairs in terror. I will die with a battle cry on my lips and fire in my heart. Time to become something else, time to turn the tide on these fuckers...

I surge up the last few stairs of the tower, taking them two at a time, certain I have, at most, a minute left, before my life is drawn to a close when the building collapses underneath me.

My rifle is held steady in my hands, cocked and loaded. Beautiful bright sunlight is streaming in through the huge windows that circle the entire tower, allowing anyone looking out, to see in all directions. I turn towards the south facing window where I can hear the helicopter's dreaded rotor blades beating ever closer towards me. I take one huge gulping breath and hold it, smash the rifle's butt hard into the window shattering the glass and providing a clear line of sight to the helicopter. I sink down onto one knee, tuck the stock of the rifle tightly into my shoulder and sight down the barrel.

I can't see inside the cockpit through the chopper's tinted glass, I don't try and guess where the fuel tank might be, there's no time to try at guessing or hoping I might hit one of them by just firing at the windows. Instead, I take a beat on the rear rotor blade. I don't know much about the aerodynamics of a helicopter, but I suspect if I can take the rear blade out it will be like trying to drive a speeding car without a steering wheel. I flick the switch just by the rifle's trigger, setting it to automatic. Then I pull the trigger and lean in hard as the rifle bucks back against me, firing off twenty rounds in less than three seconds. At the same time, I see the glint of light from the side of the helicopter as a rocket is released and starts its deadly path towards me...

The explosion is so loud I can't hear anything except for an irritating ringing in my ears. The top of the tower is just gone, there is nothing but blue open sky above me. I must have jumped about ten feet and landed in a crumpled heap on the stairs, just as the rocket hit the south side of the tower, but I can still feel the intense heat bearing down on me and have to draw my dropped coat over my head to try to prevent my skin from burning. The tower's swaying is getting really bad now and I doubt it's going to be standing for much longer but I still find myself grinning fiercely, almost belly laughing at the absurdity of what just happened. Because just before I jumped, I saw that I had hit the helicopter exactly where I hoped and the last sight

I had of it, it was spinning out of control, grey smoke billowing out of its wounded tail, and just a few seconds after the first explosion, a second, even louder one rocked the tower, but I could tell the rumble came from the ground this time. The dark part of me sincerely hoped that every one of the people inside was dead...

The next few minutes of my life are fraught with anxiety, each small step back down the tower steps is met with a terrifying groaning of metal and all the while the whole building around me is starting to crumble, bits and pieces of burning masonry keep falling off the walls above me, the last piece, a ball of fiery concrete barely missing my head and crashing onto the already burning floor below. I clutch the hilt of my sword tightly, drawing strength and courage from her where I have none left within me, and so I keep moving, keep putting one foot in front of the other, every breath wondering if it will be my last, until somehow, I am back at the bottom of the tower, just ten feet between me and certain doom if I stay a moment longer.

I lean down and crawl over the edge of the last stair, hang by my hands and drop the last five feet to the ground, my legs folding underneath me, my body rolling to the side with a thump and certain bruising to follow later. I haul myself back to my feet, using part of the remaining wall for support and stagger out of the hole where the door used to be. I am coughing and spluttering the thick smoke from my lungs, first limping, then stumbling, then finally crawling on my hands and knees. I have barely made it twenty metres from the building before it sounds a final death knell. The top half of the tower simply collapses in upon the lower half and a great gout of flame and smoke, surge up into the air in its wake, like a mushroom cloud from a nuclear bomb. For a few precious seconds I just lay on my side, staring at the pillar of rubble and flame that should have been my grave and then to the left, at a second burning mass of metal that has to be the remains of the helicopter. And for some reason I just can't stop laughing.

CHAPTER 8 – JACK, PLEASE PICK UP

In the end, the laughing turns to coughing, the coughing to retching. I lurch back to my feet and stumble away from the searing heat and smoke of the burning tower, whatever crazed mirth that had overtaken me at the astonishing fact that I had just survived the last ten minutes, has completely abated. Stinging pain in my chest as my still healing ribs have grated against the surrounding muscles after all the falling and coughing I have been doing today, has served to remind me I am still very much a mortal and Mum and Jack, as well as the others, are all still in very real danger too.

I pull the phone out of my pocket as I make my cautious way back towards the sound of gunfire in the distance. I am almost all the way at the other side of the naval compound now, the Rover has been shot to shit and is so close to the burning building behind me that I would probably melt before I could get close to it anyway. I hold down the power button on the phone, waiting for it to boot into life and as the ringing in my ears starts to fade a little, I realise that I can't hear the sound of the other helicopter now either. Since there is still automatic and single shot gunfire going off periodically, back towards the Mess Hall, I can only assume the other helicopter must have landed.

The phone vibrates in my hand and, with a sudden bright glow, the screen bursts into life. A few moments later and I am dialling Jack's number, praying that Europa haven't already taken care of him and my mother. Christ, after everything I risked to get her safe, it's almost too much to bear thinking about. I press the green phone button, put the mobile up to my ear and keep everything crossed in my head. Come on Jack, please pick up...

I am leaning against one of the worn white washed buildings not far from where I stumbled out of the collapsing tower. The world around me has shrunk to the shrill sound of a phone ringing. I have counted every ring with growing trepidation, my mind taking my thoughts down darker and darker corridors of what if's. I am starting to picture his house as a burning pile of rubble, much like the one behind me, he and my mother's heads on stakes outside, with their eyes gouged out, when his gruff voice suddenly answers the phone with a monosyllabic, "Yes?"

"Jack? Oh, thank God, please tell me you're ok?" I am gripping the phone with bloodless fingers, my hands shaking at the sudden release of panic that has been building within me, or maybe it's the shock starting to kick in from my lucky escape just moments earlier. Either way, I find myself sliding down the wall, pulling the phone tight to my ear, cupping it with my hands as though guarding a precious secret.

"Naru? Huh? Yeah, we had a few interested guests come by yesterday, asking all sorts of questions about you. Flashed what I imagine were fake police badges, waved a load of different photos in my face of your friends and your mother. I made out like I didn't know you from Adam. Just said I let you stay the night, kindness of strangers and all that, implied I liked the look of you, if you know what I mean? Anyway, as luck would have it your mother was out tending to the garden at the time, I said there was no one here but me and one of my neighbours, just an old lady who I pay to do some gardening for me. They had a poke around like they were expecting to find you hiding in one of the cupboards. I had already stashed your father's car in an old barn out the back so they never even caught a look at it. After a while I made out like I was getting a might pissed about all their snooping and told 'em none too politely to sling their hooks unless they planned on coming back with a search warrant." The casual way Jack explains his ruse that could just have easily resulted in both he and my mother being brutally murdered is enough to set me laughing and coughing again. "You're alright," I stutter out between coughs and gasps, "Thank you Jack.... Just... thank you." I have to stop talking for a moment and concentrate on just breathing before I pass out from lack of oxygen. My hands have curled back into claws, I know I am hyperventilating, close to a full-blown panic attack and I have to count slowly in my mind, seeking to control each breath in, each one out, one by one. "Steady Naru, just breathe, one, two, three. That's it slow and steady, I'm here, I'm not going anywhere." Jacks deep calming voice is reaching out to me across hundreds of miles and I can feel my body responding. Whatever danger he and my mother had been in, it was past for the time being. Still it couldn't hurt to warn him to be careful, to stay sharp. Once I can breathe well enough to speak again, I say, "Jack, don't trust that you've fooled them completely. Be ready, they followed me all the way here, they just tried to blow me to pieces and drop a building on top of me. I got lucky this time but it's only a matter of time before it runs out." A brief pause after my fevered rant, "Jack, can you still hear me?" … Then, "Yeah, I hear you. Don't worry about us, I won't ignore your warning. Are you ok?" I try to hold back another crazed cackle at that question. But despite my best efforts a disturbed snort still works its way loose from my nose. "Fuck Jack, I've used up at least three lives today already. If there is someone up there looking out for me, they are one crazy, sadistic, kuso yaro." At my words, I hear a sudden burst of gunfire coming closer than before, the fight was moving and it might just be coming my way. "Jack, I have to go, thank you Jack, just keep her safe."

I don't wait for a reply but hang up and rip the phone to

bits before crushing the sim underfoot and throwing the pieces in different directions. I slide myself back up against the wall until I am standing as straight as I can manage under the current circumstances. I dump my empty rifle on the ground, I have no ammo for it with me and the weight will just slow me down. I pull my Beretta from its holster and thumb the hammer back, point it a little before me and slightly at the ground, take a last gulping breath and step out from behind the building.

CHAPTER 9 – DEATH BECOMES HER

I follow the sounds of battle like a blood hound on a scent trail, pausing every few seconds to listen and try to get a beat on where the main fighting is taking place, as well as listening out for the smaller pockets of resistance that have veered away from the mess hall, where they are engaging with each other in a semblance of guerrilla tactics. I know enough about the weaponry that Megan and the others are using, that I can tell at least three of them are still fighting back against the automatic machine gun fire from the squad who had arrived in the other helicopter. The one that had followed me must have had the heavy ordinance on board, as I haven't heard any other explosions yet and if a rocket had hit the mess hall with all McCreedy's plastique inside, the resulting explosion would have blown us all to hell by now.

The base is isolated enough from the local population that I have no idea if anyone would have raised an alarm to the police yet. Knowing how Europa like to do things it wouldn't surprise me if the local constabulary had already either been paid off, or sent somewhere else a long way from here on some wild goose chase, so that the Europa agents could exact maximum carnage upon us all without worrying about the police coming along to spoil their fun. In the end, it might have actually done us all a favour. With one helicopter down already, I had helped even the odds somewhat, plus I strongly doubted that a single person, still alive and fighting, suspected I would have survived what just happened. If we can take the other squad out without taking too long, we might just stand a chance of getting away from here before the authorities arrive and make things any more interesting than they already are. I realise that I am the key here, no one knows I am still alive, and I aim to keep it that way, until I get close enough to make a difference...

I move stealthily, crouched low to the ground, keeping the sun behind me, stalking from building to building, drawing ever closer to my quarry. A sense of calm has taken over me, like the feeling I had in the clearing that seemed a lifetime ago. I know I am likely walking into my death, when I could have run and saved myself. This is my choice, and something about that makes all the difference. My hands have become steel and I am gripping my gun tight and steady, each step I take is purposeful, as I stalk closer to my prey, one step at a time, one breath at a time. I pour out my focus in all directions... There... The sound of a shotgun blast... A few seconds later the return fire of an automatic machine gun. It's Grim, and by the sounds of things, he could do with some help...

The soldier has his back to me, he is so busy seeking out Megan's brother, so certain that his squad mates have his back, that he fails to see the scrawny silhouette slipping silently towards him. I take each step as he does, waiting for just the right moment, as he turns his head to the left, searching for Grim amongst the maze of old oil barrels and scrap metal piled up behind the sleeping quarters where I had slept just last night. My gun is rising almost with a will of its own, my mind going blank at the dark deed I am about to commit. No time for regret or worries about the ethics of shooting someone in the back. Its simple cold calculation, I am his shikei shikko hito and he has just placed his head on the chopping block.

I fire twice, just to make sure... The first bullet glances off his shoulder and spins him to the side, his face, surprisingly young to my eyes, holds a look of shock and terror as he sees me sighting down my gun, point blank between his own. I pull the trigger a second time, watch his lifeless body sink slowly to the ground a moment later, do my best to ignore the mess of brains and skull splattered across several white barrels a few feet away from his corpse. The deed is done. I call Graham's name and see him rise up not far from where his protagonist fell. I give him a small nod, see the look of astonishment pass swiftly across his face before disappearing behind his usual dour mask-like countenance. I keep walking, straight past him. Now, where are the rest of them?...

A tense gun battle has moved inside a warehouse further north of the Mess Hall. The machine gun fire has stopped and only single shots seem to be going back and forth. Seems like the Europa agents may have been a little too enthusiastic with their ammo when they first arrived. I slide up to the main door that has been left half ajar by whoever went in last. I glance down at the footprints in the sandy gravel and by the size of the prints backing into the building, I know it's one of the women who came in here first, the larger feet of one of the soldiers pointing forwards, going in after them.

My Beretta has been emptied out on the way here, two other soldiers lie dead or dying behind me, their body's shot through with forty five calibre bullets, even now I can hear one of them slowly choking his last few breaths out into the dirt, the other is lying still, no longer moving at all. I don't recall feeling anything as I watched them fall, what am I becoming?

With no bullets left I holster my gun and draw Jack's hunting knife from the belt at my waist, glancing briefly at my reflection in the shining steel. The creature staring back at me seems more demon than human, my eyes are wild and burning with a dark green intensity, hollowed out by days of little sleep and physically pushing myself to the limit. My skin is black and grey from smoke and dust, small rivers of blood have drawn battle lines down my cheeks. I grin back at the macabre reflection, whatever has become of me, at least I will scare the hell out of the men trying to kill me and my friends. I step into the fading gloom of the warehouse, certain of one thing, death was inside this building, whether mine or theirs it no longer mattered...

I glide amongst the old shelves and pallets within the warehouse, a dark ghost, a silent shadow, wavering between the small rays of light piercing through the weather worn holes scattered throughout the building's exterior walls. I can hear the soft crunching of boots just off to the right, trying hard to stalk quietly but failing, as they step onto small pieces of broken glass that litter the floor. I suspect either Megan or Cole has laid them down purposefully, giving them a good idea of where their stalker was coming from. I am more careful, spying the ruse and tiptoeing amongst them, barely breathing now, knowing I am drawing ever closer to them.

I hear a sudden smash behind me and give up on stalking. Whoever has snuck around the soldier just either deliberately gave their position away or threw something large enough to make a distraction and lure the soldier in the wrong direction. Whatever their plan was, it has resulted in something unexpected. The soldier will be coming straight back towards me...

I brace myself for the worst and sure enough, just a moment later, a six-foot hulk of a man stomps back around the corner of the pile of stacked pallets right into my path. Without thinking, I bury Jack's blade deeply into the arm that was holding his Glock and as I leap back to avoid a crushing blow to my forehead from his other arm, I note with cold satisfaction that he has dropped his gun to the floor, but a creeping, horrified fascination takes precedence, when he simply wrenches the knife out of his arm and starts coming towards me with it held before him, dripping his own blood uncaringly on the dusty floor and treading it underfoot as I back away from him.

I reach over my shoulder and clutch at my heart and my

courage. I find the hilt of my sword, grasp her tightly and send a silent prayer to her. Naitoben answers me with a beautiful ring of steel and a blinding flash of light as I draw her forth. My would-be attacker has just gone from enraged beast to nervous boy. Why? Because he just brought a knife to a sword fight, his last mistake. He has skidded to a halt, backing away from me warily, back towards the gun. I can't allow that...

I charge at the soldier with a sudden battle cry of rage. It has the desired effect in that he has to stop and face me, but I can see that he is terrified, and so he should be. He tries to raise the knife as a shield before him but I spin on my heel and kick it from his hand sending it spinning off to the left and burying itself in a shelving post. Even as Jack's knife is spinning through the air, I am continuing my own swinging arc, using the momentum through my hips to bring Naitboen to bear with all the speed and strength I have left.

I swing her hard and fast, from high right above my head, diagonally across my body, cutting the very air in two before she finds the soldier, slicing through his body from left shoulder to right hip. He has a look of utter surprise plastered across his face as each half of his desiccated body falls in opposite directions with a wet slap. A great deal of blood and bodily organs are leaking across the floor by my feet, so I take a few steps back and bow my head, turn my cheek to avoid the awful smell and the sight of the man's insides displayed on the floor in gory detail. I flick Naitoben's blade, shaking the few droplets of blood loose that have remained stuck to her steel, before sheathing her once more in her obsidian cloak. I know I should feel utterly exhausted, but my body is singing, my blood pumping through me with renewed vigour.

At a sound from behind I turn my head sharply, clutch Naitoben's hilt a little more tightly.

"Sweet baby Jesus new girl!" McCreedy emerges from the

dark, a large iron bar held in his hand, looks like he was out of ammo too. I glance down at his feet, raise my eyebrows in surprise, so, not Cole or Megan after all. "He died well," I say, though to look at the mess I have made of him I'm not so sure how true that was. "I'd say he died pretty fecking horribly, fecking crazy Japs, you're all fecking psychos." He chokes out this sentence while trying somewhat futilely not to throw his breakfast up all over the floor. I ignore his goading and retching, walk over to Jack's knife and pull it out of the wooden post where it had buried itself, slipping it back into its sheath at my side, then track back along the soldiers blood trail and pick up his discarded Glock. I check the magazine, good, still five bullets left. "Come on," I say, "we have to find the others." I start walking back towards the front of the warehouse, hear McCreedy whisper, "Feck that, this whole thing has gone fecking FUBAR." But he still follows behind me nonetheless...

CHAPTER 10 – STILL ALIVE, SOMEHOW

I can't quite believe my ears when I step outside the warehouse, back into the hazy light of day. Wisps of smoke are blowing across the compound from the two burning piles of rubble I left in my wake just minutes earlier, but there are no more gun shots being fired. Instead, there is an eerie silence that gives the whole place a real, end of the world kind of feel to it. I squint against the light of the sun as I turn to look at the mess hall, still standing, not appearing any different from the day before. I know, without knowing why, that Megan will be inside. As to whether she is dead or alive, I am not sure which would be preferable at this stage. I still can't help feeling something inside me pulling towards her but I wonder if I can truly trust her now, so where does this leave us? McCreedy disrupts my trail of thought as he stumbles loudly out of the door, catching his shirt and ripping it on a loose nail sticking out of the wood. He begins swearing loudly and angrily, along with a few choice blasphemies. How he was still alive when I found him is a mystery to me. I give him a look of warning and hold my finger to my lips to silence him and he actually complies without arguing. Then I begin walking silently towards the mess hall, my mind alert for any sign of life stirring amongst the building's shadow.

As we reach the front of the building, I notice movement off to the left, two figures coming towards us, the first has their hands above their head, the one behind is holding a large rifle and occasionally using the butt of it to speed the one in front up. As they draw closer, I can see that the first figure is dressed in the same combat gear as the other soldiers who just attacked us, but seems a little on the small side compared to the others. He appears to be limping heavily, while his captor, I can make out now, is the tall, dark form, of Selina Cole. She is strolling behind him with a casual grace of one who knows what they are about. On seeing McCreedy and I waiting for her, she flashes a wolfish smile our way, and with it I begin to share the emotion, I think it's triumph, I think we might just have beat these fuckers.

But we still have Megan and Steve unaccounted for, something about the fact that neither one has emerged from the mess hall should be worrying me more. I turn to the dark double doors, feel a small tremble of unease pass through me, this side of the building is riddled with bullet holes, the doors themselves are shot to pieces and look like they are about to fall off their hinges. We may have beat them for now but what was the cost?

Just a few yards from where McCreedy and I are standing, Cole comes to a halt and kicks the hapless soldier's legs out from under him so he collapses onto his knees in front of us. She mouths the word 'pilot' to me and I nod my understanding. I turn back to the mess hall doors, at least what's left of them, gather myself to prepare for what might be waiting within, ready the Glock and head inside.

The devastation inside the building is something to behold. Practically every bench and table in the room has been turned on its side as a barricade, every one has been peppered with bullet holes and several appear to have been set on fire and are blackened and smoking. Large parts of the ceiling have come down and appear to have crushed several soldiers underneath the crossbeams. Two other soldiers further inside, look to have died from gunshot wounds, the putrid smell coming from their corpses, a stark reminder of how little dignity one has in the event of their death, all those bodily fluids being released back into the earth from whence they came.

I can make out Grim's sizeable form at the back of the hall, he is standing completely still, looking down at the floor like someone has carved him out of marble and left him there like that. I'm too far away to see the expression on his face, but I don't need to. I realise there is no need for me to be holding a gun, the danger from the soldiers has passed, there are none left alive beside the pilot outside. I tuck the Glock inside my belt and start making my way through the bullet ridden barricades, my mouth has gone very dry and I'm finding it suddenly hard to swallow. Whatever Graham has found I know I have to see it for myself.

Closer now, the hot rays of the midday sun are shining down on me through the huge hole in the ceiling, drawing beads of sweat from my already dehydrated body in an attempt to cool me down. I take off my coat, hang it over one of the benches, unzip my hoody and dump that on top of it too. It has kept the inevitable at bay a few moments longer at least. I carry Naitoben in my left hand, giving me the courage and strength I need to keep putting one foot in front of the other, until finally, I come up alongside Grim and find myself following his gaze to the scene that has frozen him in place.

A, a, sore o ki ni... Steve's lifeless form is laid out on the floor in front of me, stained with his life's blood, a grimace of pain the last expression he ever made, forever plastered onto his grizzled old face. Megan is on her knees, holding his hand, weeping over him silently. From what Steve had told me the night before, I understand immediately just how much his passing will mean to them both. This man had always been there for them, always offered them shelter and kindness when their own father had treated them terribly. I have nothing to offer either of them at this moment except hollow platitudes. Still, I feel I have to say something, so I tell them, "It's over, for now, Cole has one of the pilots outside. For what it's worth, Steve was kind to me and listened without judgement, he gave me food and shelter when I needed it most. He was a good man, and a hero to many. O-kuyami moshiagemasu." Megan acknowledges my words with an a weary nod. I bow my head in a moment of silent prayer and contemplation for Steve and the life he had lived, before turning on my heel and leaving the Archers to their shared grief...

CHAPTER 11 – A ONE-WAY TICKET TO HELL

Back outside, McCreedy and Cole are talking quietly, she never taking her eyes from her captive, while he appears to be trying to look anywhere else. At sight of my approach, both stop their conversation and turn to me with worried looks of their own. "We lost Steve," I say, "Megan and Graham are in there with him now." At my words Cole gets a dark frown across her face, kicks the pilot hard in the side bringing a gasp from his lips and clutching at his ribs in pain. She whispers, "Motherfuckers," before spitting on his back and kicking him again for good measure, leaving him sprawled half-conscious on the ground. McCreedy has taken a few wary steps away from Cole and her sudden violent outburst. He looks truly saddened at the news of Steve's passing and says, "Ah fecksake, he was a good bloke, solid, you know?" I nod back at his words, of all of us here, Steve deserved his fate the least.

I ease myself down onto the weather worn steps that lead into the mess hall, simply stare ahead at the empty spaces between the deserted buildings all around and for a moment my mind has gone blank. I rest Naitoben across my lap and find myself picking bits of peeling white paint from the small wooden banister beside me, not really sure what to say or do at this point.   I hear the sound of a lighter clicking and look up to see Cole sparking up a cigarette. For a moment all I can think is how fucking cool she looks just standing there smoking after all the chaos of the last hour. I realise she hasn't got so much as a scratch on her and have to hand it to her, she is the biggest badass I have ever met by a country mile. "I tort you gave up smoking those fecking things." McCreedy can't resist a little jibe at her expense, but Cole comes right back at him with, "And I thought you'd all be dead by now, looks like we were both wrong." I find myself smirking along at her dark wit, catch her eye and say, "I don't suppose you have any more of those?" My nicotine addiction has taken over and I am staring at the cigarette with a hunger only a fellow smoker can truly appreciate. "Here," she says, throwing me the pack and the lighter one after the other, "keep the rest, I don't smoke anyway." I open the pack to see there are still five cigarettes left, take one out and clutch it between my teeth, tuck the rest of the pack inside my trouser pocket. Within a few seconds, I have got the end burning merrily and I lean back against the bannisters, smoking contentedly, the nicotine rush doing wonders to steady my nerves. "Watashi no kokoro kara no kansha," I say and mean every word.

"Speak fecking English will yeh, neither one of us can understand what you keep saying" McCreedy has got his arms crossed looking at us both like someone expecting to be stung badly, almost flinching at some rebuff he thinks is coming his way. "I said thank you is all," I say, not rising to his bait. I have no interest in swapping banter after what I just went through, but I guess it's McCreedy's way of handling the shock of it all. "You're welcome," Cole returns, smiling at me, before giving Lister one of those looks of hers, he pales visibly and mutters, "Fecksake, you're both a pair of psychos, crazy fecking bitches," before walking away from us and staring off towards the sea. I raise my eyebrow and say, "Is he always this touchy?" Cole smiles back at me, showing her teeth, the last of her cigarette still clamped between them, "Always," she says, before throwing the butt to the ground and crushing it beneath her boot…

By the time I have smoked my cigarette down to the butt and stubbed it out on the stair beside me, Grim has appeared at the mess hall doors, with Megan just a few steps behind him. I get up off the stairs and move aside, my muscles aching and my backside feeling numbed from sitting on the hard wood. Grim holds the badly damaged door open for his sister, who steps out into the light of day with a look to match her brother. Dried tracks of tears are plainly visible across her face, but she shows no sign of the emotion she must be feeling inside when she speaks, "Get him on his feet." Her voice is at once compelling and commanding. Cole hauls the injured pilot back up off the floor, he gives a barely disguised whimper once on his feet, whether from pain or fear I can't tell. He would be wise to be afraid though, given the company he has found himself in.

Megan walks straight up to him, getting just inches from his face, looking hard into his eyes. At the same time both myself and Cole have moved in a little closer too, ready to react if he tries anything stupid. "What's your name soldier?" She asks him, expecting an answer and getting one, "H… Harry." The man manages to stutter out. "Harry, I'm going to ask something of you, I will only ask it once. Do you understand?" He swallows and nods at her words, his face showing his dismay and worry about what was coming. "Harry, I want you to take us back to the mountain, to An Teallach." He is already shaking his head, sinking to his knees. "I can't, you don't know what they'll do to me, it's worse than anything you could possibly think of." Megan sighs, turns her back on him and looks me in the eye. "Kill him," she orders me, "He's no use to us." I nod at the order, thinking she might be playing him, hoping the fear of death will make him change his mind, but as I make the few paces to his side, he simply closes his eyes and whispers quietly to himself, seemingly resigned to his fate.

I draw Naitoben slowly, no ring of steel to announce her, just a soft hissing as she slides free of her scabbard. I look down upon Harry the pilot with distaste. If it was me, I would have fought to my last breath, not cowered in the dirt. He deserves to die, of that I am certain, he brought the men here who tried to kill us all and since he has no collar around his neck, I can only assume he had come here willingly. I raise my sword high above my head, close my eyes for a moment, I have named myself their executioner and I am largely responsible for them coming here today. It should be me to do it, but something about the man's pathetic attitude has brought me up short. It's one thing to kill someone who is intent on murdering you and your friends but this, this would be coldblooded murder, there would be no turning back from it…

A timeless moment ensues, my mind teetering on the brink of indecision. Then, quietly, almost so softly I don't hear at first, Harry speaks, then again, louder, "Alright, alright, I'll take you, please, please don't kill me." I turn to Megan, awaiting her order. She bids me to step back. I sheath Naitoben and walk away from Harry's prone form, so close to becoming something monstrous myself, my darker side had hungered to slice him in two, to watch his life blood seep into the dusty ground at my feet. I feel sickened and relieved that he stopped me from having to make the choice in the end.

Megan motions to Cole, who drags the pilot back up once more and growls at him to stay on his feet this time. Our leader takes in the rest of us, meeting every one of our eyes one after the other, measuring us, a commander, weighing the courage of her troops. "Looks like Elizabeth just bought us a one-way ticket to hell. Given what's at stake, what we have seen of these people, I will understand if anyone wants to back out. But I figure, if we do this now, we might still have the drop on them, coming at them with one of their own choppers is the last thing their going to be expecting. Besides, this just got real fucking personal." Grim moves to stand beside her, "I go where you go." His stance is strong, his countenance a foregone conclusion. I turn to Cole, who nods once and says, "Looks like this just got real interesting, I'm in." McCreedy is still standing away from the rest of us, hugging himself like he is freezing cold, but clearly sweating in the heat of the summer sunshine. "I won't have Cole calling me a fecking sissy for the rest of my days. But I want it on record this is the worst fecking idea you've ever come up with boss." Megan smiles back at him and says, "Noted Lister."

Finally, she turns to me, and I can't help myself from saying, "What happened to the line between recklessness and bravery?" She shakes her head at me with an apologetic grimace, "We are so far beyond recklessness now Elizabeth, I don't think there's even a word for what we are planning to do. I'm sorry for doubting you, if not for you, we would all be dead right now." Cole laughs at that and says, "Speak for yourself." I turn back to Megan and say, "Are you sure about this?" Another nod, a look of steel in her eyes. "This can't just be about revenge or we are no better than them. We have to try to save as many of the servants as we can." I am imploring, hoping to speak to the better part inside her I know to be there. She hesitates only for a moment before she steps forward and holds out her hand, "Agreed." I reach out and clasp it firmly, feeling that electricity between us once more and say, "Then let's finish this." ...

We have loaded McCreedy's bag of MEMP's and plastique, minus a few bricks, on board the helicopter. Cole is sitting snuggly with the pilot, holding a pistol pressed rather unnecessarily into his crotch to ensure his continued co-operation. Having used most of the ammo and guns that the gang brought with them, McCreedy had the bright idea to blow a hole in the bases armoury and 'borrow' some of their weapons for the cause. So, I have now added grand theft larceny as well as wanton destruction of property and mass murder to my growing list of misdeeds since leaving the hospital only a few days ago. I find it hard to care though, when I think about what we are planning, in the end we are acting in the best interests of the country's' citizens, they just don't know it. Europa corporation and the people working for them were acting above the law, so we had to do the same if we hoped to stop them from abducting and trafficking more innocent people.

As I climb on board the helicopter and stare back at the destruction we have left in our wake, I feel a hand rest reassuringly on my thigh and turn to find Megan looking at me with that fathomless quality in her eyes. I can't begin to wonder what she's thinking, and I can't ask either, since the rotor blades of the helicopter are so loud even shouting would be drowned out by the noise. I only know I am glad to have her and the others by my side, so I smile back at her and link my fingers between hers, she does not pull away and instead answers my smile with one of her own...

CHAPTER 12 – SELINA COLE

We have been flying for less than an hour when the mountain comes into view. I feel something cold and hard settle in my stomach at the sight of An Teallach, growing ever larger as we speed towards it. The mountain itself appears virtually baron of any sign of life towards its peak, just different shades of brown and grey rock as far as the eye can see. From our high vantage point in the air, I can make out the small wooded area north of Dundonnell village, just as Megan had described it. Cole directs the pilot to circle us around and out to sea, making sure we come in unseen from the side of the mountain that looks out onto miles of trackless wilderness on its north face. With the helicopter bringing us back in from the north, Cole turns to the rest of us and motions me forward. I find I have been unconsciously clasping Megan's hand throughout the journey here and have to force my fingers to disengage with hers so I can move forward and speak with the dangerous femme fatale in the front seat.

Cole pulls my head in close and shouts her instructions into my ear, then motions Megan forward and does the same with her. I find I am flattered that she has asked me, over everyone else, to descend first with her, but I can't help feeling a stab of fear at what she wants us to do. Megan pats me on the shoulder, draws her newly acquired pistol and rests it very firmly between the pilots' shoulder blades, then Cole climbs through to the back and helps me rifle through the munitions, picking out all the things she wants to take with us. Having loaded up two backpacks with spare ammo and equipment, she hands me a high-powered silenced rifle, the weapon of a true sniper, with three times the stopping power of the one I had used to take out the other helicopter. I have my faithful Berretta holstered and fully loaded at my side, Jack's knife at my waist and Naito-ben slung tightly over my shoulder. I put the backpack on, then tie the rifle across my chest, leaving both hands free to grab the rope that Cole is feeding into my hands. Kuso, I can't believe I am actually going to rappel out of a moving helicopter...

The pilot gets us to within a mile of the woods, keeping us low and well out of sight or hearing from what might be waiting for us on the other side of the mountain. When we are around forty feet from the ground Cole throws her rope and bids me do the same. With my heart in my throat, I launch myself over the side of the helicopter and begin letting the rope slide between my gloved hands. Letting the leather of the gloves act as a brake, I am able to control my descent to some extent, though I still find the ground coming up to greet me with alarming speed, before suddenly running out of rope and having to drop the last few feet to the ground with as much elegance as someone weighed down with heavy objects and no experience can man-age, without making a complete fool of themselves. In short, I land badly, but manage to bend my knees and roll to the side so that I don't actually break anything when I hit the rocky terrain underneath me.

In contrast, Cole zips down her rope like the seasoned pro she is and lands with both feet firmly planted on the terra firmer, just a slight bend to her knees and an even slighter smile on her face that says she does this kind of thing all the time and if we live through this, I expect she will be ribbing me about my own landing as soon as she gets the opportunity. She holds out a hand and helps pull me back to my feet. I readjust my gear and brush myself down, taking in the lonely landscape all around us before waving that I'm ok to the still hovering helicopter, which turns a one eighty and heads further north, looking for somewhere flatter, where it can land so the others can begin unloading the rest of the kit and, hopefully, ensure that we have a means of escape if it all goes horribly wrong.

As for Cole and I, we are supposed to prepare the way for the others. I untie the sniper rifle from around my waist and check it over to make sure I didn't do any damage when I crash landed. After I have checked all the mechanisms seem to be working as they are supposed to and sighted down the scope, I give Cole the nod that I am ready to let her lead the way. She wastes no time in scouting a route and begins the march southwest towards the woods, currently out of our line of sight. I watch her feet as we go, planting my own where she has just been, feeling the extra effort every step is taking weighed down with so much kit.

Cole hasn't even broken a sweat by the time we reach a small summit that allows us to get a line of sight to the woods on the outskirts of the village. She motions me down to the ground and we crawl the last few feet to the vantage point and lay there for some time, using our rifles to scan the area ahead, looking for any signs of life or movement that isn't in keeping with the grey rocks, scrub brush and sandstone cliffs all around us.

It gives me a chance to catch my breath and as we lay there together, I can't help wondering just who this woman is lying beside me. She is definitely army or navy, maybe an ex-marine or seal. Maybe she is on leave and this is the kind of shit she does for fun on her holidays. Whatever reason brought her here, she is exuding a confidence in what she is about that is helping to put my own anxiety at ease. As my mind tries to picture what someone like Cole does in their spare time, when they are not running around with guns and shooting at people, she suddenly hisses softly by my side, taps my shoulder and points off to her left.

I turn my scope slowly to point in the general area Cole indicated and at first, I can't make out anything other than more rock and more empty space. She has gone completely still beside me, barely breathing, just watching the same spot with the intensity of a mountain lion waiting to pounce on an unwary elk. I try to follow her example, but I am finding it harder to concentrate as the rocks beneath me are becoming increasingly uncomfortable. Then, just when I think she must have made a mistake, I see it. Something moving, no, not something, someone. Now that I can see them, I follow the movement, tracking them first one way, then back again. No one in their right mind would be pacing back and forth in the middle of nowhere, but a soldier at their post, trying to keep boredom at bay and keep the circulation going? I've only been laying here for a few minutes and I can already feel my body cramping and complaining beneath me.

I edge closer to Cole and whisper, "There's just one I can see." She shakes her head slowly and advises me, "Where there's one, there'll be more." I feel my stomach clench at her words, try to keep scanning ahead of us but I can't see any other soldiers. Then, suddenly, the one I can see drops back out of sight and without saying a word, Cole shoots to her feet, tapping me hard on the back as she rises, and starts running straight towards the place where the soldier was standing only moments before.

I drag myself up and dash after her, not really understanding her tactics but just trusting that she knows what she is doing. After a fifty-yard sprint Cole drops in her tracks behind a small outcrop of scrub next to a cracked boulder. A few seconds behind her, I sink down gratefully by her side fighting to control my heavy breathing. Once again, she lays herself flat and takes up her rifles' scope, scanning for the soldier and any other potential hostiles, so I follow suit and take up position alongside her.

After several minutes of utter silence, apart from the cold wind intermittently blowing into our backs from the north and sending periodic shivers through me, I see the soldier once more, following the same pattern as before, first going one way, then back again, before disappearing from view. Ready this time, I tense my muscles and take a deep breath and when Cole leaps to her feet again, I am right behind her.

We go slightly to the right, I can't see why, until I spot the little dent in the largely flat terrain and as we draw closer, I can see that it's a sizeable ditch, some vestige of an old river that must have once run through the valley we are trying to cross. Once more we drop to the ground, once more we scan for the soldier. This time when their head appears above the horizon, I can make out their features quite clearly. It's a man with short, cropped hair, a thick, dark beard, but well groomed, I can just about see the top of his shoulders and that he appears to be wearing a dark uniform, that I could state with fair certainty, would be an exact copy of the one that the soldiers who turned up at the base were wearing. "Be ready," Cole whispers to me and I find I am suddenly full of tense energy, my body tingling with adrenaline at her warning. She swings her rifle around behind her, draws her handgun. I keep sweeping the area ahead with my rifle's scope, certain that she was right, there would be others.

"When I give the word, I want you to take him out and whatever happens after, stay down and keep to cover. Watch the cliff to the right, good place for a sniper, it's where I would take up position." My mouth has gone dry, I nod, too nervous to reply to her command, then take aim, waiting for the man's head to come back closer. I wanted to say, what are you going to do? But in the end, I don't have to ask. As the soldiers' head comes back into my rifles' sights, Cole turns to me with a predators' gaze marring the beauty of her dark features. "Now," she orders me… I obey and fire a single shot, blasting the man's head into bloody splinters, seeing it almost in slow motion through my crosshairs. At the same time Cole is already up on her feet and sprinting across the last fifty yards to where he fell, her rifle slung over her back, a silenced pistol held steady in her hands.

She sights down the gun and fires off half a dozen shots in quick succession, from my prone position on the ground I have no idea who or what she is shooting at, but I have no time for distractions, I follow her instructions and point my rifle up at the cliff to the right, spying a tiny ridge I hadn't seen earlier. I notice a small glint of light reflect off something then spot a burst of dust and rock shoot into the air just a few feet from Cole's sprinting form out of the corner of my eye. With no time for precision shooting, I switch to auto and unload the full magazine at the ledge just below where I saw the glint of light. There is a loud, creaking, cracking noise, that echoes across the valley. A moment later, the entire ledge collapses and a small human figure falls with it, spinning and smashing against the cliff face, disappearing out of sight with a pile of loose rocks raining down on top of them.

For a terrifying moment, I wonder if the whole mountain is going to fall down on top of us all, but after several minutes of stunned silence, Cole emerges from the other side of the rocks ahead and waves me over to the camp that she just took out practically single handed...

I am looking down upon a scene of carnage, as well as the headless body of the soldier I took out, there are five other men and one woman, lying cold and dead. From the equipment and gear all around, it looks like they have been camped here for some time, some kind of look-out post for protecting against people like us. Except they didn't count on Selina Cole turning up to ruin their day. I have to hand it to her; she is more deadly than anyone I have ever met in my life and a part of me suspects she could have managed this task just as easily without me tagging along. Maybe she is trying to get the measure of me, maybe she actually respects my skills, she did see me shoot down a helicopter after all, but I have learned a real lesson here today. Cole is not someone I ever want to get on the wrong side of. I imagine she could slit my throat and I wouldn't even see her coming.

"Subtlety isn't one of your strong suits is it?" Cole nods towards the pile of rubble that has buried the sniper underneath it, smiling at me like I just got initiated into her secret club. I stare back at her, dragging a fake smile across my lips, finding it hard to see this as anything but a slaughter. I swallow the lump in my throat and try not to breathe through my nose in an attempt to avoid the stench of death all around us. I look ahead towards the woods, wondering what other horrors wait for us. But the path was the path, and I was the arrow, loosed already, heading unwaveringly towards my target. And so, I nod for Cole to move on and together we leave the bodies of the dead soldiers behind us...

We move together in near silence, taking each step with measured care. Our rifles are slung over our backs for now, the dense alder trees that make up the small woodland, too close together for any long-range shooting. Instead, we both carry our handguns, silenced for extra precaution. Cole allows me to lead the way, her instinct for combat giving her some sense that the woods were more my element than hers. As we make our way ever south, I sense the change between us, here I find my mind clearer, my body moving with an animal grace, born of years spending my summer months hunting and tracking in the woods with my father and Jack.

I am listening out for any small sound, any sign of a potential patrol, when I catch something glinting high in one of the trees to our left. I hold out a hand for Cole to wait and ease myself into a better position to see and not be seen. I use the scope from my rifle to get a closer look and as I adjust the focus, the glint wavers in front of my eyes and slowly sharpens into a small camera lens. I turn to Cole and give her a thumbs up, it's just what we had been hoping to find. She moves position with me and takes a look for herself, treats me to another feral grin of her bared teeth, before taking her radio out and calling Megan and the others...

While we wait for the boss and the rest of the team to arrive, Cole convinces me to do a little recon further ahead, while she takes a closer look at the camera in the tree. We have been marking our trail as we made our way here with crosses carved into the north side of the trees, giving the others a near perfect route to find our location. We mark a safe route around the camera and, once at the base of the tree, Cole gets out some climbing equipment from her backpack, including claws that she attaches to the bottom of her boots, a decent climbing rope and a pair of exceptional gloves with tooth-like grips on the fingers. She then begins the arduous-looking climb straight up the trunk of the huge alder tree, seeking the camera from the other side. From the ground, it looks around forty or fifty feet up. I'm glad it's her and not me, after my rather clumsy descent from the helicopter, I have had my fill of heights and ropes for the time being. Instead, I concentrate on securing our perimeter for now and cut a circling path a good fifty metres from the base of the tree in all directions.

Cole has estimated that we have likely less than an hour before the soldiers we killed at the woods' edge fail to report in. From their position and the way they were behaving, like actual army soldiers, Cole reasoned that they would probably have an hourly call in, some kind of standard protocol. If luck was with us, since it was just past the hour when we struck them, it had given us a window of opportunity we had to use now. We couldn't afford to take too long here. We needed Megan's skills and we needed them soon. Otherwise we were likely to find that Europa would be very much expecting our arrival instead of catching them unawares and vulnerable...

Fortunately, we don't have to wait for long. In less than ten minutes, Megan, Grim and McCreedy, have reached our position back at the trees' base, their journey here much faster than our own, since we had already cleared the way before them of any danger.

By the time they arrive, Cole has secured her climbing rope to one of the high branches above her, in order to allow Megan an easier and safer climb up than her own had been. Still, she would need good upper body strength to get up there even so, and do whatever it was she needed to do. Like Cole, Megan has packed her own climbing gear, she also takes her laptop, and several other small gadgets and wires which she puts in a satchel that she hangs around her neck, the pouch swinging in front of her waist for easy access to the contents within. I keep my back to her, not wishing to see her struggling with the climb or witness if she falls, as there would be little I could do in either case. Instead, I watch the woods for any sign of danger, Grim joins me and takes up a defensive position a few metres to my right, as always, his first thought for the safety of his sister. I glance behind me and see that McCreedy is staring up into the tree's high branches, biting his fingernails and looking a little like a drug addict needing his next fix. If I didn't know better, I would say he was looking anxiously up at Cole rather than worrying about the safety of his leader...

I feel a small bead of sweat run down my forehead and tickle my nose. I have been standing almost completely still, listening and watching for anything that might pose a threat to our position. Every now and then I take a quick glance up at the tree to mark Megan's progress. I spare a look and see that she has finally reached the same level as Cole and has her laptop out in her hands while sitting on one of the branches. Megan has attached a thick wire to the camera and is furiously tapping at her laptop's keyboard, her face one of total concentration. I turn back to the woods, the sudden crack of a twig over to my left ringing alarm bells in my head. I don't think, I simply react to the threat and slink carefully but quickly towards the sound, using the denser brush and trees for cover, seeking out the sound's location. Another crack of a branch and then a crunch of dry leaves in the undergrowth and it's clear that a human is walking through the woods, but they aren't doing so with stealth, which is good, because it likely means they aren't out here looking for us.

I cock back the hammer on my gun and peer carefully around the tree I am using for cover, and I see him. A Europa soldier dressed the same as all the others, but he is simply making his way towards the camp that we have already desiccated, carrying a large dark duffel bag over his shoulder, perhaps full of supplies for the team that were posted there? Regardless, he can't be allowed to find them or raise an alarm when we are so close. I wait a few precious heartbeats, until he is only a metre or so from my position, then I twist out from behind the tree and point my gun right at the centre of his chest. The soldier freezes in shock at my sudden appearance and I have milliseconds to make a decision...

I have been wrestling with the darker half of my soul ever since I left the facility. But this is a pivotal moment. I know I could shoot him dead and no one else in the group would blame me, in fact it could make things more difficult and riskier if I keep him alive. I imagine much the same kind of debate could be raging behind the calculated look in the soldier's eyes. Afterall, he is seeing a scrawny young woman with a gun and might be favouring his chances if he is quick. What he doesn't know is that I am quicker, and if he tries any kind of shit like that, I won't hesitate to take him down, too much is at stake.

Barely a second has passed since I showed myself. The soldier, finally making some decision in his head, lets out a long sigh and drops his bag to the floor, then raises his hands in the air. I swallow back the rage that is threatening to take over my reason and finally manage to speak, "On the floor, hands over your head, interlock your fingers, now!" My command and my language have an impact. Whether the soldier was fancying his chances, he must now know I am not some escapee with a gun or some crazy wildling living in the woods. He nods, eases himself down on his knees, then on to his chest, puts his hands on his head and does as I asked by locking his fingers together. I keep my gun trained on him, take my radio from my belt and call in with my position and request back up. No point in risking him trying to fight me if I attempt to tie him up by myself after all. I had been a cop for a fair few years before I was taken and it was something you learned early on, never underestimate the importance of your partner.

A few minutes pass before Grim emerges from the woods, takes one look at the man, makes a grunt of approval, then sets too in sitting on his back and tying his hands behind him with cable ties. Once he has him secured, Grim hauls him back to his feet with relative ease. Then shoves him forward towards our current base camp at the bottom of the camera-tree. I pick up the dropped bag, then follow alongside him, my gun trained and ready, just in case the soldier tries anything stupid...

CHAPTER 13 – HELLO DARKNESS MY OLD FRIEND

When we arrive back at the base of the huge alder tree, Megan and Cole are already back at ground level. Our leader is sitting cross legged as we approach, her laptop is nestled between her legs, the grin on her face is infectious and I find my confidence grow with it. At sight of the prisoner, Cole makes a face that I can only guess as one of curiosity, aimed my way I am sure. I think her conscience would have allowed her to make the harder choice, but I am not quite there yet, despite everything they did to me. I am still finding it hard not to play by the rules. I still have some honour left in me it seems, but for how much longer? I am not so sure I want to think that far ahead.

Grim marches the prisoner over to a nearby tree, makes him sit on the floor and ties him to its trunk securely. In the meantime, I head to Megan's side and dare to ask just why she is smiling so hard right now. She turns the computer around on her lap and shows me the images she has been studying for the past few minutes and I find myself grinning back at her just as hard.

The computer is showing a half dozen images and every few seconds they flicker and then change to another six. After one minute, they have scrolled through around thirty different cameras that must be in place all around the facility, but not only that, Megan advises me that she has put them all on a thirty second loop. Essentially, we are now invisible to every camera that is linked to their internal network, and we also have 'eyes on' for the whole damned facility, we will be able to see where practically every soldier and guard is located, and, more importantly, where every servant is.

"This is all very exciting but we still don't know how the hell we actually get inside." Cole's pragmatic statement brings me back down to earth with a thump. Maybe this wasn't going to be so easy after all? I find my head turning to look at the guard at the same time as the thought must have come to both Megan and Cole that he will know where the entrance is but is unlikely to want to tell us willingly or without provocation. Suddenly, the hog-tied soldier has the intense gazes of the whole gang staring at him with something like hunger. I suspect he may have just shit himself, I know I would have, if it were me. Especially since Cole just drew a large hunting knife from her belt and is stalking towards him with murderous intent.

"Cat just wait," at my imploring words, using the short hand for her codename, Cole pauses for barely a second before continuing towards the soldier, not even bothering to look back. Instead she says over her shoulder, "You aren't going soft on me are you Kingsleigh?" I turn to Megan in desperation, "We can find it without him, let me see those cameras again, there were places I didn't recognise." Megan hands the laptop up to me, she hasn't advised Cole to stop whatever it is she plans to do and I know if I tried to stop her, the gang would put me down, or Cole herself would, if necessary. But as much as Megan is ruthless, I feel I know her well enough that she would not see this man tortured if she had another option.

I quickly scan through the images, until I get to the ones I hadn't recognised, feeling time slipping away from me as Cole draws close to the prisoner, whispering something into his ear that makes him visibly pale. I stare hard at the screen, trying to make sense of what I am seeing, and then it hits me. This must be the youth hostels' interior; I remember seeing the outer images when Megan had been looking at satellite photos of the area. The interior and design is in keeping with the exterior, it looks old and dilapidated, nothing like the sleek insides of the facility, which had been designed and constructed far more recently and for a much darker purpose. Also, in the corner of one of the outside cameras I can make out the front edge of the same black Humvee that dropped me off in London. A further camera shows a number of interior doors with padlocks on the outside and as the images continue flicking, I can see inside several of the rooms, there were women in them, and several were not alone. What was being done to them was enough to bring my blood boiling to the surface in a rage. Kuso yaro!

"Cat stop! Please. Just wait." Cole actually looks slightly annoyed, like I might have just spoilt her fun, but she does walk a few paces from the soldier, her knife still in hand and folds her arms across her chest. "Come on Kingsleigh, let's hear it then?" Megan commands me for an explanation, every minute counts at this point, so I quickly try to explain my reasoning.

"The entrance, it's through the hostel, maybe underneath, I'm sure of it. There may be another way in through the old mining tunnels but I have been down there and they are like a damn labyrinth. We could be lost for days trying to find a way through. No, it has to be the hostel. Think about it, it's the perfect place to take the abductees through and for paying customers to get what they want without ever seeing the real facility beneath them. And not just that, but the car that took me from here to London is parked right outside." Megan is holding her chin in thought, staring first at me then at Cole, before she makes her decision. "Sound reasoning Kingsleigh, but given the time constraints and the risks if you're wrong, we need to be sure. Caterpillar, continue, if you please?" Megan waves her arm towards the terrified soldier and Cole gives me a kind of, 'what are you gonna do?' shrug of her shoulders, before turning her full attention back on him, and tapping the side of her knife against the palm of her hand, likely thinking of a quick and painful way of getting him talking.

I don't think I can watch, it's one thing to take a life, quick and clean when it's them or you, but I haven't signed on for torture. Something about the look on my face tells Megan just how uncomfortable I am with what is about to happen. I see Cole shoving a large stick between the man's teeth, telling him to bite down, as what she is about to do is going to hurt, a lot. "Gryphon, why don't you and Kingsleigh go on ahead and scout the village for us, we will all be along presently I am sure, this won't take long." At his sister's command, Grim grunts his assent, gives me a nod and a look that suggests he is about as uncomfortable with this as I am and, together, we turn from the sinister scene and start making our way to the edge of the woods on the outskirts of Dundonnell village. I can hear McCreedy muttering obscenities under his breath as we pass him, he too has chosen to stand well clear of Cole and her dark intent, only Megan seems to have the stomach to stay close to her.

Finally, clear of the scene, we eventually reach the edge of the woods, we can see most of the village at a glance. Aside from the ruined old hostel, there is only a single, silent, shepherd's cottage, seemingly abandoned some time ago, a rusted barn, largely made of corrugated iron, and the remains of a farmhouse, just three walls really, leaning in on each other, largely covered with moss and rot. Other than the Humvee and two other cars parked outside the hostel, there are no other signs that anyone lives here anymore. The perfect cover for what is really going on inside the building and within the mountain itself.

Off to the left of the village, I can make out the entrance to the old coal mine, there are half a dozen hazardous warning signs sticking up all around it and a good deal of black and yellow tape has been plastered across the boarded-up hole that leads inside.

Something about seeing that black hole sends a chill

through to the very marrow of my bones. Of all my time spent in that hellish place, being thrown into the pit for punishment had been the lowest point. The total darkness and isolation, being led around by the pain in my collar, feeling a kind of raw hunger that couldn't be sated and a near ceaseless fear of being buried alive, underneath the mountain. My sanity is now undoubtedly questionable, given everything that was done to me, but it was in the pit when I first noticed just how fractured my mind had become, when Naru had emerged as someone else in my mind and I had accepted this new persona that had been forced upon me.

I, Elizabeth, in truth, had been born in that dark mine. I turn from the sight, more upsetting to me than witnessing what was happening back in the woods. Instead, I bring all my attention to bear on the hostel, there are people in there, right now, who are enduring their own horrors and for a change, I am in the right place at the right time to do something about it. With no signs of anyone between us and the front door I find I am not prepared to wait any longer, point to the hostel, share a nod of agreement with Grim and step out cautiously into the dirt track that doubled as the road leading straight through the centre of the village, my resolve and my purpose as one.

Before I take a second step, Cole's bloody hand slaps down on my shoulder, stopping me mid-stride. She has hold of Grim too, and we both turn around at the same instant, likely both thinking the same thing. Why has she stopped us, and how did she get here so fast? I open my mouth to begin asking her, since I know Grim will keep his own counsel as always, but Cole waves my unasked question away and draws us back into the woods, and back out of sight of the village, then pulls us both to a stop to explain. "They've got the whole damn place boobytrapped, hidden land mines filled with some kind of knock-out gas for the most part. Anyone curious enough to wander through that village without knowing where to step, will be sleeping with the fairies and waking up in your old cell I'm thinking." Kuso,

I can't believe how close Grim and I just came to the one fate I don't think I could bare to live through, being caught again. I reach up almost unconsciously to my neck and rub it, remind myself for the hundredth time the collar is definitely gone. The motion isn't lost on either of my comrades. Cole actually looks at me with something close to sympathy, while Grim puts his hand reassuringly on my back. I find little comfort in either reaction but I am grateful for their understanding all the same.

"How did you get him to tell you that so quickly?" Morbid curiosity gets the better of me and right now I want to think about anything else other than what nearly just happened. Cole raises her eyebrows and puts an 'are you sure you want to know?' expression on her face before smirking and saying, "Most people don't realise but there is a nerve cluster a few inches below the collar bone, all it takes is...." "Wait!" I interrupt her, "forget I asked, I don't think I want to know after all." Cole shrugs it off as if to say she didn't care one way or the other. "So how do we get across the village?" Grim asks, speaking for the first time all day that I can recall. Cole pats herself down and then draws out a crumpled piece of paper from one of her many pockets. It has a rather crude map of Dundonnell drawn in brown crayon upon it. She points out a dozen crosses marked on the map, most of them zigzagging along the main track that Grim and I had been about to start walking on. "There's a path," she begins, "Look here," she points, first to the rusted barn, then to the back of the shepherd's cottage, then draws her finger through the ruin of the farmhouse, before finally alighting on the hostel.

I close my eyes and let the image of the path burn into my mind, this is one thing we can't afford to get wrong, the thought of waking back up in that cell naked and collared is enough to shatter my fragile grasp of courage. I take a good grip of Naitoben's hilt, reaching within myself for that resolve I had so recently felt, searching for more strength by conjuring up images of my father and our ancestor Idoshi, the man who first made her, forging the blade from priceless sky steel, gifted to him to craft on behalf of the emperor. She's no magic blade, no Excalibur or Vorpol sword that I hold, but she's something damnably close. Without her, I know I could not have come this far, that my mind would still be a fractured mess. After just a few moments of holding her, my breathing is steady and my mind is set once more to see this through to the bitter end.

I open my eyes, hold Cole's steely gaze for a moment, there is something I have to say to clear the air between us. "I apologize, for not trusting you knew what you were about when you took a knife to that man, God knows he probably deserved it anyway." Cole gives me one of her wicked grins, more like the Cheshire Cat than any caterpillar. "For someone so good at killing people, you really are rather squemish Kingsleigh. Ah, here come the others, let's get this over with shall we?" And that was that as far as Cole was concerned, I was back in her club and part of the team once more...

We have shared the explosives out between ourselves, McCreedy has given us all a crash course in how to turn the plastique, wiring and circuit boards into a serviceable, timed IED. For all his swearing and crude behaviour, there is no denying Lister knows what he's doing and it turns out he's a pretty good teacher. That thought almost sets me off into quiet hysterics, as I consider him standing in front of a class of schoolchildren, calling them little feckers and teaching them how to blow things up. Maybe it's the fact that I am about to go into a very dangerous situation with a backpack filled with dynamite. I can't say I am comfortable with the idea of carrying enough explosives on my back to blow myself and my comrades into tiny pieces, but it makes sense that we each have a means of doing some serious damage to the facility once we get inside. It should allow us to cause maximum chaos and with any luck, we might just bring the mountain down on the heads of Kiko and the other masters, while providing us enough time to flee with whatever servants we can locate and take with us.

I can't help my thoughts turning to my old master, wondering if he was still alive after my brutal assault. I am almost certain, if he did survive having a toilet cistern crack his head open, Richard will be inside too. I owe him my freedom, if not for him, we would not be here now but I can't deny the time spent as his servant, what I was forced to do, or risk the sickening fate that Kiko had shown me laid in wait for those who continued to resist their training. I am still not sure how I will react if I find him. A part of me wants to embrace him and another part of me wants to carve him in two. My stomach is twisting into knots, I realise I'm spiralling again. Just breathe Elizabeth, I tell myself, we are so close now, just breathe... Sensing my distress, Megan moves close to me, takes my hand in hers and tells me to look her in the eyes. After a few still moments of simply measuring one another, she finally releases my hand and smiles broadly, little dimples appearing on her cheeks, something I hadn't noticed about her before. I find myself smiling in return, whatever was coming, I wasn't alone this time.

Between my friends and my sword I find the courage to stand tall once more, slip my rucksack back over my shoulders, draw my pistol and step back out onto the abandoned road leading through the village, this time following the invisible path in my head, first aiming for the barn, and hopefully not stepping on any sleeper mines in the process. The others slip in behind me, Cole stepping so close I can almost feel her breath on my neck, Megan and McCreedy come next with Grim drawing up the rear. Everyone is carrying a rifle or handgun, cocked and loaded. I can't help feeling a little silly as we weave around the village like a group of drunkards after a night of serious drinking. If anyone was watching us from a distance, I suspect we all looked rather foolish, in spite of the serious nature of our situation.

Despite my fears, we eventually make it to the front doors of the innocuous looking hostel without incident. No sign of anyone, nothing stirring and is it any wonder? We have taken out the two squads they sent after us, as well as their rear guard. It won't be so easy once we get inside though, the images I saw on Megan's laptop showed there were still plenty of guards inside the complex itself, and then there was Kiko, her barely human, demonic features have been haunting my dreams for two years, and she was in there somewhere, the dragon guarding its lair, and sooner or later, I would have to face her.

At Megan's hushed instructions, Cole and I take point either side of the hostel's main doors, while McCreedy takes out his lockpicking kit and begins working on the lock with a surgeon's skill. After just a few moments, he steps back following the sound of an audible click. Cole pats him hard on the shoulder and steps in to take his place, she takes hold of the handle, pulls it down so slowly that it makes not a sound. With a quick glance to me and a nod at my gun, she holds her own silenced pistol out before her and thrusts the door open stepping to the right as I go left, my gun trained and ready.

Two guards are sitting at a table directly in front of me, they appear to be in the middle of a game of cards. At our sudden intrusion they both turn their stunned faces our way. As I raise my gun to take the one on the left out first, I hear two sudden sharp thuds and both men clutch at their chests, one collapsing across the table, sending cards and money crashing across the floor, the other falls to the side and takes the chair with him, ending up sprawled in an unmoving heap on the ground beside his winnings.

I turn to Cole with something like awe on my face, she's even faster than I thought. With the room cleared, Megan nods at both men and orders me and McCreedy to check them for ammo and take one of their radios. While we seek to rob the dead, Grim and Cole move to two of the locked doors, then Megan takes position up outside the third. Megan holds up three fingers, then counts down silently, until she is only holding her fist in the air. At her signal, all three of them shoot out the locks on the doors and kick them open simultaneously. There is a good deal of crashing and shouting, which is suddenly cut off, then the sound of several people sobbing openly.

Meanwhile, McCreedy and I dump our ill-gotten loot on the table, having shoved the other dead guard off it onto the floor next to his friend, and divide the weaponry amongst us. I pick up an extra magazine of bullets for my Beretta and take a long refreshing swig from the bottled water that had been left, half full on the table. For his part, after scoffing a partly eaten sausage roll down in two quick bites, McCreedy begins filling his pockets with wads of twenty-pound notes, trying hard not to look me in the eye as he does so. I turn from watching his misdeed, my discomfort all too plain to see, and instead make my way over to the reception area.

As I draw close to the desk, I hear a soft whimper come from behind it. Drawing my gun, I ease myself slowly around the side of the desk and peer into the dark space underneath. A pair of huge bright blue eyes stare back at me from a too young face for this to be a guard. As my eyes adjust to the dark, I can make out more detail, I realise it's a girl, perhaps thirteen years old, she is dressed in a smart blazer with matching trousers and a white blouse, there is a little badge on her blazer that says My name is Joy, how can I help. Something about the fact they are using such a young woman for their receptionist unsettles me to my core. Seeing the familiar glint of silver shining underneath the collar of her blouse I swallow the lump that has risen in my throat. I dread to think what this poor creature has witnessed, or been subjected too already. I do my best to plaster what I hope is an unthreatening smile on my face, putting my weapon back in its holster, and instead hold out a hand to her. "It's alright", I tell her, "We're here to help, do you want me take that collar off you?"

The girl is all knees and elbows, she has hunkered in under the desk as far as she can, but at my words she unfolds herself a little, raises her hand unconsciously towards the collar without touching it, as I had done a thousand times myself. She looks me hard in the eye, not daring to hope just yet. I pull my own shirt down to reveal the mark that has been left from wearing one myself for close to two years. "See?", I say, "I can get yours off too." Sensing the truth in my words and likely feeling the same solidarity that I have for her at this moment, the girl finally nods her agreement and undoes the top button of her blouse to reveal the insidious device underneath.

I slip my rucksack off my shoulder, unzip the main compartment and dig my hand inside, locating and pulling out one of the MEMP's. I show it to the girl, explain its purpose, "This won't hurt," I promise, "but it will feel a little tingly, OK?" She nods again, so I turn the MEMP on and slowly lean in and hold it close to the girl's neck. It makes the now familiar rapid clicking noise so close to the electronics inside the collar, so I press the button on its side and the same pulse I felt sweep through my body, passes across the space between us and instantly wipes the collar's inner battery. A small grimace crosses the girl's face at the feeling but when she feels no pain following the strange pulse, she gives a hopeful tight-lipped smile and leans forward, allowing me to reach behind her neck and unlock the collar from the back as I had done to myself just a few days before. With a satisfying click, the collar comes loose and I waste no time in throwing it as far from the girl as the room's dimensions allow. Her shaking fingers reach up to her now bare neck and she touches the skin there, a look of disbelief, then undisguised joy and tears falling at the same time. Quite unexpectedly, she leaps into my arms and embraces me tightly, then whispers, "Thank you, thank you," into my ear, her quiet little voice clutching at my heart like nothing before.

I find an overwhelming feeling of protection for this child; it twines and wraps itself around the dark rage bubbling within me and leaves me at once breathless and full of a greater strength than before. I return the girls embrace, rub her back as she begins sobbing quietly against my shoulder. We stay like that for a short while, both blind to all else around us, then, when she is ready, she disengages herself from me, so I hold out my hand and she takes it, her small little fingers, gripping my own delicately, shaking with emotion, and together, we both climb to our feet.

The others are gathered around the table with three women, two dark haired and pale, the third, so fair, her hair is almost white. They are all painfully thin, all dressed in almost see through undergarments and nighties, designed to draw the eye to the more intimate places of the female form. They are all hugging each other, three more collars laid out on the table before them. I can see several thin rivers of blood pooling out from beneath two of the closed doors. I don't need to ask the fate of the men who had been within. At sight of the other women, Joy darts across the room, ignoring the three other armed strangers, and joins in their group embrace. The fair-haired woman goes to one knee and they share an emotional reunion, clearly some bond having formed between them during their time here.

I find I am searching out Megan, wondering what we are going to do with these women and the little girl. I want to go on but I can't just leave them here, what if more soldiers arrive behind us or we all end up getting captured or worse under the mountain?

Megan has already made a decision, though, I can see it plainly, the calculations having already passed through her brilliant mind. She clears her throat, taking command of the emotional situation that has suddenly taken hold in between us all. Everyone turns to her, including the freed women, "Cat I want you to hot wire one of those cars outside, take these women as far and fast from here as you can." Cole's expression wavers a little, one half disappointment, the other sudden realisation that she would probably be in more danger alone, having to protect the women on the road. We had no real way of knowing if there would be another guard post heading out of the south side of the village, since we had all snuck in from the north. There was no one else here I would trust with managing it alone. Cole was the best choice, though I would miss her presence sorely, her confidence and skill were truly something else.

Cole wastes no time in arguing the point, or making a suggestion of her own. She is a soldier through and through, taking the order from her commander without a second thought. She joins the group of women huddled together in the middle of the room, holds the shoulder of the fair-haired woman, who appears to be the unspoken leader of them, and tells them all to come with her. At her words, Joy runs back over to me, bids me to lean down to her and whispers into my ear, "There is a switch under the desk, it will open the way to the bad place." I thank her for her information, give her a heartfelt hug and tell her to go back to the others, that she needs to go and that Cole was the strongest, toughest person I had ever met, and to do what she says and she would be safe. Joy wipes the tears from her face, draws her courage around her, and marches back over to the other three women once more, her bravery making me feel even more desire to protect her and to deal with the bastards down there who had put that collar around her neck. "Cat," I say, "keep them safe." She gives me a wink, says, "Just don't go having too much fun without me," then leads the women back outside.

Within a few moments we hear an engine starting, doors opening and shutting, the crunch of tyres on gravel and the car's engine rumbling off into the distance back out of the village, sounding like it was going at high speed. I let out a breath I hadn't even realised I had been holding, then walk back over to the reception desk, check underneath and find the small black switch exactly as Joy had said.

I check with Megan, who nods before all three remaining with me prep their guns and wait for me to press it. I close my eyes, send a whispered prayer to whoever might be listening to keep Cole, Joy and the other women safe, then press the switch under the desk. There is a faint thud inside the wall behind me, then the entire wall slides almost soundlessly to the left, revealing a huge doorway leading down a flight of metal steps into total darkness. This is it, the tunnel that will take us inside the facility, where my fate has drawn me unerringly since the day I sat before Kiko for my exit interview, the wires sticking to my temples, her scrutiny sending shivers through me wondering about all the horrible things she was planning on doing to me if I failed her. If she is down there, she will be furious, but this time, so am I, and this time, I am thinking of the things I plan to do to her.

CHAPTER 14 – NAITOBEN'S FURY

Each of us has put our night vision goggles on in preparation for heading into the tunnel. It's a curious thing seeing everyone as yellow and red heat signatures, Grim particularly is giving off more heat than the others and looks like some living fire elemental from a fantasy tale. Looking down into the tunnel the metal steps appear in dark blue, radiating cold rather than heat. Something about the tunnel is sending an ominous feeling of foreboding through me. I am trying to put it down to my nerves but I can't shake the feeling that there should have been more men guarding this entrance. No one else seems to feel my lack of enthusiasm and all three of the others have already started down the stairs by the time I get enough of a grip of my fears to start putting one foot in front of the other. But by then, it's already too late…

A second, metal door, slams down from the ceiling above, cutting me off from the others. I find myself sprawled back on the floor of the hostel reception area, staring at a cold blue wall in front of me. I rip the goggles off my head and confirm with my eyes, the thick metal wall that is now barring my way. Alarms start blaring from all directions and I have no more time to think as several armed men come storming through the main doors. I roll behind the desk as machine gun fire rains down upon the floor where I had been laying just moments before. I realise I am outgunned and out manoeuvred. If I make a stand here, I will likely be dead inside of sixty seconds. I make a disturbing decision and have no idea if it will work but everything just went to hell anyway.

I pull off my rucksack and draw out the plastique brickett I had turned into a small IED at McCreedy's instructions. I reset the timer for three seconds and hurl it over my head towards the main doors of the building. I hear a collective shout of surprise from the two soldier's intent on gunning me down but they have no time to get clear, no time at all...

The plastique explodes with the sound of thunder and instantly destroys the entire front side wall of the hostel, including the two men standing in the door way. Pieces of blood and bone, masonry and plaster are littered across what's left of the room. I, myself, have been thrown a good five feet across the room by the blast, but the reception desk has saved me from being set on fire at least. I am wedged under the remains of it, sharp pieces of wooded splinters are sticking out of me in various places. I can't hear anything other than ringing in my ears and suspect I may have just ruptured my eardrum. I can't even tell if the alarm is still going off anymore. One thing I do know is that my friends are trapped down in the dark and I can't get to them. I suspect it would have taken all of McCreedy's plastique combined just to make a dent in the metal door that has slammed down between us. That only left me with one other option if I was to stand a chance of helping them. I would have to go in through the old mining tunnels and into the pit itself. My father once taught me an old Japanese proverb that says 'fear is only as deep as the mind allows'. I have been afraid for too long, its time I faced it down, looked it between the eyes and roared my defiance, instead of living with it rotting inside my mind for a moment longer.

I climb out from under what's left of the reception desk, stumble out of the ruined hostel, disorientated but alive, pieces of the wall are still smoking after the explosion, the smell of burning flesh and wood, mixing together to leave a foul aroma that I can't get out of my nostrils. Woozy and somewhat sickened, I have to pause a moment and concentrate on where I need to step. I stare hard at the ground, piecing together the route I need to take to get to the mine entrance without setting off any more traps. I am finding it hard to think straight, my bruised and battered body is singing for attention, but there is no time and this is no place to be hanging around trying to piece my thoughts back together.

In the end, I trust to luck to some degree and try my best to retrace the path we took from the woods. With each passing minute, as I weave my way across the village, I can't help feeling like there is a target painted on my back. How could we have been so stupid? What did we do that set the trap off so suddenly? Maybe there were sensors on the stairs, that if you didn't know where to step raised the alarm that you were unwanted visitors? I couldn't blame Joy for not knowing, but I do blame myself for not urging more caution before we headed inside. I realise I still have the dead soldier's radio that I took from the body resting on the table, my own having come loose when I was thrown across the room in the explosion. I unclip it from the belt at my waist, turning it on as I jog the meandering path through the minefield, slowly rotating the receiver dial, trying to pick up the frequency that they are communicating on. After cycling through a lot of white noise, I suddenly chance upon a hurried set of instructions and coded orders emanating from the radio's speaker. I can barely hear it through the ringing in my ears and can make out little useful information from what is said, but one thing is clear, they know we are here and they are hunting for us. Whether they realise how many of us have split up I'm not sure, but when they come to investigate the smoking ruin I have made of the hostel's front wall, they will realise not all of us went down the steps, plus, with one of the cars missing, how long before they head off in search of Cole and the women we freed just minutes earlier?

As McCreedy would have said, it's all gone fecking FUBAR. I can't recall ever feeling such deep-rooted anger in all my life. Every time I think we have the drop on these bastards, they show that they are one step ahead of us. Not even Megan had suspected such an impregnable trap slamming down on us like that, and its only dumb luck that I wasn't on the other side of it with the rest of them. I turn off the radio and throw it into the bushes by the side of the road, maybe Megan or Cole would have been able to work out the codes but I have no such skills at my command. Since only Cole and Megan were carrying the other walkie talkies, I also have no way of warning Cole or getting through to Megan that I am still alive. I have no idea if they have already been captured or if they're creating merry hell for the Europa corporation down there. Time to stop worrying about everyone else and think for myself. I could hot wire another car, make a run for it, even work my way back to the helicopter and force the captured pilot to get me the hell out of here. But I don't do any of these things. For some reason, I keep moving ever closer towards the boarded up mine tunnel, my fingers settling on the hilt of my sword, her untapped fury an almost palpable thing.

CHAPTER 15 – THE PIT OF DESPAIR

A few swift and savage swipes of Naitoben's sharp steel and the once boarded up tunnel is now an open invitation for me to step warily inside. A cold and suffocating wind is blowing out towards me, the smell is stale and poisonous, whipping clumps of my hair from my neck and sending shivers through me. The walls of the tunnel are old and crumbling, the wooden cross beams above my head, in place to prevent the ceiling from caving in, are creaking with ominous abandon as I step gingerly through the archway inside. I have to walk with a half crouch, the height of the tunnel, being only around five feet high, was not built with comfort in mind. The remnants of an old cart track lies rusting and rotting at my feet. I put my night vision goggles back on and follow the now cold blue cart lines stretching off into the distance, as I once followed the green lights inside the facility, heading ever deeper into the mine, deeper into the belly of the mountain and whatever doom awaits me.

After a few hundred yards or so, the cart lines come to an abrupt end and the tunnel splits into half a dozen different directions. After a few moments of indecision, I pick the central tunnel that looks like it starts to go down, deeper still beneath An Teallach, the wind also seems to be blowing most strongly from this direction. The old thoughts are creeping into my mind as I begin my descent, threatening to bring me down to a crumpled heap on the floor. The sheer weight of the mountain above me being held by a few old pieces of rotten wood, is in itself a terrifying thought, let alone that if the ceiling were to fall down on me, no one would ever know what became of me, or worse, if it buried me alive, I might have to endure a long, slow death by suffocation or starvation, whichever came first.

I draw Naitoben from her black scabbard, sensing more strongly than ever, that my grip on her is linked to the grip on my sanity. Through the night vision goggles, her beauty is almost ethereal, shining a bright shade of blue, giving off shimmering waves of colour as I turn her one way or the other. Though I feel her filling me with familiar courage and fury, it is not enough to completely keep the terror at bay, but it helps to keep me putting one foot in front of the other, and for now, that is enough...

I have lost all track of time; I have taken so many right and left turns at different intersections that I have no idea how to find my way back. I thought at first to mark the walls but figured if anyone was following me, I would be leaving them a trail straight to me that even a blind fool could follow. In the end, I decided, it didn't matter, I wasn't intending on going back. If I didn't find a way through to the facility, this would all be for nothing anyway. Every now and then I think I hear voices talking, once I could swear, I heard someone sobbing uncontrollably, had to think hard for several minutes to ensure it wasn't me. It stopped as abruptly as it started, for a long time I simply sat and listened, wondering who it could be. Total and utter silence follows, when my legs begin to feel stiff beneath me, I decide to get moving once more and drag myself back up.

'Just keep moving, that's it, one foot, then the other. Don't give up, your friends need you. Don't worry I'm here, I'm with you.' Naru's voice is like a steady drumbeat inside my head, I don't know when he started talking to me, when our minds had frayed apart once more. Something about this place, it's occupied the darkest corners of my nightmares for so long, even confronting it head on, has done nothing to mask the tickling, creeping fear that has leached inside me with every step. I find I am following Naru's instructions, even so. Just one step in front of the other, yes, I can do that at least.

It's getting hotter, sweat is beginning to drip down my face and I am finding the goggles are becoming increasingly uncomfortable, almost useless so deep in the dark, I decide to remove them and pack them away, pausing a moment to swig the last of my water and make short work of an army ration bar that I had stolen from the sack the soldier dropped in the woods. The food and water don't do much to still my tremorous body but it gives me the energy to get back to my feet and keep going a little further. My eyes begin to adjust to the darkness, I start to use my hands to check the width of the tunnel either side of me, measuring its height above me.

Suddenly the ceiling seems to disappear above me, I stand to my complete height for the first time since stepping into the mine and stretch my arms out in all directions. Nothing, I listen intently, completely still, realise I can hear the quiet drip of water. Is it me or is the darkness moving over there? I step carefully towards it, the dripping sound louder over here. My eyes straining hard to see what's there. I trip, stumble over something on the floor I didn't see, my right-hand landing in a freezing cold pool of water as I crash to my knees. I can't quite believe it, I hear Naru's chuckling laughter burst forth in my mind, he is laughing I realise, not because I fell but because he knows this place, as do I, I am inside the water cave, at the centre of the pit and, more, I know the way back to the cell block from here, I know the way out!

I had spent, in all, something like two weeks of my life stumbling around inside these tunnels in abject misery during my training. At last, in familiar territory, I find my strength returning, my mind seeking ahead of me, an arrow flying towards its target, searching for the small grate ten feet above the ground where I had been lowered down and raised back up more times than I cared to recall. 'It's left here, then right, yes, you're getting close, just round the next bend, wait, did you hear that, listen, what is that?' Naru's constant dialogue has kept the loneliness and fear at bay, but I am already tiring of his hypervigilance. I can hear what he hears, I know to be cautious. With a way out so close, I want control of my mind back. I need to have all my faculties if I am going to be any good to anyone up there above me. 'Please Naru, we are stronger as one, look how far we have come. We need to do this as me not us.' 'I have been here all along Elizabeth, letting you draw on my strength and memories when you needed. We can never be me or you, we are us. But I understand, I will be here when you need me.'

I find I have gone numb with shock at Naru's words. All this time, since I first held Naitoben in my hands, I thought I had healed my mind. Now I understand the truth. I wanted to believe the sword held some power that could fix my broken soul but, in the end, it was just Naru, silently giving me courage, strength and ruthlessness, as I needed it to survive. I want to drop down onto my knees and weep. So, I am still mad, there's no getting around the fact. What if the noise I can hear is in my head, not out there, what then? 'Do not despair Elizabeth, I once wanted to bring an end to it all when I saw no way out but you kept surviving and because of both of us, we have lead Europa a merry, bloody chase across the country and back. They are hurting, just as we are, but this time we have the element of surprise, they will never see us coming from the very pit of despair that Kiko was so fond of subjecting us too.' Naru's words are heartfelt and I realise, despite the few times he was able to take over our body, as time has gone by, I have learned to block him from full control. With sudden clarity, I am hit with an epiphany of insight. I see that, after all, it is me that is the stronger of us, because all that Naru has left is anger and pain and dark memories, but I, I have hope, empathy, kindness, and something almost indescribable, the feelings I have towards Richard and Megan, it's not love, not exactly but, it is something, well, more.

I feel Naru's grudging acceptance as our minds rub against one another, like one wolf giving ground to the other, I have become the alpha in our little pack. I hope it's enough, it has to be, I steel myself, press my hand tightly to my chest, solemnity has replaced fear, calm has replaced anxiety, and so we step, as one, deeper into the shadows, a symbiotic creature of Europa's creation, something more than the sum of our parts, something harder than the sky steel we are clutching so tightly in our hand, both lover and hater, saviour and assassin, Night's bane in truth, our purpose to cut through the dark, to blind our enemies with the light of our intent…

The sound is clearer the second time I hear it, yes, it's definitely human, though they sound like they are badly wounded. I slow my steps, even my breathing, sheath Naitoben quietly, keep her held at the ready. In utter darkness I move with a stealth Cole would have been proud of, stepping on tip toe, feeling ahead with my free hand, keeping myself close to the cave's moisture-slick walls. There it is again, closer, just a few feet away. This close I can recognise the sound for what it is, a human-being in utter misery, sobbing quietly to themselves. I am standing right over them, I could end their suffering with a swipe of my blade, it might be doing them a favour in all honesty. But instead, I reach down and gently lay my hand on their forehead, whispering whatever soothing words that come to mind. "It's alright," I tell them, "I'm going to help you, do you hear me, it's alright now." The sobbing changes at my touch and at my words becomes an outright whimper, then, a whispered outcry of desperate hope, "Elizabeth? Is that you?" The voice of my former master is barely recognizable, his mouth so dry, his body so weak, that the sounds have to fight their way out of his mouth, cracked and swollen. I find I have drawn my hand back in utter shock, Richard is alive, he has been ruined, beaten and starved, but somehow, he lives still. I can't stop the tears from falling, some of it is relief that I didn't kill him at the hospital, but mostly, it's for the awful fate that Europa has put upon him. His plan looks to have failed miserably, the people who ran this place might be crazy sadistic fucks, but they weren't stupid, in fact the savage intelligence they had demonstrated so far continued to teach me not to underestimate them.

I cradle his broken body against my own and say, "Yes, it's me, I'm so sorry Richard, for everything." My words come out stuttered, marred by my tears and choked with emotion. I am already reaching inside my rucksack, first for a MEMP, then my last ration bar. I explain what I am about to do, don't give Richard time to answer. The MEMP sends its wave of power against his neck and as I begin reaching behind him to unlock it, I realise he still has both collars locked around his neck. Rage and guilt threaten to drown me, I have no idea how much suffering he would have endured if both those collars had been used at once, those fucks, kuso yaru! Once I have unlocked both of them, I throw them angrily into the darkness, hating them for everything they represented and were capable of. Richard's sobbing thanks is overwhelming, for a time we just clutch at each other in the dark both too overcome to speak.

That I should find Richard here, now, I wonder at the cruel hand of fate that is making a mockery and tragedy of my life. Now I see another path laid out before me. I could help Richard back through the tunnels, maybe even get him to one of the cars outside the hostel and together we could flee this place. As badly injured as he is, I would have to practically carry him most of the way, but I could do it, maybe. But that would mean abandoning the others to whatever was going on above us. If I keep going, I won't be able to take Richard with me, I will have to leave him down here. Neither choice is good enough, neither option is truly a choice at all. In the end, Richard makes the choice for me. "Go," he says, his voice breaking with sadness, "you have to free them, you have to save them if you can." I doubted Richard could understand how much his words cut me, he could have no idea my friends were likely fighting for their lives up above us somewhere, he meant the other servants. Even after everything he had been through, he was still prepared to sacrifice his last hope for the sake of everyone else. I cannot see him, I can only feel at his bruised and swollen face, trying to recall how handsome he had once been. His head in my hands, I lean in close and kiss him gently on the lips, just once, a kiss of goodbye. He reaches back and takes my hands in his own and for a short time we are just two lovers, holding one another in the dark.

I am the first to pull away, I reach down beside me then place the ration bar in his hand, the last gift I can give him, such a small thing when he needed so much more, then, with a certainty of belief I tell him with conviction, "I will come back for you, somehow, I will get you out of here, just wait a little longer." He almost chokes on his own laughter at that. "I'm finished, we both know it, if you could see me, in truth you would never have put your face anywhere close to me. But I thank you all the same Lizzy. Now, go help the others, I'm not going anywhere." At the deep sorrow in his words I dread to think what a mess they have made of him, no, not they, Kiko will have been the one to do it, I am certain. My anger gets the better of me and I practically growl my next words, "I'm going to bring the fucking mountain down on top of her."

CHAPTER 15 – A TORTURERS' FATE

I am staring up at the grate in the ceiling, the door to my freedom from the unending dark, but entry into a different kind of hell awaits. I have left Richard behind, the location of his broken and dying body fixed in my mind. He had called out his love for me once more as I turned my back to him and I had stalled in my tracks, sobbed so quietly into my hands that even a bat would have had a hard time hearing me. I hadn't said it back, I couldn't, even to offer him something at the end, I just couldn't find it inside myself. Instead, I had swallowed it all down inside and told him once again that I would come back for him. Then, step by painful step, I had walked away from him, a nameless sadness hurting me more than any pain the collar had ever inflicted.

I slip my rucksack back off my shoulders and pull out the grapple and rope inside, thankful for Cole's forethought, and recalling her saying something like, "You never know when one of these might come in handy." It takes me ten attempts at spinning the thing in my hands, then launching it up at the grate, before it finally grips something hard enough to bear my weight. I am quite sure Cole could have done it on her first attempt and while fighting off soldiers with an arm tied behind her back. My skill set, unfortunately, had not included jumping out of helicopters or rock-climbing out of caves. After several tugs of the rope and not being hit on the head with a large piece of metal, I find I am smirking triumphantly in the dark. Say one thing for

Elizabeth Shaw, say she was not a quitter. With Naitoben back over my shoulder and the rucksack weighing me down, it was no boast to say that it was a damn hard climb for the first eight feet above me.

Nearer the grate, there is a small square opening dug into the ceiling that allows me to brace my feet and back and ease my aching arms and fingers. It also means I have my hands free to examine the lock, realise I have no clue how to pick it, add another skill set I'm lacking to the list, then, deciding on brute force, I unholster my silenced gun and shoot point blank at the padlock holding the grate in place. A few moments later, there is an audible clang of metal as I raise the heavy grate above my head until it slams open behind me. Not exactly the ninja like stealth I had in mind but the fucking thing was far heavier than I realised.

I pull myself up and out of the hole in the floor, scan the corridor ahead and behind me. The place is utterly silent, unusual in itself, since there is usually some poor soul screaming out their pain into the dark uncaring halls of stone. Pistol in hand, I start making my way back towards the cells, a little thrill of fear tickling at the corner of my mind as I draw ever closer to the lair of the woman who ran this place of terror. I would have to pass Kiko's chambers to reach the cell block, a turgid pressure is building in my head, memories best left buried, threatening to burst forth like the undead and tear my sanity to ribbons. Putting each foot in front of me is like wading through treacle and in the end I have to holster my gun and draw the one thing that I know can keep my terror at bay…

Naitoben sounds her battle cry, the sharp ring of steel echoing down the empty corridor ahead of me. I am able to walk with my head held high once more, my thoughts now a quiet rage rather than full of noisy fears. I can hear my heartbeat pounding in time to my steps, my breathing slowing, my focus stretching out, feeling ahead for what I know and dread to find, and then, I sense her near, Kiko, the figure of my nightmares, the beast I have to slay or die trying. She is here and she is waiting for me...

To my surprise and trepidation, Kiko has left the door to her chamber wide open, inviting me to simply walk inside. I have only been in this room twice before and both occasions have left my mind scarred beyond redemption. I feel Naru's wary curiosity, we both know it's a trap, but there is no turning back, not now, whatever else is inside this room, there is one thing that is certain, one of us would not be walking out again. I pause for just a moment, marshalling my courage, letting my anger bleed slowly into my sword arm. The moment passes, I draw a deep, sweet breath, perhaps one of my last, then step through the threshold, my sword steady and her steel hungry for the blood of our enemy...

The loud, slow clapping of my former mistress is not the sound I had been expecting to hear. When her morbid laughter begins moments later, I have the strongest urge to throw my sword to the floor and flee with my tail between my legs. But I don't run, instead I find I have frozen in place, fighting to control my horror at the scene in front of me. Megan has been stripped and tied to a cross on the wall, a crown of thorns has cut deeply into her forehead, leaving rivulets of blood running down her cheeks and dripping from her chin. There are dozens of lash marks all over her body, yet still, she has her eyes open wide, her expression at the sight of me strolling into the room one of desperate hope, despite the pain she must be enduring. "I have to hand it to you, Elizabeth, you and your friends have caused us quite a deal of trouble and I don't recall giving you permission to go galivanting around the country with that little pig sticker. Truly you have earned a most delicious punishment."

"Jibun de fakku shi ni iku!" I shout back at her, my defiance and hatred boiling to the surface. One friend lies dying in the dark beneath me, another, the best of us all, has been crucified like some twisted pagan mockery of Christ. I have no idea where

Grim and McCreedy might be but I fear their fates could be even worse. Kiko steps from the shadows of the room, she is dressed all in dark leather and buckles, creaking with every move of her body, her gleaming fangs bared and a silent hiss emanating from her lips. I stare into the demonic eyes of a sadistic predator and I can't help but feel that old pull of obedience, the need to obese myself at her feet and beg her forgiveness for my insolence.

My hand is trembling, my mind reeling, why don't I do something, anything? Her wicked grin is overpowering, each second, she draws a little closer, her sinuous body almost hypnotizing as she stalks towards me. There is something in her hand, something I know I should be paying more attention to, but I can't draw my gaze from her reptilian stare, those slitted pupils reminding me of every horror, every dishonour that she inflicted upon me. Megan is screaming at me to look out, to fight her, but I am as frozen as if I had been cast in concrete. Some part of my mind is breaking inside, and with utter abjection I discover I don't have enough to stop her, I can't...

I scream in despair, start to sink to my knees. How? How does she have this hold over me? And she knew, knew all along I could not fight her. No, I realise, with sudden understanding, I can't fight her, Elizabeth can't fight her, but Naru, Naru can. And then I see, all I need to do is surrender, but not to Kiko, to the man who once called this body his, to the only one whose dark soul could match Kiko's own. So, I step back inside my mind once more, letting Naru come forth with all his cunning and ruthlessness. Something in our sudden smile wipes the grin off Kiko's face, she has come to a halt, just a few metres from us. I am watching through Naru's eyes, see the wavering of her confidence. We glance down at the object she is holding, her stun rod, almost as long as Naitoben, it's a sleek piece of metal that can send a few thousand volts right through anything it touches. A terrifying weapon to be sure, but compared to the sword in our hands, it's a children's toy.

Naru wastes no time to give Kiko the chance to let the new status quo sink in, instead he moves us forward at frightening speed, sweeping Naitoben out to the side, then arcing her in at chest height, forcing Kiko to stumble backwards and swing her weapon out in front of herself as a shield. Sparks of electricity crackle down Naitoben's gleaming metal, setting her afire with lightning like some true magic sword of legend. Kiko cringes back from the heat and light, her free hand going up to her eyes to shield her from the blinding light. Perfect. Naru spins us on our heel, launching the next strike up and across, not going for the weapon but instead for the weak spot.

There is a wet slap, followed by a shriek of pure agony, Kiko's hand and part of her forearm are spinning across the room, completely severed from her body, sending bloody spray in all directions. She is staggering back from us, clutching her bleeding stump to her chest, her weapon dropped and forgotten on the floor. We kick it away from us, keep coming at her, don't give her an inch. She tries to speak, holds out her other arm, imploring for us to stop, to obey. We grin right back at her, the grin of a tiger that has brought it's prey to ground, and now to feast.

The next slash of the great sword is two centuries in the making. I doubt Naitoben had ever moved so fast or with such lethal intent other than by the hands of Idoshi himself. Just a moment is all it takes to slay the beast before us, driving Naitoben right down through Kiko's hideous malformed skull, out through her jaw bone, sending a handful of sharp fangs spitting forth from her mouth along with other pieces of bone, brain and blood, continuing straight through her shoulder and cleaving what's left of her already severed arm from her body at the armpit.

Her lifeless body falls to the floor in three pieces, half her head rolling off to the side leaving a river of dark red blood in its wake. The scream that is coming from my lips is primal, a roar of hatred and triumph, but it is not me that is making it. Only now do I begin to understand the true depths of Naru's brooding malevolence, his monstrous intent. For Naru has no intention of helping the others, he is already looking around the room, searching for one of the backpacks, for the explosives within. Kuso! He's planning to blow up the lift shaft and destroy the whole facility with us still inside...

CHAPTER 16 – ME, MYSELF AND NARU

I call forth everything I have to reach him, bring every moment of kindness and love in our life to hold up in front of him, remind him we are not this savage creature, this bloody warrior of vengeance. Somewhere, under all of it, a good man remains, the boy who wanted to be a racing driver, the son who wanted to make his mother and father proud, the youth who chose to become something more, to serve and protect, for the sake of others who couldn't defend themselves. 'This is how you see me?' 'Naru, please, you have to let go of this darkness inside, we are becoming the thing we hate. Please? Let me back in, let me help my friends.' 'There is nothing else for me out there, if I destroy this place, we will have beaten them and stopped them from doing what they did to us, to anybody else.' 'But what about Winters, he is still out there, you think this is the only place in the world like this, you think Europa is just this facility, how many others will suffer at his hands if we die here, if Megan and the others die here? Other than Cole, we are all there is who know what has happened here, what is still happening.' 'I cannot bare to live like this a moment longer, we are disgraced, dishonoured'...'I want to live damn you.'

There is an intense battle of wills going on between us, our body has sunk to the ground, we are kneeling before a spreading pool of demon's blood, the thought of it touching me sickens my very soul. Megan is calling to us, begging for our help, but her voice is distant, she may as well be a hundred miles away. Something is changing inside us, the weapon in our hands trembling with a new purpose, we are looking at Naitoben with a dawning realisation, sebbaku is only a swift plunge away, to end this insane tug of war once and for all. 'No Naru, I refuse, Kesshite akiramenaide kudusai... I... don't... want... this!'

There is a pressure building in my head so painful I can see sparks of light dancing before my eyes and the ringing in my ears has become the toll of the division bell announcing my doom. The beautiful sword of my ancestors is lifting inevitably before our eyes, no my eyes, god dammit, this has to stop. I recall my dream back at the base, Naitoben, shattered into pieces at Kiko's feet, and with the insight born of desperation I understand what it is I have to do.

The wail that bursts from my lips is one of utter desolation and with the last of my mental strength I wrestle control of my arms back from my darker half and swing the flat of the sword down hard against the cold granite floor, shattering Nightsbane, the morning star, the demon slayer, last of the sky steel blades, one of the finest swords ever crafted, into a thousand pieces of glistening metal...

The pressure has subsided, my mind is my own once more, Naru has gone, at least for now. But the cost, oh the cost would weigh on my soul for a longtime to come. I am holding the last remnant of Naitoben in my hand, her hilt, cross guard and a few inches of priceless steel, all that is left of her. A choked sob, a single tear drips to the floor, the sorrow of a thousand lost sun rises, for the child that will never be. And then, somehow, despite everything, I am staggering back to my feet, doing my best to circumvent the lake of blood on the floor, slowly working my way to Megan's side and trying to figure out a way to help her down from the cross. She is distraught, yelling at me to leave her and help McCreedy first. I stare wearily around the dark chamber, there are two doors on either side. I can recall with vivid and scarred memory what was behind those doors the last time I was here. The room with the box is to my left, the one with the rats to my right. Megan's heated gaze is pointing out the door to my right, my heart runs cold. Megan is babbling, telling me about the screams, that they only stopped a few minutes before I arrived.

I move in a kind of numb trance, each step closer to the torture chamber surprising me that I keep putting one foot in front of the other. The thick oak panelled door swings open at my touch as though recently oiled, showing me the horror show in all its sickening detail. McCreedy has been stripped down to his underwear, spread-eagled, his arms and legs are strapped and padlocked to the dull metal table bearing his weight. On his chest have to be at least twelve large rats, trapped inside a Perspex box, their only way out, to dig through his body and out through the hole in the table underneath him. A huge metal bowl, full of white-hot coals, is perched on top of the box, incentive to make the rats do all in their power to find an escape route. McCreedy's face is ghostly pale, he is still alive, staring at the box of rats with bulging, terrified eyes. There is a fair amount of blood trickling down the side of the box but not so much that it actually gives me some hope I can save him. I race to his side and shove the hot metal bowl on to the floor, ignoring the burning pain in my fingers, then unlatch the Perspex box and tilt it up as high as I can, until it falls off the table under it's own weight. Released at last, the rats flee across the room in all directions.

McCreedy still hasn't moved or spoken, he is looking at me with shining bright eyes, as though I am some holy spirit come to raise him to heaven. I look down at his chest, fearing the worst but to my surprise, the rats have only slashed him badly, haven't yet broken through the skin to his bones or vital organs. I turn back to him, hope and fear is warring on his face in equal measure. I nod once, "You'll live, it's going to hurt like hell though." He swallows, closes his eyes, tears falling in streams down his cheek, "Jesus, Mary and Joseph, new girl, you took your sweet fecking time, please just get me off this fecking thing will ya?" I nod wordlessly already looking for the keys to the locks. I spy a set hanging from the wall. I snatch at them and begin trying each key one after the other, first on his arms and wrists, and then on the buckles around his legs and ankles. By the time I have undone every strap McCreedy is weeping openly, praising Jesus and promising to go to confession and take holy communion right then and there. I have to shake him from his religious revelry, explain that we still need to help Megan and find Grim. In the end, he makes one final sign of the cross and, with my help and a lot of swearing, he is able to first sit up on the table and then slide his feet to the floor.

Standing stiffly, Lister begins gingerly touching and inspecting his numerous wounds. I point him over to a small ceramic sink in the corner of the room and he moves like a marionet, taking an age, before carefully turning on the tap and beginning to clean himself up. Both his and Megan's backpacks have been dumped in the corner of the room along with their clothes. I dig out a few bandages from my own pack and take Lister his clothes and his bag. Satisfied he is able to tend to himself for the time being I head back out into the main chamber to see to Megan...

After slicing through the thick rope binding her to the cross with Jack's hunting knife, Megan collapses into my arms and I have to carefully lower her to the ground, mindful of every whimper of pain that escapes her lips as her myriad injuries press against me. I help her to ease the biting crown of thorns from her head, then pull out a bottle of water from her pack and pass it to her, wait as she swigs half of it down in moments, then pours the rest over her head before passing it back empty. Next, I take out a tube of antiseptic cream from the med kit inside her pack and begin gently rubbing it into each stinging slash. She has half as many cuts on her front as her back, Kuso, that fucking bitch has whipped her more than thirty times that I can count.

By the time I have finished administering the cream to every cut, McCreedy has managed to bandage and dress himself, though at the sight of him, he looks like he could do with a blood transfusion before he faints. I tell him to sit down and rest, then help Megan on with her clothes, she cursing and swearing under her breath all the while. I estimate around fifteen minutes have passed since I first stepped into Kiko's chambers. Fifteen minutes, yet we are all so changed for it. Megan and McCreedy are a mess, they are going to struggle just walking out of here. With dawning understanding, I know I am the only one left with any chance of finding and helping Grim. I keep looking at the other door to the room with the box inside, out of the corner of my eye. Wondering but not daring to utter what I am fearing, my mind recalling the poor woman who Kiko had locked inside it when I was last here. Have they done the same to Grim? I have to know, one way or the other...

I am standing over the box, just staring at it, daring myself to just flip the latch and open it, trying my best to ignore the various torture devices lying haphazardly on a bench by the door or the chains and manacles hanging from the walls and ceiling, not to mention the small drain in the centre of the room still stained with the last victim's dried blood. Part of me wonders if this will be one last trap, that if I open the box, the ground will open up and swallow me. I have walked all around it several times already, examined it and the floor for anything that might indicate some mechanism or moving part that shouldn't be there.

Nothing, and, in the end, there is nothing else for it. I reach out slowly, carefully, barely touching the latch with the end of my fingers. I stay back as far as I can, my arm stretched out with my head turned to the side, my eyes shut, my breath held. I count down from three... then flip the latch and throw the lid back, leaping backwards at the same time. Nothing happens, the floor doesn't cave in, no poison gas is pouring out of the ceiling. I ease myself back over to the box, my feet sliding across the floor. Finally, I move my head above the open box and stare hard into the contents inside. It's not what I was expecting to find, but it's enough to send a cold shiver of loathing right through me. I reach in and take out the two items inside the box, close the lid and turn my back on the room, then stride out as fast as I can without physically running.

CHAPTER 16 – OH BROTHER WHERE ART THOU?

I place my old servants robe and collar on the table in Kiko's chambers, staring at them for a long moment, caught up in a hundred different memories of a life not of my own making. I wonder at what Kiko had intended, perhaps to strip me in front of my leader and make her watch, as I dressed in my old robe, put the collar around my own neck and become her faithful servant once more? I move away from them, no sense wondering at Kiko's intentions now, she certainly had not intended the fate that had been hers at the end. Megan has retrieved her laptop from her pack and is desperately searching through the camera images for her lost brother, her beautiful features scarred by the anxiety she is clearly feeling. The pain she must be in seems to be nothing compared to the fear of not knowing what has happened to Graham.

"What happened?" I ask the question without really thinking, Megan glances up at me briefly suddenly recalling McCreedy and I are still here with her, then turns back to laptop's screen, continuing her search, before replying, "After the door came down they sealed the corridor, we had no time, they sucked all the damn air out, created a vacuum. We all passed out within a few minutes, there was no way out. When I woke up, I was naked, hanging from a fucking meat hook in a huge freezer. The others were there too, Lister and Graham, both tied and gagged like me. That crazy bitch came for us with two of her men, she had me taken down first, whipped me bloody in front of the others, then they dragged me half-conscious to this room and tied me to that cross. Later they brought Lister in here and took him in that other room. I couldn't see what she was doing to him in there but his screams are going to be giving me nightmares for the rest of my life." She pauses for a moment, staring hard, unblinking at her computer screen, her eyes squinting, forehead frowning in concentration. Then, she draws back, shakes her head, looks back up at me, "What about you? How did you even get inside?" I run my hand through my tangled hair, half turn to the open door behind me, recalling my time in the dark, alone and uncertain if I would ever find my way out. Then, finding Richard down there, and he was there still, maybe with Megan's sharp mind we could figure out a way to help him. But first, we had to find Grim, it was possible he might still be in the chiller, but I suspected they might have had something else in mind for him and where they would have taken him. In fact, I'm almost certain of it.

I sit down beside Megan on the floor, point to the cameras that show the third floor, the labs, gesture for her to start cycling through them, then say, "I think I know where they would have taken your brother, the place where they altered me, where this whole nightmare began, on the third floor, the laboratory." She nods at that, looking pale and sickened, then starts flicking through the cameras. "As for me, I blew a hole in the hostel wall to escape with my IED. Then I broke into the mine, I must have walked for hours, I think maybe even a day or more, I became certain I would die down there, but somehow, in the end, I found my way to the pits, where they had sent me for punishment before I was given the assignment to lure Wonderland into the open. Once I realised where I was, I found my way to the hatch beneath the cellblock. I used a rope and grapple hook to climb out, not my finest hour I assure you. My friend, Richard, the one who helped us at the hospital, he's still down there, he's hurt bad, but if we can find Graham, maybe we can all leave that way, take Richard with us and blow the place up behind us." At my explanation and hopeful last words, Megan cocks an eyebrow before looking pointedly at McCreedy, then gesturing at herself. "I'm not leaving here without Graham but I don't think any of us are in any shape to be able to get out the way you came in." My head sinks at her words, she's right of course, I'm not sure if I could even find the way back if I had a week's supply of food and water. It was blind luck that I even reached the pits and didn't end up falling down a mine shaft or getting trapped in one of the claustrophobic tunnels that were so tight you had to crawl and squeeze through them with barely a breath of air held in your lungs.

I try to think, to come up with a solution, but I am so tired, the thought takes my mind to Richard, dying down there, beaten half to death, utterly alone, his parting words cutting me to the core. But more than that, my mind keeps hovering around the fact that he was the architect of this whole place, if anyone knew another way out, he would. But that would mean going back and asking for his help, asking for him to save me yet again and leaving him to die, again.

Megan is looking at me with that calculating way of hers. "You've thought of something." Not a question, a statement. Am I so easy to read? This is no place for sentimentality or regret, my leader expects an answer, so, I give it, "Richard, he designed this facility, thought he was being paid to construct a grand underground hotel, something to make him famous. When he started to get suspicious of it's true purpose, they made him a permanent 'guest', that was nearly ten years ago. If anyone knows another way out, he will." Megan and McCreedy share a look, she turns back to me and says, "The Hatter and I will figure out a way to get your friend out of the Pit, in the meantime I'm going to need you to put those on." She gestures to the robe and collar on the table and I feel my whole-body tense up, my mind balk at the absurdity of what she just said. I am already shaking my head, the thought of putting that collar back round my neck would be worse than committing seppaku.

Megan is holding out her hand placatingly, seeing the sudden panic in my eyes. "Just hear me out, look, there are still a few guards dotted around the facility on the other levels, a servant in a collar and robe will be able to walk amongst them unchallenged, is that not right?" I lick my dry, cracked lips and swallow back a mouthful of bile. Though I hate her for suggesting it, Megan's logic is impeccable, if I put those on, I could walk right past any guard, provided I was following a green light. With Megan's hacking skills, I know she has figured out a way to make the lights dance to her tune. My hands are shaking violently, my teeth are clenched so hard it hurts, I want to run away from this place and never look back, but I owe Megan and her brother a lot already, and if I do this, she just might be able to save Richard too. Kuso, mother fucking kuso!...

I have passed the MEMP over the collar three times already, it has worked it's magic and wiped it of any power but I still can't bring myself to physically pick the thing up and place it around my neck. Megan has taped my gun and Jack's knife to my back and I have slipped the familiar, itchy servant's robe down over my smalls and untied my hair so that it hangs long and limp around my shoulders. In the end I have to ask Megan to do the honours, I close my eyes and try to conjure images of blue skies and sandy beaches, but it feels more like falling or drowning as the familiar cold weight of the collar settles once more around my neck and locks back in place with a loud click. The look Megan gives me when I turn to face her is utter misery, she can see how much it has taken for me to agree to do this and the weight of responsibility is resting heavily on her shoulders, but there is still a steely determination in her eyes, like she would have commanded this of me even so. She nods once, shows me the image she has found by running back through the security footage, around an hour ago, Grim being wheeled unconscious on a stretcher onto the third floor, into one of the labs. We all knew what that could mean, that I might already be too late, but I had to go, none of us were going anywhere until we knew his fate...

The familiar corridor of the cellblock is making my skin crawl, the cold stone floor on my bare feet sending chills right through me. As I pass each cell, I check inside hoping to find someone, anyone still here, that we could help to escape with us, but each room is empty, the corridors utterly silent. Megan is sending the green lit path ahead of me, her hacking skills proving more than proficient for the task. Eventually I reach my old cell and lurch to a sudden halt despite myself. Two years they kept me here, two years of being trained, punished, feminised, locked away below the world, dead and forgotten. Is it any wonder I lost my mind? I take one last look at my old pallet bed, the little sink and dented bucket, the darker patches on the stone floor, testament to all the times I had crawled back in here bloody and beaten. The room is tiny, smaller than I remembered, I try to recall the person I was, who had existed at the whim of her masters. I needed to keep that mindset fixed in my head, if I have a hope of pulling this off...

I am almost at the lift, despite the empty cells there is still a single guard on duty. At sight of me, he turns to the lift, presses the button and moves aside, the green light ahead of me enough to convince him that I was simply following the orders of one of the masters. I keep my eyes downcast, stare at the floor a few metres ahead of me, certain if I look him in the eye, he will know my true intentions.

A moment of pure anxiety as I step into the lift, half because of my old fear of the cursed thing dropping me to my death, the other half from putting my back to the guard, leaving me completely defenceless should he decide I'm not so innocent as I seem. But my fears remain unfounded as the doors slide shut behind me and the lift begins its ascension to the third floor. Barely sixty seconds later, the lift grinds to a squealing halt and lets me out onto the level where my life was changed forever. Though I had never been conscious during the operations, I am certain it was in one of the labs on this floor that Darren Winters had the surgeons alter me for his own special brand of sadistic amusement. And now, God only knew what they might be doing or have done already to Grim. I just hope and pray that I'm not already too late…

There are two guards ahead, standing at attention outside one of the labs, dressed in familiar black uniforms and their faces hidden behind blank, metal masks, only their eyes visible beneath. I have seen no one else, the other doors along the winding corridor have been locked and seemingly empty of life. At my approach the closest guard steps forward and demands me to stop. I come to a halt at his command, keep my eyes lowered to the ground in expected supplication. I don't recognise his voice, but I hear the lecherous intent in it, when he motions me towards him, tapping his fellow on the shoulder suggestively. "Looks like we've been sent some entertainment at last Mikey boy, and a real pretty one too." The other guard nods, both staring at me with hard, cold eyes that tell me far too much about what they have in mind. I realise I won't be able to just slip past these two, I have to think fast.

Though it sickens me, twists my stomach into a tight knot, I raise my eyes to meet them, smile shyly and say, "Mistress Kiko has commanded me to pleasure every guard on this level, starting with you." I point at the man who spoke first, his eyes lighting up with mirth, chuckling under his mask. "Come on then, let's see the goods, take that old sackcloth off and show me your pert little titties." I feel sick bubbling up my throat, do my best to keep plastering a simpering smile on my lips, though every fibre of my being wants to launch myself at the man and claw those light grey orbs out of his metal fucking face. I pull the robe up over my head and drop it to the floor beside me, stand before them in nothing but my underwear, leaving very little to their perverted imaginations.

The one I pointed to steps in close, raises his mask up onto his head, wanting a sniff of me before pointing at my bra and demanding I take it off next. He is clean shaven, handsome after a fashion, with a square jaw and tight brow line under the mask, but when he leans in to lick and kiss at my neck, it's all I can do not to throw up all over him. I reach behind my back with my left hand, take a grip of the handle of Jack's knife, smile back at my lecherous companion, whose right hand has already slipped inside my panties, and for the briefest of moments, we stare hard into each other's' eyes.

Whatever he finally sees in the look I am sending back at him has given me away, his eyes suddenly bulging, his mouth opening wide to call out a warning, but it's too late for that. My arm is already travelling up between us, the sharp serrated blade clutched in my hand, is already launching at speed towards its target. He never gets to utter the warning, the ten-inch blade penetrates just under his chin, right through the roof of his mouth and straight into his brain, killing him almost instantly. Meanwhile, my other hand is pulling the Beretta forth. The second guard is only just realising something is amiss, as his friend makes a final gurgling wet cough, his body going completely limp, he drops to the floor at my feet, dead. The second guard finds himself staring down the barrel of my gun. It's the last thing he ever sees. I shoot him twice, just to make sure. The first bullet goes right through his left eye, the second in the middle of his chest, tap, tap, just like that, another man falls dead at my feet.

I bend down, pull Jack's knife out of the guard's head with a wet slurp, wipe the blood off on his uniform and re-sheath it at my back. I pick up the key card from around his neck and snap it from the cord. Then I pick my discarded robe off the floor and pull it back over my head. Dressed once more, but this time with my gun at the ready, I swipe the door card against the black sensor on the wall, the doors parting before me with a quiet swish, letting me into a brightly lit room with dozens of jars, bottles and storage units all around it's edges, the walls brilliant white, like a hospital. On the other side of the room a glass door shows a short corridor and a further, larger, thick metal door with a port hole window at the end. With nowhere else to go I press ahead, feeling more urgency, I start jogging, then running, certain that I have finally reached my destination. I ram myself bodily into the glass door, but it's locked and won't budge, so I step back a few paces and fire off two more shots, shattering the glass. I leap over the broken fragments littering the floor and charge ahead. This time, when I crash into the metal door ahead of me, the handle moves at my touch and I burst into the room, my gun held steady, my mind sharp and focussed...

My sudden entrance was clearly not expected, three people look up in startlement, two men and one woman. They are all dressed in surgeons' scrubs, surgical masks covering their faces, latex blue gloves on their hands. Two of them are holding scalpels, the other looks to be holding some kind of suction device, for cleaning up the mess her colleagues are making. Grim is lying naked, unconscious on the table, his legs are up in the air on stirrups, his genitals, still attached but shaved and prepared for something sinister. There are lines drawn on his chest, markers for where the surgeons have begun carving into him, in preparation for implants that sit on a smaller table off to the side. "Sew him back up, right... fucking... now!" My voice is ice, hard and cold, my gun is trained on all three, moving from one to the other, all the while my mind is spinning, wondering if it was these very three people who had done this to me. It's all I can do to keep myself from gunning them all down in a gory massacre, my hatred threatening to bring Naru back to the surface, no... I can't allow that, I need to keep control, but Kuso, it's the hardest thing I have ever done to not pull the trigger on these bastards.

The surgeons jump at my command and begin bustling around the room, putting down their scalpels and picking up pliers, needles and surgical thread. One of them is shaking so badly, the woman has to take the needle from him and take over, sewing Grim's chest up one careful stroke at a time. "Please try to understand, what we are doing, it's revolutionary, we are creating works of art from dull clay, the bioengineering is so advanced our patients will never have the need to take any drugs or hormones, you see not only do we alter the body inside and out but we rewire the brain too. Look at yourself, Elizabeth, you cannot deny we have made you beautiful." The gun goes off without conscious thought, the surgeon pleading with me to understand their crazed motives is now dying slowly and painfully on the floor, the bullet taking them in the stomach, their death would be a long time coming, and it would hurt like hell. "What you are doing is monstrous, you all deserve to die for it and if either of you say one more word, I will ensure it's your last." I think I've made my point, while their colleague lies groaning and bleeding on the floor, the two surgeons work urgently to put Grim back together. When the final knot is tied and they have cleaned and bandaged his wound, I scream at them to back off and make them lay on the ground with their hands on their heads. I step forward, pull the plastic oxygen mask off Grim's face and take out the long tube that has been lodged down his throat. I wonder if I should ever tell him how close he came to losing it all. Then again... Perhaps it's something I will keep to myself...

CHAPTER 17 – MAD AS A HATTER

Just minutes after pulling the tube from his throat, Grim begins to groan and stir from his enforced slumber. I shake him by the shoulders, tell him it's me, reassure him he's ok, that his sister is ok, after a fashion. At mention of the White Rabbit, Grim's brilliant blue eyes flash open and he stares in open mouthed shock at his predicament, first wincing and feeling at the bandages around his chest and then more urgently at the objects between his legs. "Gryphon, we have to go, can you stand? Can you walk?" I know I'm rushing him, demanding a lot of him so soon upon waking, but I am starting to feel like we have pushed our luck too far already, that An Teallach might have one last trick up its sleeve before we can escape. Can a mountain be malevolent? I think perhaps, in this case, yes, yes it could.

With my help, Grim blearily clambers off the table, losing a little dignity in the process, but certainly a better alternative to what he would have lost if the surgeons had been allowed to have their way with him. We stumble from the room, arm in arm. I lean him up against a wall, shut the door behind us and jam Jack's knife through the handle, effectively locking the door from the outside. Satisfied I have sealed the surgeons in their own lair, I turn back to Grim and put his arm around my shoulder once more. He is looking at me with a lazy, dumb smile on his face, like a happy drunk at a party. The drugs they used to sedate him will likely take a while to wear off yet, maybe it's for the best he isn't thinking too clearly right now but it isn't making it easy to get out in a hurry.

As we reach the broken glass door, I have to pull Grim to a halt and use the Beretta to sweep the glass shards out of the way since we are both bare footed. Once on the other side of the door, I search through some of the cupboards and lockers in the last room and find a spare lab coat that allows Grim to at least cover his modesty. He looks down at himself and laughs at the strange way he is dressed, grips my hand in his own and whispers his heart-felt thanks, leaning into me as I take some of his weight once more.

Together we head out into the quiet corridor, the two dead guards leaving growing pools of blood across the polished floor-tiles. We step over their lifeless forms, keep moving until we get back to the lift. I wave my hand at the camera above the lift's doors and at my signal, Megan sends the lift back to pick us up. When the doors open minutes later, I am taken aback to find the others already inside. Megan and McCreedy are pale imitations of their usal selves, blood loss and torture have clearly taken their toll. Richard, if that is really him, is a broken and bloody mess curled against the lift's back wall. I honestly don't think I would have recognised him if not for the lock of foppish hair covering his hugely swollen left eye and cheek. He was wrapped in a blanket and shivering uncontrollably, his teeth chattering audibly.

Grim lurches from my grasp at the sight of Megan and practically falls into his sister's arms, the two of them embracing silently, for a moment no one and nothing else in the world mattering to them. I turn to McCreedy, since he is the only one looking my way and ask, "So, what's the plan? Did he, did Richard have the answer?" McCreedy glances briefly at the tortured soul of my former master lying broken on the floor of the lift, wincing in sympathy at his plight before turning back to me and lifting up a small black tube with a red button on top that he is holding in one hand and a walkie talkie, crackling to life at his touch in the other.

Cole's voice echoes loudly across the space between us as though she is having to shout the words out in order to be heard, "I'm about four minutes out, I'll ask the pilot to try and land if he can, there are some strong cross winds up this high, this is going to be a little tricky folks." Hearing Cole's voice is like finding fresh water in the desert, and from what she said, I know where she is and what she's planning, I just don't know how the hell we are going to pull this off. My perplexed expression is enough to bring a grin from McCreedy's ghostly pale lips. "The architect, he says there's an emergency access hatch, right up in the penthouse. Looks like we're getting out of this fecking rat infested hellhole after all." And what's that for?" I ask, pointing at his other hand. "There's two of my IED's at the bottom of the lift shaft. Whatever happens next we are making sure this place goes up in smoke." Something about the fact that several pounds of plastique were sitting at the bottom of the lift shaft really doesn't help with my phobia. In the end, it takes both Megan and her brother to coax and tug me inside with them. Plus, Megan is holding something in her hands that sends a small thrill through me, it's the remnants of Naitoben, her scabbard, with the hilt secured inside, as well as a bag full of her broken fragments. She passes them to me without ceremony, I am not sure whether to curse her or thank her for bringing them, but I take them from her all the same. The doors close behind me with a frightening clang, and the five of us hold our collective breath and stare up at the ceiling above, as the lift rises higher and higher, taking us up out of the mountain's belly...

Our final destination, the eleventh floor, the penthouse. I wonder how many people have ever been allowed up here, and what horrible things were likely done to them. For this is Darren Winters' apartment, the grand fucker himself. I doubt he is currently in residence, at the first sign of trouble it looks like they took most of the servants and staff from the whole facility and left in a hurry, just to be on the safe side or maybe we just got here after a big sale?

When the lift comes to a halt with its usual worrying jolt, I practically jump out of it as soon as the doors allow, my skin itching all over and my heart beating like a racing car. For a moment, before it came to rest, I had a cold certainty that we would all plummet back down the mountain, swallowed whole back into its greedy maw. I turn to the others, a rag tag bunch of bloodied and beaten souls compared to when we first met. Megan and McCreedy limp out behind me, both having to find things to lean on to stay on their feet. Grim, having roused more from his recent drug induced slumber on the way up here, is able to help my old master up off the floor and practically carries him out of the lift and into the apartment.

Taking in our new surroundings, the five of us stare agog at the myriad ghastly paintings of human beings subjected to all kinds of horrific acts lining the walls and the twisted statues that look like the victims of Mount Vesuvius that litter the streets of Pompeii, but are currently decorating the huge open plan space we have stumbled into. "Feck me, this guy must be the biggest cunt on the fecking planet." McCreedy's crass words, for once, mirror my own thoughts, there are things in this room that can' t be unseen and just what is going on in the mind of someone who would want to decorate his home like this? He was tsu no byoki no hahaoya kuso!

Richard is trying to speak but his voice is so weak it comes out as barely a whisper. I kneel down beside him where Grim has eased him into a chair that wouldn't have looked out of place inside a gothic castle. This close, I can hardly bare to look him in his one good eye, the other is swollen so badly it's completely shut and lost beneath a huge purple and black bruise, his once perfect teeth are crooked in places and some have clearly been ripped right out of his mouth, his nose is battered and bloody, very much broken. I close my eyes to the sight, rather than let him see the horror on my face, lean in close and ask him to speak again. "There's a false wall, behind the bookshelf in the next room, I don't know the code for the door but your clever friend over there, seems capable of figuring that out I'm sure." He is gesturing to Megan as he speaks, hoping like the rest of us, that she really is the White Rabbit, that she can hack the security system one last time and get us all out of here…

Grim and I wrestle with the book shelf until it falls forwards under its own weight, no doubt dropping half a ton of shit on the floor that no one but a psychopath would want to read anyway. We have searched the whole apartment and there isn't a soul around anywhere, just more evidence of a sick mind and the tools he used to entertain his dark tastes. Megan has scoured the cameras again in her laptop and confirmed, apart from the three arseholes I locked in the lab, everyone else has either already fled the facility, is dead, dying or in this room with us.

While McCreedy and Megan work together, talking in hushed tones over the locked door barring our escape, I find, for a change I have nothing else to do except wait, so I gravitate, inevitably, back to Richard, sitting forlorn and broken, every breath or movement clearly causing him pain. I take my place at his feet, unable to look at him directly but unable to help myself from leaving his side, I end up simply leaning against one of his legs, listening to his quiet breathing, recalling many times when we had shared this closeness, though at the time I felt I had little choice in the matter, now though, now I just want to comfort a friend who needs it desperately.

After a time, I feel Richard's hand rest lightly on my shoulder, a gentle brush of my hair, tucking it behind my ear to see me better, perhaps reminiscing as much as I was, then, "I suppose you're wondering how they did it?" I barely hear him speak, even this close, but I find myself nodding at his words. I couldn't begin to guess how Megan and McCreedy pulled him up out of the Pit, given the shape they were both in, and then there was the guard at the lift, they must have subdued or killed him to get inside as well.

"The gentleman from the Emerald Isle, he waved a large amount of C4 in the face of the guard still manning the lift, persuaded him he was extremely unhinged by all accounts." "He is," I interrupt, smiling at my own joke, as I picture McCreedy playing the part of his alias, The Mad Hatter, with his usual flair for insult. "Well, anyway, he convinced the guard to help pull me up out of the dark. Your friend, Miss Archer, she rigged up a rather fiendish pulley system, after raiding the meat locker and using the rope you left behind. She and the guard pulled me up while the other chap swore and blasphemed like a well, in all honesty, I can't say I've heard anyone besides you swear quite so much Elizabeth."

I often forget how sheltered a life Richard had led before being held prisoner in this place, brought up at an expensive private school, he still struggled to utter a vulgar word despite all that had been done to him. I shake my head at the story, half wishing I could have been there, that I could have been the one to pull him out of that place to make up for what I did in the hospital. "And the guard, what happened to him?" I wonder aloud. "Well, in thanks for his help, the Irish fellow kicked him in his crown jewels and tossed him through the hole in the floor, then he shouted something down about rats and shut the grate on him. Remind me not to cross words with that one, I can't help wondering if he actually would have blown us all to bits down there if the man had looked at him the wrong way." "He's had a rough day," I reply, "We all have. In fact, I wasn't so far from doing something like that myself not so long ago."

"Elizabeth I want you to look at me," so used to following his commands I obey without question, turn to stare him in his one good eye, my wince of anguish at the state of him enough to draw a tear down his cheek. "I'm so sorry," I say the words but they really can't convey the depth of how I am feeling for what I did and for what happened to him because of me. He leans forward, the movement clearly causing him pain, but he doesn't cry out, just grunts, holds a hand to his ribs, and with the other, reaches behind my neck, sending goose bumps down my spine at the intimate gesture, once so familiar, but he is not seeking to caress, instead his still clever fingers twitch at the clasp holding the dead collar in place and with a cool flick of his wrist the hateful thing springs loose and crashes to the floor a few feet from where I am sitting. "There, about bloody time too." For a moment I pull a genuine smile to my lips as I stare back at him, the gesture is not lost on me, in fact, I think it might just be the most thoughtful thing anyone has ever done for me...

CHAPTER 18 – ON ANGEL'S WINGS

A shout of elation wakes me from a weary doze. Megan and McCreedy have been working on the door for only a few minutes but the moment I sat down I could feel the last few days catching up with every muscle in my body. Each ache and pain that I have been doing my best to ignore is working its way into my bones. The groan that leaves my mouth as I pull myself back to my feet is enough to draw a crooked smile from Richard. I blush at the warmth in that look and use the excuse of the noise to turn my back on him and head off to investigate. McCreedy is slumped against a wall, paler than I've ever seen him but grinning like a mad man. Megan is holding a fluorescent tube into the tunnel that was behind the barred door, a clean, fresh breeze is blowing into the room making everyone inside feel a little less claustrophobic. After cracking open a flare and throwing it further down the tunnel and waiting to see if any more traps lay in wait, a collective sigh of relief ensues when nothing happens.

Megan turns to me beaming from ear to ear, claps me on the shoulder, "We did it Kingsleigh!" she cries, the emotion finally showing a little in her eyes, her pupils shining bright with glistening tears, despite her efforts to remain in control. I smile back, not quite ready to celebrate until we have finished what we came here to do. But I nod all the same and say, "Let's go, and by that, I mean, isoide, koko kara seiko o suru koto ga dekimasu." She grins back at my vulgarity and calls out to Grim and Richard to join us. McCreedy grumbles under his breath as he clambers clumsily back to his feet, "Feck you say new girl?" "She said let's get the fuck out of here, you ok with that Hatter?" Megan answers for me, calling over her shoulder as she starts making her way into the tunnel. McCreedy doesn't answer, just rubs at his arms, looks down at his chest and says, "I fecking told you this was the worst idea you ever had," before turning more slowly to follow our leader, who has gotten a few metres ahead of him already.

I hold back a moment, waiting for Grim and Richard, then help Grim by taking Richard's weight under one arm each, while I clutch Naitoben's remnants to me in my free hand. "So, I guess we follow the White Rabbit," Richard whispers by my ear. I squeeze his shoulder and together, the three of us walk out of a place of nightmares and darkness, seeking the light of day, our collective hopes and fears written on every face...

It takes three of us to push the slick boulder aside that's masking the entrance to the tunnel. After years of disuse, the mechanism allowing it to slide out of the way must have almost completely seized. I suppose that's the trouble with hidden escape tunnels, they don't exactly appear on an engineer's maintenance list. But nothing was going to stop us from getting the damn thing open, not when we were so close.

The sudden blast of cold air and glorious bright sunshine that hits us as the boulder finally moves aside is just incredible. I feel like I could float away into the clouds, Kuso we are so fucking high up, must be a thousand feet up at least. The sky above me is clearer than I ever remember, a beautiful azure blue that takes my breath away. Everyone is smiling, taking deep lungsful of the clean air, all shivering in the chill wind gusting around and through us. For Grim, Richard and I, it's particularly exposing since we are all barefoot and wearing next to nothing. If it was winter up here, I suspect we would have frozen to death already.

I turn from taking in the heady views of the distant landscape to see something even more beautiful, the helicopter that brought us here. Selina Cole is leaning against the pilot's door, a lit cigarette in one hand and her MK automatic rifle in the other, she's grinning like the Cheshire Cat, she's the coolest fucking human being I have ever seen...

It takes a few minutes before we are all loaded onboard our 'metal Pegasus'. We are all running on fumes, all except Cole it seems. She takes each one of us in hand, checks we are all buckled in for the ride, warns us it's going to be bumpy as fuck, then climbs aboard herself and orders Harry to take us out. The first few seconds of flight as the helicopter gains a few metres of lift are the most terrifying moments of my life so far, a sudden gust of cold wind blowing the helicopter down, the rotor blades coming perilously close to the cliff face before Harry gains control, finally spinning and lurching the flighty machine back up above the mountain's summit.

Once we are reasonably clear of An Teallach, at least enough that we can't be blown back into its face, McCreedy holds his hand in the air like someone holding a lighter out at a rock concert, only what he is holding is one hell of a fucking lighter. At Megan's nod of command, he presses the button down, at the same instant a colossal crescendo of sound and light erupt from the mountains' side and its summit where we were standing only minutes before.

I find myself staring back, dumbfounded at the sheer ferocity of the blast. Even from the distance we have reached I can still hear a chain reaction of more crashes and explosions going off deep within the mountain's core. I'm assuming the main gas pipes that fed the whole facility must have been breached in the blast. Within minutes, half the mountainside has cracked and fallen away in waves of fiery red and yellow, mixed in with grey, brown and green.

I lean back in my chair, close my eyes, doing my best to sear the image of An Teallach's fiery demise forever in my mind. McCreedy is laughing so hard I feel like he should be wearing a top hat in truth. The others are clapping each other on the backs and shoulders, sharing in the moment, I feel a hand slide across my thigh and grip my own, I don't open my eyes to see whose it is, I don't have to…

EPILOGUE

Three months have passed since I helped the Wonderland Gang to destroy the darkness that lived below An Teallach, three months since I took the head of Kiko and nearly ended up plunging my sword into my own belly but had instead smashed her into pieces in a final moment of madness I still don't truly understand. Megan had not looked at me the same way since she bore witness to my battle with Naru in Kiko's chambers. Only she knows how close most of us came to never getting out of there alive had he actually succeeded with what he had intended. I can't blame her for looking at me askance, for realising just how truly broken I am, what I might be capable of if I lose control of the hateful soul that is intertwined with my own.

Having succeeded in at least freeing some of the other servants, it had still been gut wrenching to find out that Europa had already moved or sold most of them on before our arrival. Whether it was just bad timing or damage reduction on the part of Darren Winters and his staff when they realised, we were coming after them, we may never know.

Megan has been working on some encrypted files she managed to download from the facility's mainframe in the hope it might shed some light on where the servants, and where, indeed, Darren Winters himself, might have gone. She gets Cole to call on me now and then, to let me know how the women are doing that we managed to save, including Joy, who, by all accounts is determined to follow in Cole's footsteps and keeps demanding she train her up to be just like her. The thought always brings a smile to my face, I never imagined Cole as the mothering type, but I can tell when she speaks of her, she really is very fond of the girl, and not only that, but she has recalled her bravery to me several times about how she coped with the thrilling escape that day.

Cole explained, almost offhandedly how she had to fight her way through a barricade of parked cars and waiting soldiers south of Dundonnell village, to get the women away safely. The woman never ceases to amaze me, and if not for her, there would not have been a single one of us that would have escaped that day, of that I am quite certain.

From all accounts, it sounds like Grim got away with just a few thin scars around his chest and a dim memory of the embarrassment of me seeing him naked, he remains tight lipped on the subject regardless, as always. McCreedy has reportedly taken his time under the mountain rather more badly, however. Cole told me he has been drinking himself into oblivion most days, telling everyone except her to go feck themselves. She seems to be the only one he listens to, so she makes a point of visiting him at his home in Ireland every few weeks to try to dry him out and trade insults in an effort to remind him he's part of something and worth more than a few nasty scars on his chest.

As for me, I have returned to Jack's place in Norfolk, taken him up on his offer that it could be my home, at least for the time being. I still have bad dreams so have taken to sleeping in the clearing in the woods throughout the summer. There's something about sleeping under the stars that's doing wonders for my anxiety. Gunner spends most nights sleeping alongside me. I am ever grateful for his silent company and have little fear that anyone will be able to sneak up on me with him on guard duty beside me, though that doesn't stop me sleeping with my adopted Beretta fully loaded in my hands each night.

By day I split my time between running around Jack's five acres of fields and woodland, building up my fitness levels, making sure to practice my shooting and martial arts for a few hours each day. I have also asked Jack to teach me blacksmithing in return for helping out around his property. With his help, I am working on remaking Naitoben from the shards and fragments that Megan managed to gather for me. I know she will never be the great sword of legend that I once held, but I hope to at least create something worthy of the Yamamoto name.

I haven't been able to reach Naru at all since that day, but I can still feel him somewhere inside me waiting, coiled like some deadly serpent around my soul. There is a heady kind of power there, begging me to grasp at it, to help fight against the nightmares and anxiety I feel on an almost daily basis, but filling my days with so many distractions is helping to keep me from going down any more rabbit holes for now.

Then there's Richard, he almost refused to leave the mountain at the end, whispered to me there was nothing for him if he came with us, that he just wanted to see me get away safely. I called him a damn fool, of course, reminded him that I was his companion, that though I might not be able to give him what he wanted, I could still be his friend. God knows, in many ways I need him as much as he needs me. Over the months since coming here, he has recovered more slowly than me, small wonder, given the beatings he was given on top of what I did to him at the hospital. He seems to have taken on a very melancholy air about him, spending most of his days in quiet contemplation, reading one of his books or drawing the natural world around him. I worry about him constantly, when I am not worrying about my mother or myself. Just this morning I walked in on him in the bathroom, he had been holding his razor in such a way that I knew all too well. I swore at him in some of my best Japanese, grabbed the razor off him and threw it in the bin. Tomorrow I am going to get him an appointment to get his teeth fixed, with the monthly stipend Megan has been sending me as a fully-fledged member of her team I can afford it, perhaps it will make him smile for me once more.

My mother appears to be well settled here, spending most of her days sitting on the little bench on the front porch or tending to the allotment. She still gets scared and confused most days, but each of us have our ways of calming her down or re-assuring her. I tend to take her for a walk in the woods, since I always find it so calming for both of us. Jack has a great way of distracting her with finding interesting bugs or creatures to draw the wonder from her childlike mind. I have found Richard at times reading stories to her by the fire, her face enraptured by some children's story he found in Jack's small library of old books he stores in the attic.

I am expecting Cole later this week, she says they might have found something, a possible lead, something about other sister companies to Europa called Gannymede and Callisto? From what Cole says this might be the lead we need, the one that will put Darren Winters within my reach. In the meantime, I am thinking of spending the night with a good friend, perhaps I can find some other use for his clever fingers, and help take his mind from darker deeds, what are friends for after all.

THE END

Printed in Great Britain
by Amazon